THE TROUBLE WITH TRYING TO SAVE AN ASSASSIN

MURDER SPREES AND MUTE DECREES, BOOK TWO

※

JENNIFER CODY

The Trouble with Trying to Save an Assassin, Copyright 2022 Jennifer Cody
Amazon Edition

All rights reserved. This book or any portion thereof may not be reproduced or used in any manner whatsoever without the express written permission of the publisher except for the use of brief quotations in a book review.

This book is a work of fiction. Names, characters, places, organizations and incidents are either products of the author's imagination or used fictitiously. Any resemblance to actual persons, living or dead, events or organizations is entirely coincidental.

Formatting and Cover Design by Tammy Basile, Aspen Tree E.A.S.

Editing by Shannon, Aspen Tree E.A.S.

ACKNOWLEDGMENTS

A big thank you to my entire team for keeping up with me on this one. Thank you to my alpha readers, Carol, Cameron, and Tessa and to my beta readers, Nicole, Tammy, and Tracey.

Thank you to Shannon for your editing skills! You rocked this one so hard, and I am so grateful for you!

Thank you to my PA, Tammy of Aspen Tree E.A.S., for keeping me going, listening to all my ramblings, and giving me joy when others try to steal it.

Thank you to my Beardo for your unwavering support. I am lucky to have you.

THE TROUBLE WITH TRYING TO SAVE AN ASSASSIN

Romily:
You know what I'd like to know? Where the hell my romantic, how-we-got-engaged story is. Am I going to get it any time soon? Where is my big ass diamond?

Unfortunately, all that romance-novel level relationship-angst gets put on (indefinite) hold when my beloved son, Bellamy, is targeted by who knows who, poisoned, and then abducted by a wolf-ish person I kinda like. Am I going to get my kid back? You betcha. The question is, how many people does Fox have to kill first?

The Trouble With Trying to Save an Assassin is a 60k M/M Paranormal Romance with plenty of sass, gore, and questionable decision-making skills (and now there are tiny tables too).

NOTE FROM ROMILY

Dear Reader,

First of all, I didn't end the last book on a cliffhanger. So many readers thought I did, but I swear I didn't. You saw how Fox was with the cherub rescue; I figured the one in Roswell would go about the same. I can't believe you would assume my cliffhanger like that.

Also, congratulations on making it to book two! If you're confused by the magic and mayhem thing, so am I! I'm new to the whole supernatural-people-exist thing, so let's figure this whole paranormal world out together.

Also important, this story will reference information I discovered when Fox narrated his version of our meet-cute, *Fox Recruits a Mute Boy (And Falls in Love)*. If you haven't read that one, you can get it on Amazon for 99c USD or for free by signing up for Jennifer's newsletter at the bottom of the home page on her website www.jennifercodyauthor.com. You'll get two emails after signing up, and the second will have the password for the short stories tab on her website.

Reminder: I am mute. My official medical diagnosis is mutism due to anatomical damage. I'm disabled, and I live in a world that does not accommodate me. The only way to survive in this world is either with rage or humor. Guess which way I choose to live.

If you got to the end of the last book and wondered about what I'd been reading, might I suggest looking into Eden Finley and Saxon James' hockey books (MM), Keira Andrews' pirates (MM), and Thea Harrison's Elder Races (MF). Do I look like the kind of guy who discriminates against vaginas? I'm not, and if you're the kind of reader that does, just don't read the Thea books.

Ok, let's talk about the motherfucking hellfire I went through because I decided to adopt a whole person.

Your Friendly Neighborhood Mute Boy,
    Romily Butcher

P.S. This story contains some descriptions of graphic violence, just like the last one. There's mention of torture, but don't worry, Bellamy is fine.

CHAPTER 1

Once upon a time, a mute boy got engaged to a murderer. Oh wait. He didn't. Because his murderer never presented him with his diamond engagement ring. Ever. Not for months. *Months.*

Who waits months to give their boyfriend an engagement ring they bought on the second date?

Arlington Fox does.

Why, you ask?

Who knows? Not me. And it's uncouth to ask why we're not engaged yet. My adopted son—

(It's a whole story, and honestly, if you're reading this one without having read that one first, it's on you if you get lost. I'm terrible with details and can't imagine trying to recap for you. Just, like, go read the first book. No wait, I can recap: A Reaper and a mute boy met in a diner. Shenanigans and body parts happened. They adopted a whole person together and fell in love. The end. No, you're right, you should probably just go (re)read the first book.)

—Bellamy Jones made sure that core value was hammered into my brain, so I'm not allowed to ask where the fuck my romantic how-we-got-engaged story is.

And this is not ok because we finally, *finally* have time to meet our wedding planner for the first time, *and we're not even engaged yet.*

I might be a teeny, tiny bit annoyed, but only because I really want to show my diamond off. It's supposed to be huge. What? Ok, fine—I'm also slightly annoyed by the time that has elapsed waiting on my romantic engagement story.

"Who names their kid Furion?" the kid I didn't name asks.

My boyfriend and his future step child both have their phones in hand, prepared to read whatever I have to say because I'm mute and group text messaging is my main method of communication. I could have replaced my text to speech device, but it gives me a little thrill every time Fox or Bellamy have to read what I say to other people.

Listen, I'm mute *wiggles eyebrows*. I don't have a voice. When someone cares enough to give me a voice using their own, it makes me melty and gooey on the inside. I crave that feeling, and my boys give it to me in abundance. So no, I haven't chosen a robot voice over theirs, thank you very much.

This coming from the kid someone named Bellamy? You realize I would never make fun of a guy whose name makes me think he can kick my ass, but I have zero compunction about turning your name into a nickname for shits and giggles, right? Bells. Church Bells. Gargoyle Light. Alarm Bell…I could go on. Should I go on?

"I've had girlfriends who shortened it to Bells. Darcy calls me 'Bam Bell' on occasion. I'm immune to name teasing."

Darcy calls you Red. Wait. Are you sure he's calling you Bam Bell and not just saying 'Bam! Bell' as he comes?

Bellamy purses his rose red lips, stares at me with his lavender eyes, and runs his hand over his messy ginger locks. Understanding crushes him as his extremely freckled cheeks turn bright red. It takes him a moment, and he looks out the window of the cab we're currently occupying as he speaks in his smooth, genteel accent. "I'm not sure why I never put two and two together."

I pat his knee to comfort him, and then because that is not enough, I pull him into a tight hug, blind-typing, *There there, Papa's here.*

"I swear I'm not an idiot," Bellamy whispers, squeezing my hand.

We're a touchy family. And yes, we are a family, even if sometimes

Bellamy prefers to pretend we aren't. He pretends less and less with each week that passes.

Fox reaches past me and flicks Bellamy's nose. "We don't disparage *ourselves*," he grunts.

We save that for the people we murder.

Fox reads my text and kisses the side of my head. "That's right."

Bellamy puts a handkerchief to his face to stem the bleeding coming from his nose.

My eyebrows feel like they're trying to crawl into my hair at the sight of the blood. I point to Bellamy's nose and then to Fox and drop my jaw to express my absolute shock at this unprecedented development.

Have I mentioned that I am the best at non-verbal communication? No? Well, I am. It comes with the whole having-to-use-body-language-to-make-my-point thing.

Fox shows his surprise with an almost-frown. He's stoic by reputation, and we're in mixed company, so his external presentation doesn't reflect his obvious internal turmoil. Obvious to me, obviously.

Bellamy glances at the person driving our cab and gives me a subtle, mute headshake.

He's right, of course. We don't know which cab company owns the car we're in, and if the cabbie works for the Avatar of Evil, Santanos, then letting on that something is wrong with my kid's personal protection ward isn't the best idea. Santanos has a vendetta against me for taking Bellamy away from him about two months ago, and he would definitely take advantage of this new development if he found out about it.

Me: *Can you have Dakota meet us at the wedding planner's office?*

Papa Smurf (aka, Tag, one of Fox's fathers): *I can. The question is, should I?*

Me: *Fox just gave Bellamy a bloody nose.*

Papa Smurf: *Look at that, Dakota's schedule just cleared for the day.*

Me: *This is why I text you and not him.*

Papa Smurf: *I'm the get-shit-done parent.*

Me: *I aspire to be just like you when I grow up.*

Fox lightly pinches my hip and arches a brow at me.

I huff out my amusement and pat his cheek.

You excel at getting shit done.

He gives me a that's-right grunt and turns his attention back to the front of the cab. My man isn't gorgeous or outstanding in the looks department. He cleans up well, but most of the time he's scruffy in that needs-a-shave-and-a-shower kind of way. Some people can get away with that look; Arlington Fox is not one of them. His black hair looks like it could use a stylist, and he's let what was probably a fine clean cut grow out past his ears. His brown hazel eyes see everything important: me, magic, the enemies lurking in the shadows…

Yes, we have enemies. See previous recap for reasons why.

And while he's not classically handsome or modelesque (his body would be marketable except for all the scary tattoos and scars—no seriously, under his clothes he looks like he's part of the mafia or mob or something), what he lacks in overall facial attractiveness he makes up for in confidence and competence.

Drool.

Confidence is sexy as fuck, in case you've forgotten or you're randomly reading book two without having read book one, in which case there's something wrong with you and you need to go to the hospital immediately. You can tell them I sent you. It'll be fine.

Anyway, Fox is sexy, and I love looking at him, but I adore watching him work. I've learned recently that I have a kink for competence, even if that competence is in killing people. Fox is really, really, *really* good at killing people. It's a little ridiculous how good he is at it, but with approximately three thousand years of experience, one would expect that level of skill.

I should probably be embarrassed that I'm meeting our wedding planner with a chubby just from looking at my boyfriend, but let's be honest, it's way more embarrassing that I can't brag about the ring currently not on my finger or tell the guy we're meeting all about how romantic Fox was when he proposed.

Fox squeezes my hand, making me aware that I've apparently decided to use him as a stress ball, so I squeeze him harder just to let him know that I'm not ok with planning a wedding when I'm not engaged.

Oh, and the Bellamy thing.

I look over at my personal assassin/bodyguard/adopted son, who's still staring unseeing out the window as he contemplates all his life's choices and remembers how bad his taste in bed partners is, and I lick my thumb and wipe away a spot of dirt on his freckled face.

Huh, didn't come off.

Bellamy startles as I start scrubbing at the spot.

"What the hell are you doing?!" he exclaims, pulling away from my parental love and care.

Obviously I double down, grabbing his chin and forcing him to face me as I lick my thumb again and wipe at the dirt marring his perfect face.

"Stop it! That's disgusting! Why are you second-hand licking me?!"

Fox points at Bellamy's other cheek. "Missed a spot."

Bellamy gasps and jerks himself free from my attention. "Those are freckles! They don't rub off!"

I give him a skeptical look and bring my thumb up to lick it again.

"No, no, no! Keep your spit in your mouth!"

I swear it was dirt.

"My face is not *dirty*."

See what an amazing parent I am? No kid of mine is going to spend his emotional effort self-flagellating about their past emotional entanglements. Brooding and moody isn't sexy on Bellamy like it is on Fox.

Bellamy jumps out of the car, and for a split second my brain panics about his ward, but then I realize we've arrived at our destination and take a breath to clear away that weird reaction. Romily Butcher isn't the panic-mode type—that's me, by the way. Sexy, slender, curly blond hair and brown eyes. Usually you find me wearing a thousand dollar suit, which is what I'm wearing today even though we aren't working yet.

I follow Fox out on his side and slip my hand into his, facing the high rise where the wedding planner's office is.

Across the street, the high rise where Annette Killian keeps her offices looms over me like a protective older brother. I literally have a chip in my hand that tracks my movement and serves as a means of engaging in commerce. She's my sugar daddy, but her whole organization is my big brother.

I've embraced my conspiracy-theorist's-wet-dream lifestyle.

Thunder suddenly cracks above us, so I ditch Fox—no need to get my perfectly tailored suit wet—running for cover just as a downpour of rain hits the sidewalk along with my future father-in-law, Dakota Patervulpis. I stare at the humans on the sidewalk who suddenly start running for cover, screeching about unpredictable weather patterns and how bad the weatherman is at forecasting. Not a single person looks at Dakota, a huge man with long, black hair and the body of a giant, who literally just superhero-style landed on the sidewalk *from the sky*.

I still haven't figured out how magic remains hidden from humans when magic users do shit like this all the time. Random rainstorm? Blame global warming! It's not like global warming doesn't already do enough; now we're letting it take the heat for angry thunderbirds showing up.

And, yes, Dakota looks pissed.

"My son gave you a bloody nose?" Dakota booms, storming toward Bellamy.

Bellamy braces for impact with the most adorably resigned expression on his perfect little face. No, I might not have anything to do with his biology, but the parental pride is strong in me. I can totally take credit for how handsome he is since I've been the one feeding him for a few months.

PSA: do not let that man cook. Somehow he made it to thirty-five years old without having the slightest understanding of how a stove works. It's shameful really. Even I, a twenty-one year old, who was basically raised by the foster system and then left high and dry and homeless, can operate a stove. What my kid lacks in skills amazes me sometimes.

"Yes, Grandpa Omp. It was an accident. I'm fine. But my ward needs a checkup," Bellamy explains as Dakota grabs him into a tight hug and shoots Fox a worried frown.

Dakota rumbles and lightning strikes two different lightning rods above us. In case you're wondering, no, Dakota isn't naked. Unlike his son, his clothes shift with him. There's something about being only a quarter thunderbird that makes it so that Fox's clothes don't shift with him. I can't say I have any complaints about that.

I might have complaints about Dakota, but I would never say those aloud. *smirk* *eyebrow wiggle*

My blue haired, Fae, soon-to-be father-in-law, Tag, saunters out of the building and grabs Dakota's arm. "Come on, darling. Come inside; you're causing a scene."

THE TROUBLE WITH TRYING TO SAVE AN ASSASSIN

Dakota gives his husband a wicked grin and dip-kisses him right in front of the front door, inches away from Bellamy, and close enough to me that I can basically feel their love in my dic—heart. In my *heart*.

I'm not turned on by two of the hottest men alive kissing like they're about to go find a private corner; you are. These are my future in-laws.

Well, they're two of my future fathers-in-law. I have two more around here somewhere.

I turn to Fox and press in close, pushing my chubby into his leg since he's taller than me and our hips only line up when we're forcing them to.

Fox's hands grab my hips and he looks down, giving me a minute shake of his head even though he's definitely pushing his leg into my dick.

I'm getting mixed signals here.

"I'm not sure how I feel about you getting turned on by my fathers," he murmurs.

Two hot men kissing is a turn on. It's better if it's you and me, but I'm allowed to appreciate your genetic donors since they created you.

Fox decides to stop the conversation with a kiss, which is hot, but it's not like I can't pick up the thread of the conversation with just a glance at my phone, so I'm not sure what his goal is.

Besides kissing the love of his life, obviously.

"Oh no, I think I'm about to have a relapse of bloody nose. I think I'll just go find the bathroom—"

"WHO HURT MY GRANDBABY?"

The boom of Bear's voice pulls me out of a perfectly wonderful street makeout, and I turn to face one of Fox's other fathers. Bear is the human donor to Fox's genetics, and he lives up to his name. He also looks like Thor and Captain America had a baby with Superman.

Don't look at me like that. I am not a comic book person; mixing up universes is almost a rite of passage for non-comic book people.

Bellamy goes limp in Bear's arms. Looks like he's given up the will to live. I don't know what he's complaining about; parental love is the second best kind of love.

Pulling out of Fox's embrace, I smack my kid's butt and point sternly at his grandfather.

Bellamy sighs, rolls his eyes, and hugs Bear back. "Hello, Grandpa Bear. I'm fine."

Fox's last father, Amos, the demon that birthed him, pulls Bellamy out of Bear's arms and takes his chin in hand, examining the small traces of blood around his nose and his ward, probably. "Interesting. How much nutmeg have you been consuming?" he asks, strangely concerned.

"Nutmeg?" Bellamy asks just as confused as I am.

Dakota abruptly stops turning Tag a bluer shade of horny and focuses back on Bellamy. "That could be it. How much nutmeg *have* you been eating?" he repeats.

Bellamy shakes his head and looks at me, the person who feeds him almost every meal cooked at home.

Don't look at me. I don't bake in the summer.

I send that message to the family group text that includes Fox's fathers, and every man standing here blocking the way into the building looks at their phone when it buzzes a notification.

Bear nods. "That's valid."

"But then where is he getting enough nutmeg to disrupt a council spell?" Tag asks, fisting his hips in frustration.

Dakota frowns with the same thoughtful look that Fox gets when he's concentrating on something—

I look at Fox and smile brightly because his fathers remind me of him in the best ways.

Fox sighs at me and shakes his head. "Bellamy gets a frou-frou drink from the same cafe several times a day."

I widen my eyes at our son, showing him my shock and disappointment.

Several times a day??? Without me??? What have I done to deserve this kind of disrespect from my own child?! I thought I raised you better than that!

Bellamy scowls at Fox. "You really want to tattle on me, *Oppa?*"

Fox raises his eyebrows, glances at me, turns on his heels, and walks into the office building.

That's not suspicious at all.

I follow Fox, typing out my questions in rapid fire messages.

What is he talking about?

Does Bellamy know something I don't?

Why are you avoiding me?
WHAT DOES HE HAVE ON YOU???

Fox stops in his tracks, turns around, pulls me into his arms, and does that thing where he tries to shut me up with a kiss. Honestly, I'm mute. I can't be silenced with kisses. Distracted by them, yes, but not silenced.

Gawd, he's so smexy.

I grind my actively interested cock into him and try to squish the clothes separating us out of existence. Someday I will figure out how to avoid letting him turn me on in public spaces, but today is clearly not that day.

"You two are disgusting and should be banned from public spaces."

I pull out of the kiss with Fox just in time to watch the back of a cushy chair fly through the door into the offices of Steelhorse Event Planning, LLC.

"That was your wedding planner," Bellamy deadpans, bending around us to get a peek at the flying chair.

"Was that a hover chair?" Bear asks, also staring through the glass at the person in a flying chair.

They're now speaking to one of the people inside who looks like they might be about to pee their pants.

The chair has a set of footrests like a wheelchair, but it looks way more comfortable than any wheelchair I've seen and…

It. Flies.

Or hovers. It's a hover chair. Holy shit! *It's. A. Hover. Chair.*

Tag drops his arm around my shoulders and pulls Bellamy into a side hug too. "As interesting as that is, I think the problem with Bellamy's ward is more pressing. I've already canceled our appointment with Furion, so let's go take care of the Bellamy issue."

Disappointment and relief decide to battle it out inside me for which one will win. On the one hand, I don't have to meet the wedding planner before I'm engaged, on the other: hover chair.

Oh well. Next time for sure.

CHAPTER 2

Fox owns a triple wide brownstone with more tables than any one person actually needs, and as we enter the home, I grab the parcel that was left on our doorstep and use a box cutter I keep handy on the tape, pulling out a miniature coffee table complete with coasters and a bowl of fake fruit. I set it on the matching full-size coffee table that came with Bellamy when we adopted him, which Fox put two steps in front of the sliding glass door that leads to the garden (there's another door attached to a mudroom we usually use to get in and out of the back garden).

So far I've bought matching miniature tables to decorate ten of the tables in the house.

Fox silently evaluates my newest addition while his parents and Bellamy get settled in the living room.

When I'm done setting up the mini-table, I straighten up and shoot Fox a megawatt smile, urging him to praise my effort with my non-verbal communication skills.

In our own home, Fox emotes much more freely, and he gives me an approving nod. "I don't know where you keep getting these things, but don't ever stop. They're perfect."

He's said that a couple of times now, but it bears repeating every time I add to our decor. Plus, I like that he's letting me do this for him. We both know he could jump on the internet and google miniature furniture, but he lets me do this for him and I love everything about that.

I do have amazing taste.

"You absolutely do," he agrees, pulling me in for a hug.

We're still at that honeymoon stage of love where we're in each other's space as much as possible. I keep telling him we have all of eternity, and if he keeps touching me, I'm going to get bored of him, but so far he refuses to listen to my dire warnings. It probably doesn't help that every time he touches me I get a little turned on, and apparently he can smell that.

Fox's genetics are unusual even for non-human people. He's part fae, part thunderbird, part human, and part demon—not that kind of demon, it's a species, not a religious metaphor.

Demons are from a totally different dimension than Earth and mainly use blood magic, which is why they've been, well, *demonized* by humans. They aren't any more evil than humans are, and trust me, I've been around some truly evil humans. I would take Amos on a bad day over any of them on a good day.

Amos is Fox's demon father, in case you forgot already. I know, keeping track of the names and people is hard, so I'll keep reminding you when it matters, because I'm nice like that.

Fox puffs a breath against my neck, licks my skin, and then pulls back before I can drag him upstairs to our bedroom. He gives me a knowing wink and a smirk, taking my hand and pulling me to the conversation in the living room discussing how to fix Bellamy's ward.

Honestly, I thought Dakota could just zap it back to normal.

Clearly my understanding of how magic works hasn't really improved much in this department. To be fair, I spend a lot of my time walking into strange places and sitting down to watch Fox murder people. Don't side-eye me; we know I have a weird kink for Fox's skills, and besides, he only kills people who need to die in order to make the world a better place.

Ok, in order to fix the imbalance of good versus evil in the world. It's off by, like, two percent, and Fox is actively working to restore the 90:10 balance.

"No-no, Tag. Don't—goddammit," Amos cusses, throwing up his arms and stomping to the bay window. "You *can* just let Dakota handle it," he grumps under his breath.

Tag cringes as he steps away from Bellamy, and my jaw drops. I snap a picture of my son because he needs to see this and because I need a record of it for future blackmail.

We've been home less than five minutes and you've turned my beautiful boy into a smurf! Undo it. Undo it right now!

Tag grimaces at my message as Bellamy bellows at the photo I sent to the whole group—I don't mind sharing the goods with my family.

And Annette.

Daddy: *What happened to my favorite sugar grandbaby?*

Me: *Tag did something.*

Daddy: *ROTFLMAO! He's not allowed to use magic!*

Our First Child: *Is he actually not allowed and I've been victimized by a magical criminal, or are you just giving us all false hope?*

Papa Smurf: *False hope. I have never been convicted of a magical crime.*

Me: *That doesn't mean you haven't committed any.*

I snap another picture of Bellamy, who scowls at me.

Me: *Exhibit A.*

Bellamy's hair is as blue as Tag's now, but so are his freckles, which makes me have to hold back my laughter. At least I can't mistake them for dirt now. His lips are as blue as Superman's shirt, and his lavender eyes are now glowing like he's radioactive.

Tag sighs and reaches for Bellamy. I can't see what really happens because I can't see magic, but it looks like the color melts off my adopted son and flows back to Tag, who huffs in annoyance. "See, it wasn't permanent."

Bellamy looks at himself in his camera and sighs. "Please don't ever use magic on me again," he orders Tag firmly.

He's adorable when he tries to get bossy.

Tag wraps an arm around him and kisses his temple. "No promises, baby."

"If you're done, my love," Dakota interrupts, beckoning me with one hand while taking Bellamy out of Tag's arms with the other.

I walk to Dakota and take his hand and immediately get a static electric shock.

"Ground yourself, boys," he instructs us as his starry black eyes go blank and he accesses his magic.

I grab the nearest metal object, which is the poker for the fireplace. Bellamy grabs one of the other tools—no I don't know the names of the fireplace tools. I'm not an expert on luxury tools and, yes, a fireplace poker is a luxury item because it means you have a fireplace, i.e. a home. I've only recently acquired an actual home, and that came with my boyfriend, and no, I am not quite used to the whole roof-over-my-head thing.

It's only been like eight weeks. I'm allowed to take my time getting used to not being a homeless squatter.

Dakota's brow furrows and his focus comes back to me. "Your ward is fine, but the connection to Bellamy's has been severed. He's no longer under your protection as an Acolyte."

"What do you mean? I'm still his Acolyte. I didn't quit." The note of panic in Bellamy's voice is hidden behind his usual cool tones, but I've been living with him for months, and I know my kid; he's upset about this.

I release Dakota's hand and take Bellamy's, assuring him with touch that he's mine no matter what the magic that connects us does.

"No, I saw that. You are still his Acolyte. The magic that connects you to his ward has been severed. I've seen this before; hell, I've done this before. If you consume enough nutmeg on a daily basis for a sustained period of time, it will erode your magical bonds. I used nutmeg therapy the last time someone cursed me.

"The problem is it destroys any magical link you have, not just the one you want destroyed. We caught it before it eroded the Acolyte bond, but even that one is frayed. It will eventually recover if you stay away from nutmeg for a couple of months; the ward will return as the Acolyte bond heals, but there's no magical fix for nutmeg poisoning."

He gives Bellamy a concerned frown. "Unfortunately, the only bond that survived is the one with Romily. I saw you had a few bonds with weapons and a blood bond—those are gone. You will have to reforge them."

Bellamy glances at me—*guiltily*—and nods to Dakota. "Thank you, Grandpa Omp. I'll reforge the ones I need."

Dakota gives him a hug and kisses the top of his head, then the huge man engulfs me in a hug and kisses my hair too. "Take care of him; he lost a long standing bond with someone important to him," he murmurs in my ear before releasing me.

I can't respond vocally, but I do nod as I step back and side-hug my kid, holding him fast as the rest of the fathers hug and kiss all of us before leaving us once again.

As soon as they're gone, I turn to Bellamy and spread both my hands in front of me, indicating that I'm ready to hear about this bond that he's lost.

He gives me a confused look, so Fox clarifies for me because he's my soulmate and gets me. No, not my literal soulmate; that's not a real thing that I know of. He just gets me and always has.

It could be because he's an empath and slightly telepathic, though we haven't really discussed the limits of that yet.

No, really, it just hasn't come up in detail. We are really busy people and when we get down time, I usually have better uses of my hands than texting out endless questions. Do you even know how long it takes me to have a conversation? A long ass time, so don't look at me like that. I'll eventually get around to having the long conversation with him about his empathy and telepathy.

Right now, I'm just going to take advantage of it.

"He wants to know to whom you were bonded and what we need to do to reforge that bond and the ones to your weapons," Fox explains for me.

I shoot Fox a sappy smile because I love him so much.

Bellamy purses his lips in a thin line before shaking his head. "The bond to the person is not important. It was accidental and doesn't really affect my life now. I have three weapons that I am bonded to, and I do want to reforge those bonds. Darcy helped me with those bonds, but I think I would prefer using someone else this time."

Totally reasonable considering that he is getting over a small crush on the man. Darcy is ok as a person, and I think we could even be friends if I wasn't one-hundred percent loyal to Bellamy and Darcy wasn't so bad for him. Unfortunately, Darcy isn't interested in my Bellamy and is a total asshole about it, so we can't be friends until Bellamy has found his forever person like I have mine.

"I'll make an appointment with one of Annette's people. We'll have to go to California. Charlie lives in the Sequoia National Forest." The smirk on Fox's lips and the mischief in his eyes makes me wonder what he's hiding from me, but I know that look; he wants me to be surprised.

Bellamy blinks at Fox. "There are hedge witches on this side of the continent."

"Charlie is the one we want," Fox insists as he taps his phone and it rings on speaker.

He walks to the only table in the house he had any decor on before I came to live with him. It has two sticks and two rocks on it, and what proceeds is the most bizarre phone call I have ever witnessed.

The phone stops ringing and someone on the other line whoops twice. Fox whoops back and hits his sticks together a couple of times before smashing one of them on one of the rocks.

What comes back from the phone is barking, maybe? Some loud banging like sticks being hit together, and then a hollow echoing sound like someone is yelling through their hands.

Fox returns that with more rock banging, a couple of barking yells and a weird yipping sound. I have answered Ylvis' infamous question: What Does the Fox Say?

Fox says, bang bang, clack, whoop-whoop, yip-yip-yip-yipeeeeeeeee, aroooooo. It's a little embarrassing to watch until Bellamy grabs one of Fox's sticks and starts banging on the rocks, then he too aroooos into the phone.

Now it's just really bizarre.

The answer that comes back is just befuddling—a scream like a woman dying in the woods.

I am disturbed.

The love of my life is not and neither is our kid.

Then Fox hangs up the phone and nods to Bellamy before turning to me. "They're going to fix Bellamy up; all we have to do is show up."

I blink at him to convey how bizarre witnessing that display was, and he smirks at me, bends a little and kisses me to distract me.

I'm totally distracted.

CHAPTER 3

My phone buzzes just as I'm getting to the good part of my current read. It's the 50% sex scene; you know what I'm talking about. We spent thirty percent of the book playing will-we-won't-we, and then twenty percent getting ready for the yes-we-will, and now we're at the gonna-do-this-thing, and I am here for it.

Except I'm not because of the text that comes in from the depot.

Messengers of Evil: *Bill Barnum. Under the bridge at 125th Street between Kaiser and King. 2:20 p.m.*

I breathe in through my nose and out through my mouth and get my fancy ass up from where I'm reclining on Fox's chest while he snoozes on the couch. Well, he's not snoozing now because of the message from the source of all evil—ooh, I'm changing the depot's contact info in my phone to that!

I dip down and kiss his lips before snapping at Bellamy and pointing at the chair he's currently occupying.

"Do I look like I have a death wish?" He asks, shaking his head at me, wide-eyed like my instructions are ridiculous.

I grin at him and pat his bouncy, ginger curls instead of texting him to tell him he's a good boy. I'm just glad we're on the same page about his safety.

He huffs at me, but notice how he doesn't pull his head out of the way or reject my parental love. In fact—

I bend and kiss his forehead right smack in the middle and make some clicking sounds in my mouth when I try to mime, *Love you*, to him.

Bellamy snorts and shakes his head. "I know, you ridiculous person."

He doesn't wipe my kiss away, and when I turn to look at Fox, I have to smile widely and do a little butt wiggle because Bellamy is slowly learning to accept that he's stuck with us forever.

Fox pulls me in for a quick kiss and presses his forehead to mine, slotting our noses together. "I'll be there shortly."

I resist the urge to blind type that he should take as much time as it takes to send me a nice dick pic. I have some on my phone, and I will never get tired of getting them from him, but I really don't need another one.

Need is a strong word. Like, I need food. I don't *need* another dick pic. I might want filet mignon, but I can survive on last night's leftovers. I might want a dick pic, but I can survive on the ones I already have saved on my phone.

I peck his lips and step back, heading to the door to put on my combat boots, because we're going to be under a bridge, and I do not want my loafers ruined by the muck if there is any.

Outside, the cab that took over transporting me on official depot business waits for me. Before I cross the line of the wards, I check in with my gargoyle friends, patting their stony forms as I pass them at the gate to the property. I stop just inside the wards and scan the street in both directions.

I'm not in any danger from much of anything, but ever since I was caught in a drive-by shooting that one time, I haven't left the property without properly assessing my surroundings. My gargoyle friends don't have the kinds of protections I do, and I don't want them to get hurt. The last time a few of them ended up shot up, and it was awful.

Ok, yes, I was a little more worried about Fox, who was also shot up. Let's just say I'm still not any good with first aid to bullet wounds. I'm fine with bloody massacres, but I'm no one's first choice for dressing bloody wounds. I accept this weird dichotomy of my character just like I accept all my other idiosyncrasies. Self-acceptance is an important step to living a happy life, trust me.

Since the street lacks any ominous lingering vehicles, I step out of the ward, followed by the chorus of church-bell sounding goodbyes from my friends, and make it safely the last few feet to the cab awaiting me. I've streamlined this process, patting Jostein's shoulder to let him know I'm ready. He already has the address because I demanded the depot assign me a cabbie and then send him the address because I can't speak and they should accommodate me as Fox's Harbinger.

In case you forgot, that means that I go to the murder places first to give his next victim a chance to say their last goodbyes. I've heard that other Harbingers sometimes have to chase down their Reaper's victims, but Fox has cultivated such a reputation that most of his victims don't bother running.

Yes, I know. The system is whack, right?

The good guys literally take out contracts on the bad guys and assassinate them. This isn't even a secret part of the organization. If you are evil and know about magic, you know that if you do too much evil and upset the balance of good versus evil you will have a contract taken out on your life by the good guys. And even though the bad guys know this happens all the time, they still persist in going overboard.

It's insane.

We also kill regular ol' humans. Actually, Fox kills more humans than non-humans. I didn't know when we first hooked up that I would be not-explaining to a bunch of evil regular humans that they were about to die because of their heinous crimes. I didn't know then, but I do now, and I don't care that they have no idea why they're dying. I only care that the balance is restored.

I have way too much empathy for the victims to have any mercy left over for the victimizers. If that makes me a little bit psycho, I'm ok with that. I lived through two mass murders committed by regular ol' humans before meeting Fox during my third mass killing, and no one has ever accused me of coming out of those traumatic events with a normal outlook on life. A sunny disposition suits me just fine; pay no attention to the delight I take in watching a Reaper work; it's normal to find the love of your life attractive when they're in their zone of expertise.

My phone buzzes as Jostein chauffeurs me to the murder spot, and I grin at the message from Fox. It's totally a dick pic. I love this man more than life, and his dick is a thing of beauty. Even though I literally had it in my mouth not an hour ago, getting a pic makes me squirmy and horny for another round.

Me: *We should compare cocks soon.*

Me: *We could hold them up together.*

Future Husband: *Then what?*

Me: *We slick them up with lube to make them shiny and attractive. We can admire how they look pressed against each other.*

Future Husband: *I do enjoy how you admire my cock.*

Me: *My cock would probably want to kiss yours a few times. Maybe rub up on it.*

Future Husband: *More.*

Me: *I know you love how my balls feel against your cock. You would look so hot frotting against my balls until you couldn't take another stroke without creaming, and then I'd grab our cocks together and jerk us both until your eyes roll up in your head and your breath catches and your entire body flushes as you come all over my cock and hand.*

Future Husband: **cum covered dick pic**

I love this man.

I'm also hard as a rock with no relief, but Fox's sex drive is like five times more needy than mine, and badly sexting is how I keep him satisfied while my puny human balls recover enough to dick him down again. We've learned that we do not have the same sexual stamina, which makes sense since Fox isn't more than a quarter human. Apparently thunderbirds have one of the more rapacious libidos among the paranormal population.

Thankfully, my Fox is very forgiving of my human weaknesses, and toys exist.

Our First Child: *Things I didn't ever want to be included in……*

That text appears right below the picture of Fox's cock covered in cum.

I check the message thread, and yep, my wonderful future husband sent me a dick pic in our family thread and not our personal thread. I stare at it for a moment, trying to decide if I'm embarrassed or not. Either way…

Me: *We should probably be less inclusive.*

Future Husband: *…*

Future Husband: *I'll keep that in mind next time.*
Our First Child: *Nice cock even if you're missing some balls.*
Future Husband: *Thunderbird reproductive organs are internal.*
Our First Child: *Not sure I wanted to know that.*
Future Husband: *Incubi don't have testicles at all. You might've drawn the conclusion that Amos is incubus from my lack. He isn't, but you could have gone that route too.*
Our First Child: *You'd think I would know that about incubi considering how many times I've seen Santanos naked, but there was literally always a head between my line of sight and his cock.*
Me: *I wouldn't complain about that.*
Our First Child: *I'm not.*
Shudder.
Santanos, the Avatar of Evil, is one of the original incubuses spawned by Lilith, a queen of hell, and Bacchus—yes, the one who is the mascot of Mardi Gras. Aaand now I know that the man doesn't have balls either. I'll take things I never wanted to know for three hundred, Mayim.

The taxi comes to a stop just before a small bridge going over a drainage ditch, and I grimace at the muck awaiting my combat boots. Jostein got me here just in time, so I pat his shoulder and get out, adjusting my vest and jacket as I alight onto the sidewalk. With a sigh, I step onto the muddy bank of the ditch and carefully step down.

The mud immediately slides out from under my shoe, taking me with it on an eternal surf down the embankment. I windmill my arms to keep from falling straight on my ass in my thousand dollar suit and somehow manage to keep my feet until I hit the bottom of the ditch, at which point I fly head first into a trickle of ditch water leftover from the last random rainstorm to hit this city.

It was probably the one from this morning that Dakota started.

I push my face out of the mud, frowning in disgust as it squishes between my fingers, and get to my feet, staring down at the ruined mess of my royal blue suit. I blow out a slightly annoyed breath, sending bits of muddy water flying out in front of me. My tailor is going to give me the stink eye. He does not like when I stain my clothes. I mean, I don't either because it means I have to pay for the cleaning service, and he's not exactly cheap.

Anyone else think I've got the most interesting luck on the planet? Well, it's true. Look, I know I'm covered in mud and muck, but I guarantee you that something cool is about to happen. My luck always balances itself out. Probably going to get laid or something equally hot.

A cackle echoes from under the bridge, catching my attention as a man with a devil-may-care smile on his face steps out from under it holding the head of a gray-skinned…well, I don't know, do I? I've only been on the job for eight-ish weeks. I don't know about all the possible non-human people yet. The head has ashy gray skin and long black hair.

The guy carrying the head has long silver ropes of coiled hair held back by a purple headband. A jagged scar runs from just above his left brow all the way to his right ear, splitting his face in half with skin several shades paler than the warm bronze of the rest of him. He's wearing leather—not like modern leather, but like fantasy video game leather with buckles and straps and gauntlets. The man is wearing *gauntlets!* And he's carrying a sword like Fox's in the hand opposite the one holding the severed head.

What did I tell you? Something cool, right?

His bright blue eyes crinkle with humor as he steps into the light and laughs at me. I don't blame him; if the situation was reversed, I would totally be laughing too. I shoot him a bright, sunny smile and wiggle my fingers at him to say hello before pointing at the head in his hand with a wide-eyed, questioning look.

"Ah, yeah, you'll have to let the little fox know this one belongs to the wolf," he winks. He waves his hand in a circle and some pink particles surround him then disappear, taking him with them.

I glance up the side banks of the ditch where there's a couple of humans snickering at me. They didn't even notice the man who literally disappeared right in front of them, but they sure can see the man dripping mud from uncomfortable places.

Magic's fun, isn't it?

That's sarcasm, by the way. It doesn't translate well in text, so don't blame me for having to explain. I can't vocalize my sarcasm like the verbal, so sometimes I just have to let you know it's happening.

"You ok?" one of the humans above me asks.

I send her a thumbs up and trudge toward the bridge, because even though I suspect that the man with the head stole Fox's kill, I still have to go in there just in case.

The stench of rot hits me hard as I approach the dimness of the under-street tunnel, causing me to retch into the mud. I can handle a lot—I don't even get queasy at the scent of blood—but this is very similar to what rotten turkey smells like when you try to cook it. I can't be the only person who's accidentally left a chub of ground turkey in the fridge too long and only realized it after I started cooking it. Yeah, no, the smell made me throw up then too.

It takes me a few seconds to get the retching under control before I manage to get a good enough look in the tunnel to see the corpse that belonged to the head that the "wolf" took. Have you seen *Coraline*? The bad guy in that children's horror movie is a woman who is half spider. I have found her real life counterpart. Minus the head, obviously.

The leftovers of the person in here look like a giant black spider with a naked, gray human-ish torso. I mean, where's a person who's mostly spider going to find clothes?

There isn't anyone else in the tunnel, so I make a quick escape, retching again as soon as I get out. That smell is just the absolute worst. I would rather live on a chicken farm surrounded by mountains of chicken shit (which is just awful in every way) than ever have to smell rotten-cooking-ground-turkey ever again.

"Romily."

Do you know how weird it is that my dick responds to his voice even as I am wiping the remnants of vomit off my lips? It's wrong and weird, but I should probably resign myself to wrong-and-weird being my new normal, right? Because Fox's voice does it for me every damn time.

I turn toward the love of my life, who eyes me with a steely gaze that makes me squirm, because I know he thinks someone did this to me, and he's not at all ok with anyone messing with me. Offering him a reassuring smile, I point toward the tunnel and make the *crrrrck* noise that accompanies miming cutting someone's neck.

Fox, of course, immediately understands. "Bounty hunter got here first?"

I shrug and nod. I don't know if the wolf is a bounty hunter, but he could be.

Fox doesn't react except a slight twitch of his eye before he turns on his heel and marches straight into the tunnel. He disappears into the shadows for zero-point-two seconds and returns with a stoic scowl.

Yes, I know that sounds like an oxymoron, but you haven't seen his face. He's super stoic, but somehow there are just layers of stoicism, and right now the layer is scowl. My Fox isn't happy.

"Did they push you into the mud?" he demands with as much anger as he has ever expressed in a public setting.

As I shake my head he smacks his hand at me as if he's going to actually hit me. Of course his hand bounces off my ward—*I haven't been consuming unprecedented amounts of nutmeg.*

"So you fell." The anger in his face immediately dissipates into a twinkle of amusement, and the twitch in his eye becomes a twitch at the corner of his mouth. This is his amusement layer of stoicism.

I huff and wildly express my shock and dismay that he would laugh at me for falling face first into the mud. The. Mud. Does my ward even protect against microbial terrorists that could give me some weird illness that might hospitalize me, and then I could die because it's such a foreign bacteria that the doctors can't figure it out before it eats my brain, and also where is Dr. House when you need him???

I could die of brain eating bacteria, and Fox is laughing at me. It's internal laughter, but I can see it on his face!

I narrow my eyes at him and point without touching him—obviously I won't expose him to the brain-eating bacteria. I love him. I would never do anything to harm him.

That's not to say he won't do stupid things like grab my muddy pointed finger and step in close. "Home."

I will never not love the sound of that word out of his mouth. The no-longer-homeless mute boy loves knowing he has a place he belongs.

CHAPTER 4

*B*ellamy's deeply red, perfectly groomed eyebrows find their way to his hairline when he sees me walk into the brownstone covered in drying mud.

"No! Do not take a single step more. Take off all your clothes now. Do not walk through the house like that. No."

In case it isn't clear from his fulminating protest: Bellamy is fastidious about the cleanliness of our home. Fox has a thing about his tables; Bellamy swiffers like the world might end if there's dust on our floors. I have never snuck out to the garden in white socks and then casually strolled through the house until he noticed the bottoms of them, and he has never attacked the floors with a steam mop after seeing the bottoms of my dirty socks. Nope. Never. Certainly not once a week since I figured out he wigs out about clean floors.

I push my ruined jacket off my shoulders and drop it to the floor. It clinks, hitting the floor jewelry first. Dammit. My shinies are dirty! Nooooo!

I drop to my knees to rescue my silver lapel chain.

Bellamy makes a noise of protest in his throat but kneels in front of me and starts taking my jewelry off my clothes. "I'll clean it, just get it off," he growls as he collects my cufflinks.

I go still as he takes off all my diamond jewelry, including the collar chain, earrings (these are a new addition; I got myself magically pierced with a healing charm so I didn't have to wait six to eight weeks to change out my earrings), and pocket watch. He even remembers my tie pin and the bracelet that Annette got me.

As soon as he has all my jewelry, he takes them to the kitchen and puts them next to the sink.

I stand and start stripping out of my muddy clothes, because as much as I love tormenting him, I actually agree that a naked walk to the bathroom for a shower is better than traipsing through the house in muddy clothes. He returns just as I'm pushing my trousers off my feet and crosses his arms, standing in my path when I try to head to the bathroom.

"All of it," he insists, glancing down to my briefs.

I look down at my underwear and dramatically roll my eyes at him, because I don't see any muck on them.

He points to a tiny spot of brown that could be anything and isn't necessarily mud on my hip. "Off."

Fox doesn't help at all because he doesn't have an insecure bone in his body and isn't upset by the idea of Bellamy seeing me naked. Don't get me wrong, he's possessive as hell, but he's not jealous or insecure.

Sighing, I strip out of my underwear and give Bellamy an are-you-happy look.

He grimaces and nods, then his face clears and the barest hint of a smile edges the corners of his eyes. "Who knew I'd get to see both your cocks today."

Fox's head whips around. "You swore not to bring that up again."

Bellamy snickers as he tosses all my dirty clothes into a pile. "I guess I lied."

I laugh, huffing silently as I grab Fox by his shirt and drag him with me up to our bedroom. I vaguely wave around the room to let him know he should undress and join me in the shower, then I head to the bathroom, starting the water for us.

As soon as it's steamy, I jump in and get to scrubbing as much of the muck off me as possible, starting with my poor face. Theoretically, I'm all for mud wraps and spa therapies that include clay; I haven't actually ever gone to a spa, but it sounds nice. Maybe a little boring unless I'm allowed to read a book.

Still, I could be my own company for a while. I'm very used to boredom. That's one thing people don't really realize about homelessness—the hours of nothing to do, the never-ending, soul-sucking boredom that's only punctuated by the scramble to survive. Desperation isn't a good cure for boredom, and I always preferred the boredom to the desperation.

Fox's arms slide around me as I am rinsing the (expensive) shampoo from my hair.

I grin and finish rinsing before wiping my face and opening my eyes to the best person in the world. Sliding my arms around his neck, I lift myself up to kiss him. Fox pulls me in close, turns off the water, and slots in for the kiss, taking his time to thoroughly ravage me. He pushes me up against the cool tiles, lifting me just enough to press our dicks together.

He growls his approval as I give in to the urge to frot against him. His strength isn't bulky, but my man has no problem lifting me off my feet and holding me at exactly the right place to maximize dick contact between us. He loves my mouth and spends ages enjoying the slide of our tongues before he takes his lips away and kisses along my jaw, sending shivers of pleasure through me.

I reach between us, panting and ready to come, but Fox captures my hand before I can jerk us off.

"I want you inside me before you come," he grumbles into my neck, sucking a hickey into my skin.

I whine, but I'm not actually protesting. I just want my orgasm; I don't care how he makes it happen.

Ok, my whines aren't verbal, but he understands what it means when I pinch the skin over his ribs. We've developed non-verbal signals over the past few months. It's one of the best things that comes from true intimacy. We can read each other, especially when one of us has to rely on clever body language to communicate clearly.

His deep, dark chuckle freezes me in my tracks and almost sends me careening over the edge into orgasm. "Not yet, Romily."

He's obviously not playing to win; he knows that my name + his voice = spontaneous combustion.

He grips the base of my dick hard enough to bring me back from the edge, staring into my eyes and taking me hostage until I gasp a hard breath, finally able to hold back. I give him a single nod, which earns me a wicked grin. He backs away and turns, giving me his ass as he sets his palms against the tile.

"In me," he demands, and can I just say that dominant bottoms are totally my thing now?

When we first got together, I didn't know he would be this commanding as a bottom. I thought we would switch things up, but in the weeks since we finally got each other naked for the first time, he's been the most demanding bottom I could have imagined, and I am so, *so* here for it. Gods, this man drives me crazy in the best possible ways.

I grab a condom from the stash we keep in here for shower sex and roll one on before lining up and pressing into his hot, wet channel. I hiss at the perfection of how he takes me every time. He's not as tight as the first time; regular use has trained those muscles to relax, but he's still got the most perfect ass in all the world.

He doesn't wait for me to start a rhythm. He pushes back until he has my cock as deep in him as it can get, then he grabs one of my hips, keeping himself braced with his other hand, and starts a rhythm that gives him the maximum amount of pleasure he can get from me.

This is my Fox, taking what he needs and giving me everything I could have ever asked for and more. It takes me an embarrassingly short amount of Fox's intensely erotic taking before I shoot off, tapping him hard in the universal signal of *I'm-coming-right-now-!*

Fox groans as he suddenly freezes and shoots his load onto the shower wall. His channel flexes around me—yes, I know that's not something humans can do, but Fox isn't human, is he? Plus, it feels like I'm being served the most decadent dessert after a luscious, rich meal, and I will never say no to Fox's orgasms pulsing around my cock, dragging out the pleasure of coming together with the love of my life.

Just as we're regaining our breath, my cock slips out of Fox, leaving the condom behind. I don't even bother with stifling my laughter as Fox grimaces at me and pulls the condom out. He rolls his eyes and tosses the condom into the trash on the other side of the curtain.

My huffing laughter turns wet as I restart the water and pull him into the spray. He can't help but join my joy, smiling softly and pecking a kiss to my smiling lips.

Since he's always so good to me, I give him the good part of the shower spray and grab his shampoo, reaching up to wash him when he's ready. This is one of my favorite parts of showering with Fox. Yes, the sex is always grand, but the intimacy of him letting me wash his body feeds my soul.

I can't tell him that I love him whenever I want. I have to make him feel it, and these little acts of service are how I do that. Fox's way of showing he loves people is by doing stuff for them; he feels loved when I do things for him, and he knows that acts of service are not my main love language. Mine is the giving and receiving of gifts all the way. So he gives me little and big things and I do stuff for him, and we both fill each other's love buckets up that way.

Yes, of course I also give him gifts; I can't help it. The little mini tables all over the house are evidence of my love. And yes, he is forever doing stuff for me, like washing vegetables when I'm cooking and opening doors. We fit well together, and Bellamy fits in with us too.

I know it's weird, but he does! I accidentally adopted him, but really, he belongs to us as much as we belong to each other. We're a family, a found family, but a family nonetheless. If anyone messes with one of us, they're messing with all of us, which is why I'm really anxious to get Bellamy's weapons re-bonded to him. I'll be happier when my kid isn't relying on mundane weapons to defend himself and has his ward back to full strength.

Fox cups my jaw in his hands, pulling me out of my distracted thoughts. I have, uh, definitely managed to wash his hair. Yep, very clean. Ignore the mountain of suds; that's how I always do it. He insists, in fact. I've told him he doesn't need that much shampoo and that it's a waste, but he keeps telling me that he only feels clean with like six inches of suds on his hair.

Yep.

"I'm sure Bellamy has an itinerary for us by now," he assures me because he can read my mind.

Well, and my emotions, which is easier for him. I'm sure my current parental worry is distinct from other forms of worry. This is why he's my fated mate: he gets me. He understands me even when I can't give him my words, and that is a gift I will never take for granted.

I lift up and kiss him again, then push him back into the spray and help him get the shampoo out of his hair. Then I help him condition without even daring to think about the Bellamy problem.

See what a good boyfriend I am.

While his hair is soaking in the conditioner, I wash his body up, including a sensual, soapy jerk off that makes my dick twitch, but I just don't have his refractory period. When I finally get him all clean and shiny, which is ridiculous because I'm pretty sure he took a shower this morning and that this shower was supposed to be for me, he takes his turn with me.

I'm living in the lap of luxury, and his name is Arlington Fox.

CHAPTER 5

After we dress and head back downstairs, Fox sits on the couch and pulls me onto his lap where I belong, and Bellamy hands me my phone, which was in my jacket when I dropped it to the floor. It shines like he cleaned it and smells like disinfectant.

Happiness suffuses me, and I smile brilliantly at him, wiggling as I get back my ability to make the words.

Thank you for cleaning my phone, kiddo! You're so smart.

Positive reinforcement works wonders according to some of the parenting sites I've visited while Bellamy was looking.

He needs to know that I take my responsibility as his parent seriously; I only visit parenting sites when he can see my screen.

"You're welcome," he replies, far too dignified to roll his eyes, but I can see him struggling not to.

He cracks me up.

"Tell us what happened," Fox suggests, squeezing my hip where his hand rests on it.

There is plenty of seating in the living room even with the twelve tables in here, but my seat is always on Fox's lap, and since this is the only place I really want to be, I encourage his submission to being my chair by wiggling my ass on his dick while I type. He enjoys it.

THE TROUBLE WITH TRYING TO SAVE AN ASSASSIN

Bellamy huffs because he doesn't have a lap to sit in.

I stop typing out my narrative and look at my son, then at Fox, and because Fox is actually everything a mute boy could possibly ask for, we both look back at Bellamy and Fox pats my lap.

"If you're jealous, you can sit on Papa's lap. I can handle it."

Bellamy goes from pale and freckled to red as a beet in half a second. "No. Absolutely not."

I open my arms and make gimme hands at him, patting my lap.

I didn't realize my kid could turn that shade of red. He's almost purple. Surprisingly, it compliments his red-orange hair and definitely brings out how purple his eyes are.

"No, thank you. Please just tell us about what happened," he insists, shaking his head vehemently as his genteel accent intensifies; my son falls back on politeness when most people would be at a loss for words.

I like that about him.

"Romily's lap is always available if you need it, son," Fox adds as I grin at my phone, typing out the long explanation for what happened when I got to the bridge.

Typing out whole stories takes time, and my boys have a full conversation that I have to ignore before I finish typing it out. It's nearly a thousand words. It's almost a whole short story. I could publish it if I was so inclined.

side eye

As soon as I send it to their phones, they stop chatting about whatever and both read my short story. It's *very* similar to the middle of chapter three if you want to go back and reread that.

"Ah, that's Tala," Bellamy hums and gets a grunt of agreement from Fox a few moments later.

They finish reading my amazing story that helps them identify the person who stole Fox's kill, and then Fox gives me a kiss on the neck because positive reinforcement works for me too.

"Tala is—" I cut him off with a wave of my hand because I haven't yet reached fifty points in my guessing game, and he's not stealing something that's kinda obvious to me. I could get two whole points if I get this right.

He's a wolf-shifter, right? Or possibly a werewolf in a weird traditional way, like he's connected to the moon or something? Like the werewolves that attacked you in the library?

"Not like the werewolves that attacked me in the library; that species originates from hellhounds. Tala is a different branch of shifter," Fox explains, pausing to let Bellamy pick up the rest of the explanation.

"Luna wolf is what they call themselves, because they have a preternatural connection to the cycle of the moon, but it's not related to their ability to shift forms. They can do that at their own leisure," Bellamy finishes.

"Their connection to the moon is more spiritual," Fox cocks his head to the side as he stares at me. "Do you want to guess or a hint?"

I widen my eyes at him then shake my head as I type. *Hint. Do gods really exist?*

Fox and Bellamy both look unsure, but Fox replies. "We don't really know if there's really a God, capital g. There are very powerful beings that have cults, but spiritual connections form over time and often fail, which is why cults come and go."

Ok, so give me a good hint.

I'm wasting time, but this entertains me, and life is better with plenty of joy, amiright?

"I got this," Bellamy interjects with a small smirk. "Some humans think that Mother Earth is sentient and worship that sentience as such."

I basically let my fingers think this out for me and then send them the whole paragraph.

Gaia, right? So like Final Fantasy Gaia, probably, but then we're talking about the moon, so Luna? Who is that goddess? Nyx? No, she's nighttime? Maybe. Ugh, romance books are not the best at giving me an education in mythology for real. I'm going to call the spirit of the moon Luna, then, and assume that the connection is like Gaia cults. So Luna wolves worship the spirit of the moon? I bet it's a fertility thing, isn't it? It's always about sex.

"I love how intuitive you are," Fox chuckles, kissing my cheek.

I smile brightly and wiggle to reward him; he should always kiss me every chance he gets. I've been training him for two months to habitually give me the affection I need to sustain my contentment, and I'm reaping the rewards for all my hard work every day.

"The spirit of the moon is called Luna by the Luna wolves, and yes, they do associate it with their fertility because they are on a strict lunar cycle. Their heats and ruts only happen during the new moon," Bellamy explains.

I gasp and clutch my imaginary pearls.

Bellamy shakes his head with an amused smile, because even though he protests vehemently to many things, he still thinks I'm hilarious. "I listened to a theory of evolution about this from a scientist who decided that Luna is a strict feminist. Luna wolves established their spiritual connection to the moon hundreds of thousands of years ago. It's been a part of their biology since the beginning of the written historical record. The theory posited that during the new moon it's more difficult to find the females in hiding because of the lack of natural light, so Luna made the wolves cycle around the time of the new moon so that females who didn't want to be pregnant had a chance at escape when consent wasn't one of those things that people much worried about, if you know what I mean."

That's kind of awful to think about.

Fox hums softly. "Interesting. It makes sense as a theory if Luna is a conscientious spirit. There's no evidence of that, and it doesn't take into account the fact that the females are significantly larger than the males."

Bellamy leans forward, invested in this conversation now. "No, it does. If Luna is a conscientious spirit with a bond to all Luna wolves, and the very first feminist, so to speak, then it would have influenced the females to breed stronger than the males so that they would have a higher chance at fighting off males in rut. Females are the solitary ones and the males are the social ones. So you have bands of males seeking out females, and if the female is caught, she still has a chance of escape if she is bigger than her counterparts, even if she's outnumbered. Even in the early days of the historical record, the males were pack oriented and the females were solitary; things have become more civil now, but they're still divided this way with one female leading each pack of males and mainly letting them do their own thing."

This is utterly fascinating. I've heard about human evolution because it's part of standard public school curriculums, but this is the first time I've thought about the evolution of other people.

So Luna wolves are werewolves, but they're not like the legends. Their fertility cycles are associated with the moon because of a spiritual bond they have with the spirit of the moon. Also, there are academics who study the history of non-humans!!! How do I get a degree in non-human history? Are there universities for this kind of study?

I would totally rock being a historian. Of course, now that I'm thinking about it, all I have to do is live long enough to become an expert on history. Fox has literally forgotten more than history books could ever hope to remember. He's thirty-six hundred years old! And someday, after I'm done being his Harbinger, Fox is going to make me immortal like his fathers did for Bear.

"Yes, there are universities you can study at. They aren't like human institutions, though. They have different learning programs and usually require a significant amount of travel and dedication," Fox assures me. "If you decide that's something you want to do, we will interview some schools to find one that will fit you."

Travel?

Bellamy clicks his tongue. "You can't be considered educated by non-human standards until you have spent a year studying in at least five different dimensions, planets, or realms."

Sounds expensive.

Prohibitively so.

"The council pays for free education for every person who wants to dedicate their time to learning. As a community, we believe education is a universal right," Fox assures me.

I raise my brows at him because I like the idea of that, but from what I can tell governments usually have a difficult time finding funding for universal rights like healthcare and education.

He snorts and kisses my temple. "Wait until tax time comes around."

Yep, that makes sense, but I'm fine with it. I have so much surplus it's ridiculous not to pay my taxes.

My phone buzzes in my hand along with both Fox's and Bellamy's.

Source of All Evil: *Time off approved for Thursday through Monday.*

Immediately upon reading that, Annette texts us as a group.

Daddy: *Why are you going to California?*

Me: *My son has to see a person about re-bonding his weapons to him.*

Daddy: *We have hearth witches on this side of the continent.*

Future Husband: *We're going to see Charlie.*
Daddy: *I'm not paying for that.*
Future Husband: *I am.*
Me: *Is Charlie expensive?*
Our First Child: *Charlie is the best of the best at this particular form of witchcraft and thus the most costly, but worth the price.*
Future Husband: *Exactly.*
Daddy: *I don't disagree.*

I take a deep breath to remind myself that it's ok to spend a lot of money on things that are high quality, even if we can get things that are ok quality for significantly less.

Me: *Do we have an itinerary?*
Our First Child: **attachment**

I open the attachment Bellamy sends the group to a PDF with our flight details, noticing we're taking Annette's private jet, and stand. We need to be at the airport in four hours and no one is packed. I glare at Bellamy, communicating my displeasure at the short notice.

He wipes a grin off his lips with the back of his hand and stands with the type of grace I will never have no matter how long I live; my son is very well trained and kind of amazing.

Of course, no sooner does he take a few steps than he runs into the new table Fox installed three days ago. We're both still getting used to it.

"Son of a bitch!" my eloquent and classy son exclaims as he sprawls over the table sideways.

When I say Fox installed it—it is literally the only table in this room bolted to the floor.

"Language," Fox immediately chastises Bellamy, making me swell with pride because he only just beat me to it.

Bellamy's phone buzzes with my message.

Me: *Gentlemen don't cuss in mixed company.*

Bellamy doesn't even pull himself off the table before checking my message, because he values my words more than his own comfort.

How could I not love these men?

My kid stands and pointedly looks around. "Mixed by who?"

I silently laugh, snagging him around the neck and kissing his cheek.

"Or are you calling Fox a girl?" he asks, because I totally left my beloved boyfriend open to that.

Fox snorts. "I don't identify as feminine."

We've talked about this. My future husband is capable of getting pregnant because he is technically a gender that cannot be spelled by English letters. The word sounds like an alien language because it's in the language of the demons and that species of people have extra vocal capabilities that humans cannot even begin to mimic (and in some cases, hear). That being true, Fox identifies as male-ish for the purposes of gender assignments in human languages.

You identify as <inhuman pronoun noise>, which is your cisgender, which makes this mixed company because we're not <inhuman pronoun noise>.

Yes, this is the hill I will die on to be right.

Fox makes the inhuman pronoun noise he's capable of making because he's a quarter demon and kisses me. "Of course you're right."

I smile widely at Bellamy, showing him all my pretty teeth.

Bellamy gives in and rolls his eyes, shaking his head. "I'm going to take the equality stance and say if I can cuss in front of one adult I can cuss in front of the other no matter their gender."

Damn. He's got me on that one. I will never argue against equality.

I guess we're going to have to institute a no cussing rule.

Bellamy glares at his phone like he's deciding if he can weaponize it, and Fox chuffs in my ear, and I decide maybe it's time to head upstairs to actually pack before my son decides to start sneaking me massive quantities of nutmeg.

Who'd have thought that would be his hill?

CHAPTER 6

I'm sitting in the first class lounge of the airport, because that's who I am now, and I'm trying to read, but the (forty-year old) guys in my (trashy, sweet, perfect, contemporary m/m romance) book have just gotten fake engaged, and I'm now distracted. My mind keeps wandering to how Fox is going to propose. We've only been together for eight weeks, but when you know who you're going to be with for the rest of your very long life, you just know, and it's ok to skip to the good parts as long as you're not actually skipping the *important* parts.

Like communication and getting to know each other and testing out chemistry and maybe asking about how your potential partner feels about vacations.

In case you're wondering, Fox is so old that vacations aren't important enough to him to bother planning. He's also set a limit that I can't vacation without him unless it's a staycation, at least not until we've been together long enough to need time apart. His parents still haven't instituted separate vacation plans, so I'm not sure we'll ever get to the point where we need separate vacations (yes, his fathers are my only example of a real life healthy marriage, so I will be taking notes, just saying).

So, having spent eight weeks living together and discovering that we are very well matched in every way except the whole libido thing—and we are working a plan of action on that like the bosses at relationships that we are—I'm flummoxed that my immortal life partner is dragging his feet with popping the question.

My finger needs a huge diamond, thank you very much.

Why yes, I could propose to Fox, but I didn't buy him an engagement ring; he bought me one, so it would be weird for me to take a knee and ask for my engagement ring. I'm not against going against tradition, but I'm kind of a princess and definitely want my Reaper-in-shining-armor to present me with a ring in a romantic way.

Call me old fashioned.

What's that pointy princess cap called?

Google has the answer for me, so I text Fox because I won't be reading the rest of this book until we get on the plane.

Me: *Fox! I need a hennin. And possibly a dragon.*

Fox: *Do you also need a knight in shining armor?*

Me: *No, I have you.*

Fox: *Reaper-in-black-leggings?*

Me: *You're getting sassy.*

Fox: *Bad company corrupts good morals.*

Me: *Come here so I can corrupt your morals some more.*

Fox: *Two minutes.*

I look up as a man dressed like a leather Dom takes a seat across from me carrying a highball glass with him. He's wearing skin tight leather pants that have one of those detachable cod pieces and a motorcycle jacket with something questionably shirt-like under it. He has dark russet eyes framed by black guyliner, light brown skin, black hair with a streak of red coming off the widow's peak, and a smirk that would make the most hard and fast straight dude-bro question his sexuality.

"You're Fox's Harbinger," he says, crossing his knee-high spiked boots and leaning back in his chair. "I heard you talk about as much as he does."

I arch a brow at the guy, asking without words, *Who the fuck are you?*

The guy chuckles and holds out his hand, leaning forward. "Gavin Montero, Harbinger for Julia Ross."

Oh hey! Another Harbinger! I've heard about the reputation of Harbingers and how I'm setting the bar too high these days. Apparently all other Harbingers pale in comparison to my awesomeness.

He points over his shoulder to a woman with long black and blue braids sipping a martini at the bar. Her mahogany skin shines under the muted lights and her wide smile conveys an internal happiness that just makes me want to get to know her better. She dips her chin in greeting but remains sitting at the bar, wearing the same uniform Fox does when he's working: black yoga pants and a black A-shirt with a hundred pounds of guns and ammo strapped to her body.

Also, holy smokes, Julia is *hot*. Like, at least as hot as Fox is.

I pull up my notes app and type out a message to Gavin, shoving the phone in his face so he can read it when I'm done.

I really thought it was just Fox, but I think I have a kink for Reapers. Is it the blatant weapons or the happily-I-will-eviscerate-you aura?

Gavin laughs and moves from the chair across from me to the seat next to me on the sofa. "It's everything about them, I think. So, you really are engaged to Fox, then?"

I huff and show him my naked finger. *No. The ring hasn't arrived yet. We special ordered from our jeweler.*

Trust me; I've looked. Fox has a lot of hidey holes, but unless he found a new one to hide the ring in, we haven't gotten that special order ring yet.

Gavin and I both look up as Fox enters the lounge, and he clicks his tongue after taking a sip of his amber drink. "Lucky boy, you are. I wanted Fox the moment I laid eyes on him, but he's never been emotionally available, and I'm demi-romantic enough for that to bother me."

I can see how Fox's stoicism might come off as aloofness to a demi-romantic. It would be difficult for anyone, except me of course, because I'm amazing, to form a close bond with Fox if he doesn't want them to, and I cannot imagine Fox wanting anyone as clearly dominant as this guy. Two doms don't make a right. That's how the saying goes, I'm sure of it.

Gavin winks at me, giving me fuck-me eyes. "I'm not demi*sexual*, but again, he never gave me a hint he would have been down to get tangled in the sheets with me."

I smile at Fox as he narrows his eyes at Gavin and then spins to find Julia at the bar.

Julia stands up to greet him, and although the lounge isn't huge or busy, I can't really make out their low conversation as she hugs him and he stiffens like he doesn't know how to give the best hugs ever.

He does. I've been on the receiving end of his wonderful hugs for weeks already, so watching him do this to Julia makes me silently laugh.

"It's like he doesn't even know what a hug is. I know he was hugged as a child; I know Dakota and Tag. Tag brags about him all the time. How did he never learn how to hug properly?" Gavin ponders, thoughtfully sipping his drink.

Watch this.

I show him my phone, stand up, and saunter over to my Fox, giving Julia the wait-a-moment finger as I insert myself between them and hug Fox.

Of course my boyfriend wraps me up tight in his arms and pulls me flush to his body. He buries his nose into the crook of my neck, drawing in a long breath and the scent of my skin. I give him a moment to just enjoy being held by me, then step back, peck a kiss to his lips, wink at Julia, and head back to Gavin, leaving Fox to talk to the other Reaper if that's what he wants to do.

Gavin's brows rise toward his forehead, surprised and impressed by my display. "That is a man attached to his future fiancé."

I sit close enough next to Gavin that our shoulders press together as I type my response and he reads it.

He can hug. He just isn't a touchy-feely kind of person with anyone but family.

"It bears repeating: lucky boy. If he ever treats you wrong, I'll have Julia kick his ass. Just say the word." He pauses and side eyes me with a smirk. "Or type it."

I grin at the joke as my heart decides to include him in the circle of my people. I do so love a man with a sense of humor.

I have an assassin son if I really need to make a point, but thank you for the offer.

"Oh, yes. I'd heard you claimed Bellamy Jones. Not a moment too soon, either, because he was on our list that day. We were literally around the corner when the text canceling his contract came in."

I widen my eyes at Gavin, shocked that anyone would want Bellamy dead, even the depot. *What did he do to deserve getting reaped???*

Gavin shrugs. "He was Santanos' assassin. He killed enough people to get on the depot's list."

Speaking of my red-headed assassin, where is he? He was supposed to meet us here.

Me: *Where are you?*

Our First Child: *Avoiding being seen with you.*

Me: *That doesn't work for me. Come meet the Harbinger of the Reaper who nearly killed you.*

Our First Child: *That doesn't motivate me to come out of hiding.*

Me: *Did I tell you that I found out I can subscribe and save on bulk orders of Grape Nuts through Amazon?*

"Gross," Gavin whispers beside me as Bellamy materializes out of the shadows and sits down across from me in the seat Gavin just vacated.

"You're only supposed to use your internet powers for good," Bellamy complains, giving me a disgusted expression.

Eight boxes delivered every four months. It's like they knew that occasionally you get constipated.

"Pretty sure that cereal doesn't cure emotional constipation," Gavin hums, and stops abruptly, eyes landing on Bellamy's sky blue shirt with the words, "Mini-Me" printed on the front. He looks at my shirt, which is the same flattering blue and says "Me" and then looks back at Bellamy's before chuckling and shaking his head. "Where did you get those shirts?"

My sugar daddy made them for us!

Bellamy glances down at his shirt and flashes a disgusted expression. "Annette thought it would be funny, and Romily can't be reasoned with."

"Annette is your sugar daddy." Gavin arches the most perfect dommy brow at me and then slides his gaze to Bellamy. "And did you thank her for showing you how special you are to her?"

Oh. My. Gawd.

Bellamy blushes the deepest red I have ever seen, and I've seen him beet red, and looks away like he can escape the leather Dom's scrutiny if he can't see it. Also, holy shit, Bellamy would be the most amazing sub! You can see this, right? It's not just me?

Me: *Bellamy needs Gavin to make him behave!*
Daddy: *Or a Collin—actually I think a Collin would be better for him.*
Me: *Who's Collin?*
Daddy: *Gavin's cousin. He looks like a pirate most of the time. You can't miss him.*

I look around just in case I have missed him, but I don't see anyone that looks like a pirate.

"He's not here," Gavin laughs.

"Who?" Bellamy questions, looking at me with his phone in hand and an annoyed expression because he *hates* missing out on parts of the conversation because he was excluded from my text messages.

I check the message thread I used with Annette and grimace, screen capping it and shooting it to Bellamy.

Bellamy twitches when he reads the screen cap and looks around like I did even though he heard Gavin say that Collin isn't here.

Gavin chuckles, deep, dark, swoon-worthy, and deadly. "Boy, my cousin was in Nevada last I heard. You have a thing for pirates?"

Bellamy, genteel southern boy that he is, blushes hard, takes a sip of his own glass of something bubbly and clear (I bet you anything it's hard seltzer glammed up for the first class lounge), and takes a moment to formulate a response. "I do believe everyone has a thing for pirates these days."

Oh my fuck; he's falling back on his southern politeness.

Gavin gives him a slow, sensual once-over. "I'm far more interested in the cabin boy."

Whew, if I was Bellamy and also not totally into Fox, I would be in Gavin's lap already. He's…whew.

I glance at Fox, seeing my lover glowering at Gavin. Well, as close to a glower as Fox gets in mixed company. That would be any company that falls outside the parameters of his definition of family.

When I look back at Bellamy, his eyes go wide for a split second before his entire face shuts down and he stands. "Excuse me," he says with a polite bow then spins on his heels and marches to the bar.

I open up a new contact card and type in Gavin's name in the company line and give him a nickname before handing him my phone so he can add his information.

THE TROUBLE WITH TRYING TO SAVE AN ASSASSIN

When he hands it back, I start a group message with him, Bellamy, Fox, and Annette.

Me: *He's a ridiculous child and definitely needs a firm hand to make him behave.*

Daddy: *Did you just include Gavin and Bellamy in our conversation?*

Me: *And Fox. Bellamy complained that I wasn't using group messaging.*

Daddy: *NO ONE TEXT ANYTHING!*

Our First Child: *I did *not* complain.*

Daddy: *Ok, I've added Collin.*

Unknown: *Why have I been added to a group message?*

Potential Bellamy Tamer (aka Gavin): *Because Fox's Harbinger doesn't speak aloud, Annette is his sugar daddy, and they think you and I should get together to tame a brat named Bellamy.*

Future Husband: *Julia wants in on the conversation.*

Bellamy: *I want out. Stop trying to hook me up. I am *not* a brat.*

Piratey Potential Bellamy Tamer (aka Collin): *I am *not* a hookup.*

Unknown: *Is Bellamy the cute redhead blushing next to me?*

Me: *Define cute.*

Potential Bellamy Tamer: *Yes.*

Future Husband: *Aren't all kids cute when they're asleep?*

Me: *WE NEED TO FIND OUT.*

Our First Child: *I'm not a child!*

Sexy Momma (aka Julia): *Alas, I'm married. How do I get my husband on the hit list so I can bang the red-headed stepchild of a past lover?*

Me: *He has sex with women when there's an attractive man involved. You might just ask your hubby for a threesome.*

Sexy Momma: *That requires admitting I want to have sex with my husband...*

Future Husband: *Aren't you married to one of the Gordons?*

Sexy Momma: *Yes. The prick.*

"Jamie Gordon is who she's referring to, and he's actually one half of the set of twins that take turns being on the council to represent evil. It's his brother's turn right now, so he's been driving Julia crazy being home all the time," Gavin explains and leans over to speak quietly in my ear. "Hmm, I didn't realize that Fox and Julia had been a thing. That's interesting."

Given that Fox is thirty-six hundred years old, it would be ridiculous to assume he'd never had past lovers.

Julia is hot as fuck, and Fox has good taste.

Gavin reads that, staring at me in mute shock (*snicker*) for a moment before responding. "I'm a catch and a half."

I giggle at his fake offense and pat his arm.

I'm sure you are.

"The other half is Collin on occasion when we meet a truly troublesome, high maintenance sub," he expounds, leaning in close enough that his breath sends a shiver down my spine.

Hey, I'm taken and monogamous, but I'm not immune to a hot guy in my ear.

Fox sees this and his mask of stoicism flashes with possessiveness. He sets his drink on the bar, marches over to me, picks me up, and sits with me in his lap across from Gavin, giving the man a stoically intense glare.

I smile like Fox is my very own Christmas present and kiss his jawline.

You're beautiful when you get possessive of me.

Fox glances down at my unsent message and pecks my temple, but he doesn't say anything because that would undermine his reputation. If there's anything I've learned about my future husband, it's that his reputation matters to him because it keeps the chatter down and the targets too scared to run. It saves both time and energy, and since he invests all that saved time and energy into me, I am happy to help him maintain his stoic, badass, quiet reputation.

"Good morning, Fox. I adore your little Harbinger. Where did you find such a delightful man?" Gavin asks, blatantly flirting, though I can't tell if he's flirting with me or with Fox.

Fox stares at him for a moment before turning away from Gavin to me. His dark hazel eyes hold the full volume of his passion for me and flash with fire—literally; Fox has the fires of hell in his eyes on occasion; I haven't yet figured out why it happens, because I've seen it happen in the throes of passion and when he's struggling to kill an assignment, and even once when he was playing cards with Bellamy.

He presses his lips to mine, sweeps his tongue across the seam of my lips, and then mauls me in the sexiest, most possessive display of *mine* I've ever experienced.

Damn, I love being the love of this man's life. He never lets me feel unwanted, and since that's how I felt for most of my life, it's a cozy security blanket to have wrapped around me now.

You try spending the first eighteen years of your life bouncing from home to home and see how well you respond when someone stakes their claim. I belong to Fox, and I will always want him to show me that. Security is a thing, and my last therapist explained that when we (humans) feel secure in our relationships, we paradoxically feel more independent from the people we love. So yeah, I make Fox feel secure, and he does the same for me, and as a result we're both mentally and emotionally healthier.

When Fox has made sure that Gavin knows to whom I belong, he pulls back with a smug look in his eyes and sits back, holding me as he observes the room.

I return my attention back to Gavin, not even bothering to hide how much I want to fuck Fox right now, and answer the question he asked Fox, who is probably going to ignore the other Harbinger now.

We met in a diner. How do you know Fox?

"I was briefly his Harbinger about twelve years ago. I think we lasted three weeks before I met Julia. I sent him Collin, but my cousin only lasted a few months," Gavin shrugs, tossing his glance at Fox before adding. "Fox isn't like most Reapers. Whereas Julia loves people and will sometimes choose to pass on a contract after meeting the person, Fox doesn't care who he's sent after or what they've done as long as he gets to kill them."

I didn't know that Reapers could choose to let some people live. Huh. I'm not saying I'm the epitome of moral excellence or anything—clearly, I'm not —but before meeting up with Fox I was pretty sure murder was almost never the answer to life's problems. Now, I'm just happy I get to watch him because he's just so sexy when he kills people. Oh. Oh dear. I wonder...

I quickly type out my question and shove my phone in Fox's face. *Do you kill people because you know it makes me horny?*

Fox stares at me as he slowly takes the phone and types out his response. *I didn't realize that murder made you horny.*

It doesn't! Well, I mean, not specifically murder. You're just so good at it that I get hot and bothered when you're working. Competence is my kink! Don't judge me.

Fox hides a smile by burying his nose in my hair and huffs out a quiet breath. "I would never," he assures me.

Of courses he wouldn't when he has his own weird kink, and I'm not talking about the tables.

CHAPTER 7

I finish two novellas on the flight to Bakersfield and start a third. When the plane starts its descent, I'm wondering if I'm an antihero like the villain in my book. Seriously, he's just a little bandit thief, but he could be so much more. I haven't gotten far into it, but I do find it hilarious that he's ready to bang his hot hero nemesis. I mean, I'd totally bang a kinda bad good guy.

I glance at Fox as I put my phone down. I'm totally already banging a kinda bad good guy.

Fox is reading a paperback I lent him. I stole it from a library, but that just makes me a little like the antihero in my current book: banging the hot good guy and theft. I have zero qualms about petty theft and theft for survival. It's an attitude I adopted when the system failed me, and you know what? I recognize my faultless imperfections and forgive myself for not adhering to society's ethical standards. Maybe someday I'll feel bad about stealing a PNR from a library, but today is not that day, not when Fox is halfway through it and completely absorbed by it, and I get a little thrill from having given him something he likes, filling up my love bucket.

He reaches down and adjusts his dick, so I look over his shoulder to see what's got him chubbing up—snicker. It's a m/m, shifter-shifter pairing, and the sex scenes in this book are hot. Just saying. And of course Fox agrees if his chubby is any indication.

"I think this writer must be part of the supernatural community," Fox murmurs, shuffling back through the pages and pointing out the description of one of the MCs. "Rabbit shifters look exactly like this in their human form."

I raise my eyebrows to show my surprise. I shouldn't be surprised that non-human people have mundane careers like being authors, and to be fair, it's pretty cool that they include true elements of the community in their writing. Of course, now I have to watch out for more truths in the fictions of my PNRs.

This is going to be so fun.

Bellamy falls into the seat beside me and takes my hand as soon as he's buckled. He's pale and shiny from perspiration, and his hand is clammy in mine. He just spent about ten minutes in the toilet cubicle, and if the way Fox reaches over and puts his hand over both of ours means anything, I suspect my son might have gotten a little air sick. He didn't do this last time we flew, and he hasn't said anything, but he's clinging to me, which he really only does when he needs the comforting assurance that only his family can provide. It's also possible that he drank too much before the flight and ended up a little sick from that.

The captain comes over the intercom letting us know that we're about to start the approach, and then our ears start popping from the change in air pressure as we descend and hit the runway. Bellamy doesn't release my hand until we've come to a full stop, and then he's the first out of his seat when the fasten seatbelts light goes off.

Most people would have to pay exorbitant fees to move their weapons across the country, but I have some very powerful friends in the supernatural community, and guess what, gargoyles really like helping out their friends. I don't know the details because I can't fluently understand the gargoyle language, but somewhere around here, the gargoyles are dropping off Bellamy's weapons for us. They apparently have methods of travel that make them excellent couriers.

When we disembark from the plane and head inside the small private airport, there's a normal looking girl standing to the side holding a sign with Fox's name on it. He walks right up to her, and without a word between them, she hands him a set of keys and literally pops out of existence right in front of the people around us. I assume not all of them are members of the community; this is a private airfield, but not one exclusive to non-humans.

Seriously, how is it even possible that people don't know that magic exists? We are *not* at all subtle about its usage.

My battery lets me know that I have ten percent life left after sending that message to my boys.

Fox cocks his head at me with a curious look. "What are you talking about?"

The delivery woman just disappeared right in front of my eyes. It wasn't like she slipped away and disappeared, she just popped out of existence in front of all these humans.

I dramatically wave at where the woman was like, *Can't you see what happened just now???*

Fox's eyebrows twitch like they want to come together in confusion, and I am about to get a little insecure like maybe I'm hallucinating and the woman is still standing there, but no, my hand passes right through that space; she's definitely not there.

"Humans can't see magic. It's a blind spot for them. You've been part of this world for two months and didn't know that?" Bellamy asks, throwing Fox a *look*. "Oppa. You failed."

Fox's confusion clears and he almost frowns. "He likes to guess, and he didn't ask."

Oof. I'm torn.

Fox is right, and it's sweet of him to leave me to my own devices; he knows me so well.

But so is Bellamy because I honestly would never have guessed something as simple as a blind spot. I am really intuitive—funny how good a person can get at reading other people's nonverbal expressions when they have to learn to exaggerate their own—but I'm pretty sure that particular explanation never would have crossed my mind. I'd have thought up a whole world-wide conspiracy to keep me specifically in the dark about magic before guessing *blind spot*.

Gawd, humans as a species are stupid.

It's like we intentionally evolved to be the most vulnerable prey on the planet. We are literally weaker in every way than most non-human people and then, like we're not handicapped enough by that, we go and make ourselves blind to the fact that predators that will literally eat us even exist. As a species, we are one bad coping mechanism away from extinction.

Why hasn't some other smarter species taken over the world yet? I feel like humans could have benefited from a nanny when we were growing up.

Bellamy chuckles and a smile plays at the corner of Fox's lips, and those two things are the best things in my life except my jewelry. I mean, I'd give up my jewels for either of these men, and we all know how much my jewelry means to me. Though they would have to be in a hopeless situation where there is zero chance of either of them fixing it themselves before they die. And since Fox always resurrects after a death, it would have to be a pretty extreme death for me to give up the jewels that *he bought me*.

Anyways, the point is, I would, in fact, under certain circumstances, eventually, give up my jewels for either of them.

"You out number us," Fox almost chuckles, kissing the side of my mouth.

I mean, ok, that's valid too. Humans are also considered predatory. We could potentially win in a war simply by swarming. It's unlikely we would do that, but we could. And evolutionarily speaking, we are persistence hunters and evolved to be able to just out walk our food sources, so yeah, I guess we could potentially be dangerous to non-humans in the long run. We just wouldn't ever give up.

Ok, so the supernatural nanny idea is probably unnecessary, even if as a species we've evolved ourselves into significant disadvantages.

As I am considering humanity, Fox leads us to the parking garage, unerringly finding the vehicle that goes ooo-whoop when he hits the button on the key-majigger.

Key-majigger is a valid noun. Do I know what the thingy is called that remotely unlocks cars? No, no I do not. I live in a city where I don't have to learn to drive to get around, so it's never been important for me to learn about car stuff.

I enjoy the view as Fox puts the luggage in the back, I smack Bellamy's butt as he climbs into the back seat of the small SUV, and I hop in the front passenger seat. Fox gets behind the wheel and wow. I did not think Fox could get sexier, but *dayum* that man knows what he's doing.

I think I'm a little gobsmacked that he can drive. And he's good at it. He backs us out of the parking space like it's nothing and then follows the directions of the maps app without missing a beat. It's kind of amazing.

Listen, when you live in a place where the majority of people with driver's licenses are professional drivers, it's a surprise when you see a layman getting in the driver's seat of a big ass car. I mean, I know Fox isn't a normal human, and he probably learned to drive on a model-T or something, but the man is as good as a professional. Better maybe.

I type out my deep and meaningful feelings for Fox and send it to the family chat because Bellamy hates being left out of the conversation.

"You are the sexiest man alive. I love you. As soon as we get to the hotel I'm going to fuck you into the mattress you competent, sexy beast. Watching you drive is as captivating as watching you kill people, but I would never say that aloud. I'd make Bellamy say it," Bellamy reads aloud, because distracted driving is dangerous.

"You are the worst parent ever," Bellamy groans. "I only got us a double queen room because we're only staying one night."

"Call the hotel to add a king to our reservation," Fox instructs him with a subtle laugh in his tone. "I've grown out of my exhibitionist phase."

"That's a lie," Bellamy calls him out. "You literally sent me a dick pic and a cum pic today."

I shoot through a message.

"It's well past midnight."

I snicker at making him contradict himself with a dad joke and start typing again.

"Yesterday, then," he huffs, exasperated.

"Why am I arguing with myself? Stop it, Bellman. Damn it, I didn't want you to know I call myself Bellman. I need to shut up, but I just can't. Oppa, you're my hero. Papa, you're my favorite parent—"

Fox's snorts, but Bellamy powers through the message I sent with the most deadpan, monotone voice he can manage.

"I will forever be grateful that you adopted me. It was the best day of my life when you stole me away from the Avatar of Evil."

Bellamy sighs. "Sometimes I wonder what life would have been like if Oppa had chosen a sane person to love."

I send him my response.

"You'd be poorer for having never experienced his love."

I cackle at the conversation he's having with himself and a wash of love pours over me from the fact that he hasn't refused to read aloud anything I've sent him. He knows how special I feel when he lends me his voice, and even when I'm teasing him, he puts up with it because he loves me. And yes, children, this is what love does. It's far more important as a verb than it is as a noun, take it from someone who relies on actions to make my family feel loved.

I reach back and squeeze Bellamy's hand, holding it firmly as I turn my attention back to the road.

My phone dies and my charging cord isn't worth getting out, even if I could figure out how to use the car to charge it.

Bellamy grumbles about the ridiculous people he got stuck with, but he doesn't let go of my hand until we get to the hotel, even when he's on the phone with the front desk arranging his own room so I can show Fox how sexy he is.

When we get to the hotel, Fox pulls into a huge parking lot and manages to park like the expert at everything he is. Hot. Fox just slides this huge SUV into a space between two other cars, and I might have a little chubby in my briefs because holy hell, competence is sexy, and Fox has it in spades. Also because one of us got an orgasm in the last few hours and it wasn't me. Speaking of…

Me via Fox's Phone: *Does it count as joining the mile high club if there's only one orgasm? —Sugar Baby*

The Competition (HA! Fox's nickname for Annette is perfect, just like him!): *Did you have sex in my jet???*

Me via Fox's Phone: *Only if fellatio in the restroom counts as sex.*

The Competition: *You realize the seats recline into beds, right? You don't get to join the club with a dirty toilet encounter.*

Me via Fox's Phone: *Damn. I'll try again on the way back.*

The Competition: *Recline *handclap* the *handclap* seats *handclap**

Fox turns off the engine and looks at me, immediately doing a double take. A smug grin teases the corners of his mouth when he not-so-subtly notices my chubby. "You liked that, didn't you?"

"Oh dear lord. Stop flirting over a parking job," Bellamy complains, jumping out of the SUV in a hurry.

I ignore Bellamy's outburst since it's definitely the job of parents the world over to embarrass their kids with their love (the TV assures me this is true).

You're just so sexy all the time.

I grab Fox around the back of his neck and pull him into a kiss that shows him exactly how much I love him. Or at least how sexy I think he is. It's a passionate kiss, and let's be real, passion isn't always about love. Sometimes you just gotta use your body to tell your man that he's sexy as fuck.

Fox gives me a heated look when I pull back, and for just a few moments, we stare into each other's eyes like we're the only two people on the planet. My eyes and expression say, *I fucking love you*, and the bulge in my pants says, *I love fucking you*, and I'm so glad I get to make good on the promise in my kiss.

CHAPTER 8

Banging on the door of the hotel room wakes me up, but Fox is already up and dressed, so I let him answer the door and stubbornly pretend that I'm completely undisturbed by the noise. No, I am not a morning person if I have any choice in the matter. Sometimes I have to get up because the Source of All Evil doesn't care how much sleep I've had if someone needs killing, but otherwise, I try to make all my mornings as late as possible. I enjoy waking up to a nooner, if you know what I mean.

"He's still sleeping?" Bellamy's voice interrupts my almost doze.

Fox grunts from the bathroom.

Bellamy pokes my shoulder. "Wake up, Papa." He still sounds like he has to force my title sometimes, but it's only a matter of time before it comes naturally to him.

I crack an eye open because: positive reinforcement.

He straightens when he sees my eye open and smirks down at me. He's wearing a polo and light cargo shorts with hiking boots that look like they've seen a few miles of trail. My combat boots are what I'll be wearing today, because I don't have hiking boots and I'm not about to walk through miles of mountainous forest in new shoes.

That's right, we have to hike to get to Charlie today. Anyone want to guess why? Yeah, I have no idea either. My current suspicion is that Charlie's magic works best in seclusion surrounded by nature. I think they might be a hermit, but the whole communication through banging rocks and howls tells me that Charlie definitely isn't human. I haven't asked yet, but I have a guess about what Charlie is. No, I'm not telling you until I meet them, because even I don't want to admit what I'm considering.

It's...far-fetched, and a little embarrassing considering I know almost nothing about cryptids that aren't the main characters of exciting eroticas and swoon-worthy romances.

Bellamy holds up a large cup of fancy coffee. "Toffee nut latte with a double shot of espresso."

I throw my blankets off and grab the coffee, sipping it like the lifeline to consciousness that it is.

"I got us breakfast." He points a single finger toward the dresser where a bag that smells like breakfast burritos sits.

I reach over and pat his knee, thanking him for the coffee and the breakfast, then my morning needs become pressing, so I make my way to the bathroom where Fox is running an electric trimmer over his scruff.

I pinch his butt on the way by and then take care of my bladder, shooing him over when I'm done so I can wash my hands and brush my teeth. By the time I'm done and have the water going for a quick shower, he's finished with the trimmer and joins me, because why not. We dither just long enough for a quick frot—no, I am not going to pass up the opportunity for an orgasm with the love of my life just because someone is waiting in the next room for us—then we both barely run some soap over the important parts because we had a long shower last night and don't really need more than a quick scrub down to wake up.

I am not about dry skin from showering too much. It's already a challenge to keep my body soft and supple without the added stress of dry skin from too much washing. Plus my curls really are best the second day after a shampoo. My new stylist insists I use thirty dollar shampoo and conditioner and gave me a whole schedule for taking care of my hair.

I still sometimes get vertigo from having gone from squatting in a random college student's apartment to having a pushy stylist I see every three weeks and a bossy tailor who thinks it's a crime whenever I get blood on my suits. I still don't have the nerve to more than look at the tuxedo I bought from him. He might actually attempt murder if I get blood on it.

After we finish showering, Fox and I go back into the bedroom where Bellamy is watching—? I think he's watching reruns of—oh yeah, that's reruns of *Gilmore Girls*. Is there a weird southern thing about that show? Like, I've noticed an interesting trend among people from south of the Mason-Dixon line and this show. I'm not the only one who's noticed how invested people in the south are in that show, right?

Movies and TV aren't my thing, but to each their own, I guess.

Ok, look, I've been wearing suits almost every day for the last eight weeks, and as much as I love them, and I really fucking love them, I am also in love with this baby-soft pair of jeans I managed to rescue from Bellamy when he started tossing out my thrift store clothes. Do you know how many washes it takes to make jean material soft like butter? More than I have ever managed in my entire life, that's how many. I rescued these from his cleaning, and I realize that they could fall apart at any moment, but they are going on my lovely ass right now, and if this is their last day on earth, I am going to revel in their comfort.

Bellamy makes a noise like a dying cat as I pull them over my moisture wicking briefs—we're hiking; I will not have a sweaty imprint of my asscrack on my pants, thank you very much.

"I thought I threw those away," he protests as politely as he can.

I shoot him a wink, grabbing another article of clothing that I rescued from his purge of my street clothes, as he oh so politely calls them. Thread bare it may be, but it's also the only sleeveless shirt I own that won't leave me with a farmer's tan from being outside all day.

It's possible that I may not have put in any effort to update my leisure clothing since I started spending so much time in my suits.

Bellamy scowls at my outfit, and I can see him silently plotting how he's going to get rid of this outfit as soon as I'm out of it.

These pants are super comfortable, and I haven't worn this shirt since you moved in, so it was still in my clean clothes drawer.

"I went through that drawer," Bellamy points out, arching a brow.

Fox's arms come around me from behind and he snuffles my neck to fill his lungs with my scent. "You can always borrow one of my shirts," he hums contentedly.

Bellamy sighs. "That would be preferable to what you're currently wearing. At least we know his have a layer of protection to them and aren't on the way out."

He doesn't even wait for me to consent; he just grabs one of Fox's black A-shirts from the drawer where Fox stashed his clothes. He hands it to me and forcibly rips my shirt off my body. Literally. I will never even be able to consider wearing that shirt again. I frown pathetically as he tosses the remains of it into the trash can.

Rude. I could have gotten one more wash out of it.

It's a weak argument, but it's *hard* to let go of the things from my old life, because I know those things work in a worst case scenario. The things I own now haven't yet proven themselves should the bottom fall out of the life I'm currently living. I know that I'm the adaptable one and the things are not what will make or break me, but dammit, you can't logic away an emotional bond like the one I've forged with my stuff.

Bellamy very suddenly wraps his arms around me in a crushing hug. "I'll replace it with something more durable," he promises.

Awww. I'd lose all my shirts if it means my kid will give me bone crushing hugs under his own impetus.

I pull on the shirt he gives me, and yeah, it's too big, because Fox might not be bulky, but he's bigger than me. Swoon. Boyfriend shirt.

I grin at them both and pull the A-shirt down enough to flash a nip. When I release the fabric, it stays well below my nipple without even being caught on my non-existent pec—I'm not buff; I'm sleek and soft and pretty. This is definitely a case of opposites attract.

Fox fixes my shirt and pecks my lips before squeezing Bellamy's shoulder affectionately on his way to divvy up the breakfast Bellamy brought. We eat with minimal conversation, mainly because mouths and hands are too full of huge food-baby size burritos. I eat like a quarter of mine because I really do not want to squat behind a rock or something later.

Before we start hiking away from indoor plumbing, we will be taking a toilet break.

Even when I was homeless, I never actually had to shit anywhere but a toilet. I really don't want to break my winning streak on that. I do not get people who choose to do the whole roughing it thing for funsies. I like my luxuries, like flushable toilets, thank you very much.

Bellamy and Fox both acknowledge my insistence, and after Fox and Bellamy grab their hiking backpacks, we hit the road. No one asks me if I want a hiking backpack, and let's be honest, it's kind of sexy how they both decide to spoil me. I can carry my own stuff, obviously. I spent years hauling my own duffle bag of stuff around, so yeah, I absolutely can haul a hiking backpack up a mountain. The fact that I don't have to? I'm definitely living my best life with my two best men.

CHAPTER 9

It takes about an hour to get from our hotel to a parking lot in Sequoia National Forest, where we debark from the SUV. We spend a little while loosening our limbs and using the facilities, and then Fox shuffles us back into the truck and we drive another hour on barely maintained camping trails until we reach the end of one. Fox and Bellamy don their backpacks, we hydrate, and then off we go, hiking northward.

Fox takes the opportunity to teach Bellamy about the forest, and I listen, of course. If I get lost in this place with no backpack of supplies, it will be helpful to know the edible plants from the ones that will give me a rash from touching them. Apparently I should be wearing long sleeves to avoid exposure to plants that are toxic to human skin; well, Bellamy should at the very least, because my ward will probably keep the bad plants off of me, but since we're here because his ward has been destroyed, he should have covered every inch of his skin, and he did not.

Where's his *Assassin's Creed* outfit when he needs it?

I think I've gone soft living in the lap of luxury (aka Fox). It only takes two hours before I am ready for a break. Eight weeks ago I could literally pound the pavement all day without feeling the bone deep exhaustion that my limbs are currently protesting.

I smack Fox's arm and grab his wrist, pulling him to a stop. I want to dramatically collapse to the ground, but I haven't checked it for creepy crawlies, and doing so would just negate the drama, so I resist. I lift my shirt and wipe my brow, because while the weather is fairly mild, after two hours of hiking, I'm hot and in need of a cool down and water.

"We've only got a couple more hours. Do you want a long or short break?" Fox asks, because even though he is slightly empathic and sometimes telepathic, he doesn't always use those powers. Apparently it can be nightmare fuel to be always on, and I think we can all sympathize with him on that.

I bring out my phone, which has full bars even on the side of a secluded mountain in a national forest where only satellite phones should work—gods, I love working for Big Brother.

I think I need an hour to cool down, rehydrate, and have a snack.

Fox nods once, and he and Bellamy put their backpacks down. Bellamy spreads a thick blanket out on the ground, and Fox starts unpacking a picnic of food items in plastic containers that did not come from our kitchen. I catch his attention with a wave and give him a confused/curious look, pointing at the picnic.

A soft smile crosses his features. "Athair made us food, and Pater popped it over while we were in the shower. I had room in my backpack anyway."

As much as his parents often exasperate him, he loves them. Also…

Why did we spend hours in a jet when we could have just "popped" on over? Also, why are we not "popping" on over to Charlie's place instead of hiking?

"Teleportation isn't a reliable form of transporting people. It takes significant mental effort to teleport anything and—"

I hold up a frantic hand to shut him up.

I didn't know this would be a prime opportunity to guess! Don't take the little joys in my life away!

He presses his lips together and gives a subtle shake of his head, disappointed in himself for almost ruining this for me. He retrains his focus back on his backpack, pulling out a gallon of water. If we're transporting water for three people, doing it in actual gallon jugs is less plastic waste than water bottles, and that was my contribution to this venture, besides the actual organization of the luggage and carry-ons. We do still have a water bottle each, but we can refill it from the jugs we brought.

Ok, so, teleportation takes mental effort, which means that it's probably visual. I bet you gave Amos a mental picture of our hotel room, didn't you?

Fox nods his affirmative, which is odd because he's usually more emotive when it's just the three of us.

I look around suspiciously, trying to see if someone is watching us.

"Don't," Bellamy warns almost under his breath.

Neither of my boys are tense or look like they feel threatened, but Bellamy's word confirms that we are, in fact, being watched at least. That thought sends a shiver up my spine.

"Go on, Papa. What else do you want to guess about the magic of teleportation?" Bellamy asks at a normal conversational volume.

Ok, I guess we are ignoring the whole being watched thing.

So, the person teleporting needs a clear mental image of the destination, and if the thing being transported can't think for itself, I'm guessing it's much easier. Oh I'm giving myself 4 points for this if I'm correct: animals are impossible to transport because you can't make them think of the place they're going and humans are difficult because if the mental image isn't the same for all parties it's going to fail somehow.

Fox hands me dessert first. "You earned all four points," he murmurs.

I open the container with my prize in it and my mouth waters at the homemade blueberry ice cream on a lemon tart. I love my in-laws. They never fail to make me feel their love. Oh, you're probably wondering how the ice cream hasn't become a melted mess. The parentals' chef is a brownie, and they use magic to keep their food optimal until consumption. The ice cream won't melt in the bowl, only in my mouth.

Magic does have some amazing benefits, doesn't it? Are you jealous of my fancy-ass magical lifestyle yet? Trust me, I know the feeling.

Bellamy just stares at me in open-mouth awe.

If I had a voice I would be cackling, but since I don't and can't, I settle for huffing my silent laughter at him, like I always do.

"How on earth did you intuit that?" my son asks, like he doesn't know my habits.

*I *handclap* read *handclap* all *handclap* the *handclap* time *handclap*!*

No, I have not, in fact, started using emojis. Ok, before you get all in my face about that, I want you to really think about how many names of emojis you know and what it would be like having to read my words aloud if I used them. Trust me, I have cut out the possibility of being misinterpreted by spelling them out.

All y'all who want audiobooks need to think about these things…

"Which book have you read with teleportation limitations like this?" Fox asks with stoic curiosity.

I wave him off and shake my head.

I haven't read a book with this kind of teleportation, but experience with a lot of different types of paranormal worlds has given me plenty of creative fodder to work with. All I really needed was the hint about sending Amos a mental image of the hotel room.

My ice cream and lemon tart are gone just in time for Fox to hand me a gourmet sandwich. Let's just be honest, the difference between store bought gourmet and store bought not-gourmet is just how expensive the ingredients are, and yeah, spend more, get more, but not enough to really make a big difference in the quality of the sandwich.

However, this isn't store bought. The fathers' chef made this bread, smoked this turkey themselves, and the gardener grew these tomatoes and lettuce. Honestly, this is the best kind of gourmet—homegrown, homemade gourmet. It would surprise me if Chef Trellis hadn't made the mustard and mayo themselves.

I would be making porn noises over this sandwich if I had a voice. It is delicious and better savored with my eyes closed just so I can experience the taste profile without distractions. When I open my eyes after studying the first few bites, it's to a heated look from Fox, and I can't help getting a little horny for my future husband. I wag my eyebrows at him and then shoot him a salacious wink. Fox makes an almost inaudible noise in the back of his throat before lifting his hands to his mouth and…

He barks twice, yips, and then, "Arooooo."

Sadly, this is the person I took one look at and decided, this is the one; this is the man I'm going to marry someday.

Bellamy snorts and rolls his eyes, picks up a small rock from the ground and chucks it into the forest in front of us.

Fox takes my sandwich away and then drags me to my feet and pulls me into the woods. He finds a convenient tree and lifts me up as he pushes me against it. I wrap my legs around his waist as his mouth meets mine, and his frenetic energy sends us both spiraling into the heat of a sweet kiss and hot frot.

He reaches between us, pulls his dick out, and pops the button on my jeans open. He tears the zipper down, pulling my dick out and grabbing it up with his. The zing of pleasure sometimes shocks me when he does this, like it's so much better than masturbating even though it's just a hand.

Hard and frenzied, we both thrust into his hand, letting the pleasure build between us as quickly as possible. Sometimes a man just needs an afternoon quickie, and Fox is always happy to oblige me. My balls draw up and the tingles begin low on my spine, arcing up my back and over my entire body as we both make a mess of his hand together.

It's sexy as fuck and hot as hell, but also my lunch is in danger of attracting flies and I really don't want to waste it, so when my wonder of a man yanks his shirt over his head and cleans up our mess after only a couple of minutes, I'm not sad about that. At least not until I get a good look at my jeans. He *popped* the button right off and *tore* the zipper down without managing to unzip it.

I blow out a totally unrepentant breath at the mangled mess of my jeans and glance up at Fox, spreading my hands with a flourish to display the results of his enthusiastic *amore*.

The corners of his lips twitch in amusement, because of course he doesn't regret ruining my favorite jeans. I shake my head at him like I can't believe he wouldn't take my plight seriously, but then he knocks his head back toward our picnic area and takes my hand.

I don't know how it's been eight weeks and I still get butterflies when he takes my hand. He's my favorite person on this planet, and I hope I never lose my excitement at his touch. Have you ever just gotten lost in the wonder of your partner? Sometimes, I look at Fox, and yeah, I can see how very average he is physically, but all that normalcy is completely overshadowed by the wonder that exists below the surface, and I just get lost in him.

He entrances me.

And the more I get to know him, the more I have to focus on. Like right now, he's pulling out the extra set of laces I put in his backpack along with a pen knife. He sinks to his knees in front of me, and without a moment's hesitation, he starts poking holes into my jeans. What feels like moments later, he laces up the front of my jeans, and I look like I'm sporting the most colorful codpiece ever. It's just my underwear under the laces and the fact that I have a chubby from having Fox this close to my dick.

Does my dick know there's a knife close to it? Yes, and it thinks the fact that Fox would never accidentally hurt me is sexy as fuck.

"That's not at all indecent," Bellamy comments, arching a brow at the front of my barely-repaired pants.

I shoot him a brilliant smile just to fuck with him. Smiling brightly for no reason at all is a great way to throw people off their game. Besides, it makes me look like I'm up to something.

Bellamy narrows his eyes at me.

Something light hits me in the back, startling me.

I turn around, searching for what hit me, just in time to catch a pebble to the chest. Fox's quick reflexes grab it, and he studies it for a moment before licking it and tossing it back into the forest.

Bellamy throws a stick and yips.

Just what the actual fuck is happening here?

CHAPTER 10

At midafternoon, Fox stops near the peak of the mountain we've been zig-zagging up. In front of us is a wall of trees and boulders, and if I didn't absolutely trust Fox to the depths of my soul, I might question the sanity of dragging my lovely butt up the side of a mountain to be halted by an impenetrable wall of nature.

Bellamy also doesn't seem to have any trust issues, and in fact actively encourages the strange behavior of his Oppa by picking up a couple of sticks and banging them together like he did when Fox made that weird phone call.

Fox starts throwing small rocks at the wall like we are now reduced to using pebbles to siege nature, except that we didn't start with any good siege equipment. We're using pebbles from the start because that's the prepared people we are.

This is going to end well.

Loves of my life. What the actual fuck are you doing?

Fox checks my message, and since Bellamy's hands are full of sticks and he can't look at his phone without stopping his banging, Fox reads the message to him before answering.

"Asking the forest nymphs for passage."

Yeah, no. I would never have been able to guess that.

JENNIFER CODY

I mutely convey my next question, pressing my lips together, widening my eyes, turning my palms upward, and jerking them apart as if to ask, *How does this work?*

Fox scoops up another handful of forest floor and picks out the pebbles, throwing them at the rocks and trees. "We get their attention, and when they see us, they either let us through or they don't. We were invited."

So obviously they're going to let us through as soon as we've managed to get their attention.

So stick banging and throwing rocks at trees is supposed to get their attention?

"We have to use their connection to nature or they won't bother with us," Bellamy explains after Fox reads my message.

I give them both a flat look. They are ridiculous.

So we just need something loud and natural?

I don't even wait for them to respond to that. I point to Fox and then to the sky because my man is a fucking thunderbird and he is perfectly capable of calling up a thunderstorm. Something loud, natural, and very attention-grabby.

Bellamy and Fox exchange a look that says they both agree that my idea is far superior to theirs. My kid drops the sticks and then steps up next to me while Fox retreats toward the wall of nature. He looks up at the sky and magically a thunderstorm begins to build up above us.

Unlike his father, it takes Fox a little bit of time to build up the storm. Dakota can call up a thunderstorm with a blink and banish it with the same. Fox, on the other hand, takes at least half an hour to build up the storm. The hairs on my arms stand on end, and then lightning cracks above the trees, striking Fox's upturned face or possibly emanating from his face; it's hard to tell when things are happening at lightspeed.

A downpour blankets the forest after that, soaking us within half a minute, and then, like pulling Fox's ass cheeks apart (*I *handclap* am *handclap* watching *handclap* him *handclap* work; it makes me horny*), the boulder behind Fox just cracks down the middle and parts, revealing a glade full of—

Oh wow.

I rush forward through the opening, coming to a stop right in front of a nine foot tall sasquatch.

Holy shit.

I'm so glad I didn't make a guess on this one. I wasn't thinking sasquatch at all.

I wildly wave at them, unable to hold back my absolute delight at this turn of events. *Sasquatch!* All the unusual noises make sense now!

I turn on my heels and run back to Fox, throwing myself at him because he totally deserves a hug and all the positive reinforcement for letting me have this surprise. I kiss him all over his face and jump out of his arms, turning back to the group of sasquatches, who've been silently observing my overwhelming, enthusiastic excitement.

I wave, this time with a bright smile, clutching Fox's wrist.

The tallest of the group steps forward, speaking to Fox with a series of barks, yips, and howls and including some foot stomping, a thrown rock, and some stick banging.

Fox responds with more of the same, and then Bellamy puts in his two cents, and can I just ask, How did Bellamy learn the language of the sasquatch? Seriously. Fox has been around the block a time or two, or thirty-six hundred times. Bellamy is only thirty five, and I rescued him from Santanos just two months ago. When did he have time to learn Sasquatchish. Sasquatchese? Saskatchewan? No wait, that's a province in Canada…

Point being, did my kid spend time with the Skunk Apes of the Appalachians? And does he have an accent if he did? I think this is important to know! Does Bellamy have an accent in Sasquatchian?

One of the smaller sasquatches makes a break for it, running at me and snatching me up, hauling ass away with me thrown over their shoulder. I look back at Fox, who visually tracks my abduction while continuing to converse with the big sasquatch.

Bellamy barely glances at me before I am all but gone.

Well, at least I know I'm perfectly safe, even though it's a little strange that the little one decided to just take off with me and thought bum-rushing me was the best way to accomplish that.

Before I can get too far into that thought, the sasquatch tosses me off their shoulder into a soft bed of fresh leaves and grass inside a teepee-like structure where a whole gaggle of smaller sasquatches have gathered. The one that carried me here squats in front of me, eyeing me as I sit up and rearrange myself to face them.

"Do you have YouTube?" they ask in perfectly unaccented English.

I type out a response and show them my phone. *I do and I am willing to share, but you have to answer a couple of questions.*

"Ok? Why are you texting?"

I roll my eyes and point to my throat and shake my head.

They shrug. "How am I supposed to know you're mute? No one tells me anything."

I'll tell you whatever you want, but first! Do you call yourselves sasquatches or forest nymphs or what?

"We aren't forest nymphs. We're called the Mountain-Big-Tree-Sequoia-Forest-People. We have neighbors in Yosemite called the Mountain-Giant-Tree-Redwood-Yosemite-People. We describe ourselves by where we make our homes. If my tribe moved to Washington, we would change what we call ourselves to the Mountain-Glacier-Volcano-Danger-People, or something like that."

They shrug.

Interesting. What's your name and are you a child? I'm Romily, by the way. I'm not a child.

I'll have to put on the safe search settings for YouTube, depending on if this small person is a child and if the rest of these small ones are as well.

"I'm Less-Furry-Rabbit-Chaser-Berry-Nose. I'm a teenager. I let People-Who-Are-Not-My-Tribe call me Poppy."

Sounds good. I will call you Poppy unless you want me to call you Less-Furry-Rabbit-Chaser-Berry-Nose.

"No, it doesn't have the same ring to it as it does in my native language." And then Poppy demonstrates their name with a yip, hitting rocks together twice, an almost subvocal growl that makes the hair on the back of my neck stand on end, followed by a scream that sounds like La Llorona weeping on a river bank. They're right, typing out their name does not have the same ring to it as their name in their native language.

I'm also afraid to ask what the other kids' names are, so I pat the nest beside me and bring up YouTube. Fox will come rescue me when he's ready.

POPPY ISN'T SHY about taking control of the playlist for YouTube and focuses almost exclusively on Bigfoot videos, but about three videos in, Fox appears in the space we're occupying and knocks his head backward for me to come out. Poppy gives me huge, begging eyes, and tugs my phone out of my hands, and what do you know, I can't take their YouTube marathon away.

I leave them with my phone and steal Fox's right out of his pocket. The first thing I do is send out a group message to all the people who matter to let them know I am temporarily attached to Fox's phone.

Me via Fox's phone: *If anyone wants to get in touch with me (Romily), I am currently on Fox's phone because a Mountain-Big-Tree-Sequoia-Forest-People teenager has commandeered mine for YouTube after abducting me right out from under Fox's arm. Did Fox try to stop the teen? No, he did not. Did our lovely son, who's supposed to be my actual bodyguard? No. In fact, he didn't do much more than glance at me while I was stolen away from them.*

The Competition (Annette): *Awww. I'm torn! How am I supposed to choose between my sugar baby and sugar grandbaby?*

Chris (Bear): *Why would you have to choose between Romily and Bellamy? My grandson did nothing wrong.*

Fated Mate (my phone, obvs): *I wouldn't have hurt you!*

Red-Headed Step-Child (Bellamy): *It's impolite to use someone else's phone to interject into a conversation, and I question Romily's decision to include his own phone in this group message.*

Me: *It's rude to talk about someone behind their back. We do it in front of their face so they know what we're saying about them.*

McQueen (Dakota): *New phone. Who dis?*

Drama Demon (Amos): *OMG DID YOU LOSE YOUR PHONE AGAIN?*

Papa Smurf (Tag): *That wasn't Dakota. I'm sitting in his lap.*

McQueen (so, not Dakota, then): *If Dakota is the guy who used to own this phone, someone needs to babysit that dude. His situational awareness is the worst. I literally reached into his pocket and stole his phone while he was talking to me.*

Drama Demon: *I WILL FIND YOU. I WILL TAKE MY HUSBAND'S PHONE BACK AND THEN I WILL EAT YOU!*

McQueen: *Kinky.*

Me: *I don't know who you are, but you accidentally stole a phone that belongs to 1/10 of the council, and he's only kinda good, so maybe replace the sim card as soon as possible.*

Drama Demon: *BELLAMY IS OFFICIALLY MY FAVORITE.*

Papa Smurf: *Go find Dakota's phone before the thief destroys the sim card. Bring them home for dinner. I'm sure Trellis has a recipe that would suit them.*

McQueen: *Oooh. I've always thought Nantaimori was sexy!*

I do a quick google search of that term, because I know a lot of interesting kinks, but that's a new one for me. It's sploshing with sushi/sashimi, and the pictures of it are gorgeous; you should definitely google it.

Me: *You should definitely do that and send me pics. Also, there's a kid in this group chat, so no more of this. Poppy, do not look that word up.*

Poppy: *Too late. *vomiting emoji**

Me: *This group chat is officially closed. Text Fox if you need me.*

I turn my attention back to Fox, who is staring at his phone like he might regret every life choice he's ever made that led him to that conversation. I pat his chest and give him a sympathy hug.

His hands grip my hips and quietly, just the barest whisper in my ear, he says, "We have to find Omp's phone before Pater does. I do not need another step father."

This is the problem with having an open polycule of immortals for fathers.

We don't know that that person is male.

"He said 'nantaimori.' That's the male version of the kink," Fox replies quietly.

I guess he's not wrong about that.

How do we find him?

Fox takes a slow deep breath and releases it. "We create a rumor that Dakota let Bellamy borrow his phone because of Santanos' stalking, and we make sure that Santanos' people hear the rumor. Then we rescue whoever they find and get the phone back."

We are the good guys, right?

Fox's lips twitch, and he presses a kiss to my lips. "Most of the time."

CHAPTER 11

So it turns out Charlie is the shaman of the Mountain-Big-Tree-Sequoia-Forest-People, aka Bigfoots, which is apparently also ok to call them. They think it's funny that humans have whole shows dedicated to finding evidence of Bigfoot and then turn around and decide the evidence they do find is inconclusive. It's become a thing for Bigfoots to stalk the shows and videos done about them; sometimes they even participate for funsies.

Fox and I join a circle of Bigfoots surrounding Bellamy and Charlie, who sit opposite each other in front of a small, smokeless fire. The Bigfoots all have small rocks or sticks in hand and are scraping small divots into the ground with them, creating a susurrus around the two participants in the ceremony.

Charlie brings the three weapons that Bellamy favors—his sniper rifle, a shorter sword, and a normal length one. Look, swords are not my thing. I don't know the names of swords, but the normal one looks like what you would expect to see in a King Arthur-Merlin movie—also, I cannot be the only person who wants to see an MM version of that, right? Someone needs to get on the Arthur-Merlin fanship and make this happen for me. I also take book recs if you know of something that already exists.

Ahem.

So Charlie brings the three weapons that my kid favors and passes them through the smokeless fire. They set the weapons to the side and take Bellamy's hands in theirs, passing Bellamy's hands through the fire too. My son's skin bubbles up with blisters almost immediately, and he pulls in a hissed breath but doesn't jerk his hands out of Charlie's, which is impressive even if I'm a smidge worried about him. Charlie then places the weapons in Bellamy's hands and guides them through the fire again.

I can't help it; I tear up at the sight of my Bellamy's pain. Yes, he's mine. Of course, I am willing to share him because he deserves a big family that loves him, but yes, it hurts me to see him go through the pain of this ceremony to get bonded to his weapons. Surely there's a less painful way of doing this.

Fox takes my hand and squeezes it, leaning in close. "Magic is all about balance. He has to experience the same torment his weapons will inflict if he wants to bond with them. Their experience has to be his experience and vice versa. It's never painless to bond to a weapon because weapons inflict pain."

I guess we're lucky he doesn't have to die to be able to kill people with bonded weapons.

Charlie sprinkles some pink dust over Bellamy and the weapons, the fire flares up, and when I blink away the flares in my eyes, the weapons are hanging in mid-air, deadly ends pointed at Bellamy.

Fox's arm comes around me at the same moment both swords pierce his heart and the gun fires.

I jerk, almost getting away from Fox as a mixture of fear, grief, and anguish choke me. Fox tackles me to the ground and wraps all his limbs around me as I reach for Bellamy.

Charlie flings dirt—the shaman throws fucking *dirt*—at Bellamy. The fire flares up again, burning my outstretched hand with the heat of it, and when it dies back down, the weapons are scattered around Bellamy, who's hunched over, gasping.

If I had a voice I would be screaming. Screaming at all of them. *That's my Bellamy!*

"It's ok, he's ok. He's bonded again. He knew this would happen. I should have prepared you. It's ok. He's fine," Fox chants quietly in my ear.

Charlie pats Bellamy's head and stands before stomping out the fire with their big, hairy foot.

Bellamy grabs his weapons, returns them to the backpack he carried them up the mountain in, and turns toward me. He looks like a murder victim, not even exaggerating. There is blood all down his front from where he was just stabbed and shot. He's not gushing blood, but he is definitely still actively bleeding. His already pale skin looks ashen, and he's gaunt around the eyes and cheeks. Somehow even his hair looks like he died.

I elbow Fox and scramble out of his arms, grabbing Bellamy's shirt and ripping it open to see the damage.

I've seen this man naked on multiple occasions; I've seen his scars, but now I see them in a new light. There's two long silver scars that run from his elbows to his wrists and dead center in his chest is a crater that's obviously a bullet wound, but now, examining the latest bullet hole and the diamond shaped wounds from the swords, I want to vomit because I understand how he got the other scars.

This is the second time my kid has gone through a ceremony like this; it's the second time he's let his own weapons give him mortal wounds. Without magic, my Bellamy would have died doing this. I can't. I just cannot. This is—I *hate* it.

I grab Bellamy's face in my hands and make him look me in the eye, telling him with just my eyes that he is never, ever, *ever* doing this again. I would have vetoed it if I'd known he had to die to bond to his weapons. I tell him without words, without my messages, *Never again. Never. You will never put me through this again.*

Bellamy gives me a tired smile and leans his forehead against mine. "You can say that, Papa, but you're the one who's marrying an immortal. Have you already forgotten that we have to die to become immune to death?"

I grimace at him and click my teeth, and then it hits me that without his ward he's completely vulnerable to real death, and I shoot Fox a panicked look. We have to fix this. We have to fix his ward or have the fathers make him truly immortal or *something* because we live a dangerous life and I cannot lose Bellamy to it.

"I'm thirty five years old, and I've only 'died' a couple of times. I'm pretty sure I can keep alive long enough for my ward to fix itself. You don't have to do anything more drastic than leave me home for a few weeks."

I snort, take the rest of his shirt off and ball it up, pressing it against his no-longer mortal but still bleeding wounds.

Fox kneels in the grass next to me, pressing our sides together. "We have to get approval for an extended period of non-activity, or you will lose your Acolyte status. Technically you are training to be the next generation of Reaper to replace me. When I sign off on your promotion you become a Reaper."

I didn't know that, and by the surprise on Bellamy's face, neither did he.

"I read the document that explained Acolytes, and if I recall, there wasn't any mention of being a Reaper-in-training," Bellamy says, reflecting my own thoughts on the matter.

Fox almost sighs, but he controls his breathing too well to give away his exasperation in front of non-family people. "There was a council meeting when rumors of your failed ward reached Santanos' ears. The representative of evil challenged whether you could remain an Acolyte without a ward and was pushing to have you delivered back to Santanos. The challenge forced the good representatives to clarify the purpose of an Acolyte and what would constitute the dereliction of duty. I was told twenty minutes ago of the changes to your status."

I wrap Bellamy up in a protective hug, staring at Fox with a challenging look. It's not directed at him; it's directed at the whole fucking world that wants to take my son away from me. I will fight anyone for custody of Bellamy.

One side of Fox's mouth lifts into a half smile that he doesn't even bother to suppress before he leans in and kisses me. "Of course we aren't giving up our kid."

Bellamy sighs, but he has long since surrendered to our parental love. "Thirty-five years of keeping myself alive doesn't count toward my life-skills at all, does it?"

I kiss his cheek, Fox kisses his other, and I shoot him a bright smile.

"Now you're getting it," Fox murmurs.

Bellamy gives up, leaning his head on Fox's shoulder. "Fine, but can I please get some food, a nap, and a couple of stitches?"

As if we would withhold anything our kid needs. What kind of monsters does he think we are?

CHAPTER 12

Source of All Evil: Ferguson Appleby, 161 Kings Canyon Rd, Fresno CA. 04:15 AM
Me: *I'm pretty sure I'm on vacation until Tuesday.*
Source of All Evil: *Time off approval retracted.*
Me: **flat glare* Why?*
Source of All Evil: *The reason for the time off was fulfilled.*

I glare at my phone screen, trying to decide how to respond to that. How is this government entity capable of being both unreasonable and hard to argue with? Argh.

I glance over at Bellamy, who is currently cuddling his weapons on the bed in our hotel room. Don't worry, I snapped a photo of him sleeping with his lovies, and yes we are keeping him close in case something happens with his wounds.

I reach over and turn his phone over, lighting up the message that the depot sent to his phone. As I'm a wonderful father, since the message delivered silently, and because I have learned my lesson about trying to shake Bellamy awake, I set the alarm on my phone to the arooga of a ship, turn the volume all the way up, and put it on the dresser well out of reach.

I strip out of my pajama pants in the bathroom and turn on the shower, stepping in as soon as it warms up. Unfortunately the walls are not thin enough for me to hear what happens when my alarm goes off a few minutes later, at least not until the bathroom door swings open, letting in the loud cursing of a southern gentleman. The door closes quickly, and Fox steps into the shower with me, shaking his head at me.

"Romily." He sounds like he's chastising me, but the only real effect his tone has is taking my dick from plump to hard.

I grin at him and poke him with my dick, batting my lashes innocently up at him.

He leans down and brushes his nose against mine. "You have to sleep."

Oh.

Well, if that's what this is about...

I peck a kiss to his lips and pat him over his heart, conveying that everything is fine. No, I didn't sleep, but I think that's a perfectly reasonable reaction to seeing a member of my family stabbed and shot. We know I don't do well with bullet holes in my people; of course, I'm going to have some trouble sleeping when one of them is shot.

"You better not be fucking," Bellamy interrupts as he swings the bathroom door open.

I quickly turn Fox around and push my pelvis into his ass and throw the curtain open, waving wildly at Bellamy.

Fox immediately starts moaning, deadpan as you like. "Oh. Ah. Hah. More."

Bellamy puts up both his hands, blocking our lower halves from his view. "Why would you open the curtain? I just need my toothbrush!"

Fox moans again, smirking at Bellamy as I giggle, digging my now interested cock into his ass crack—honestly his voice just makes me wish I was actually fucking him.

I point to the door and make the shooing motion.

Bellamy grimaces at me. "I'll be in my room."

I shoo him again, close the curtain, and take all my Fox-induced lust out on my man's ass.

∽

SOURCE OF ALL EVIL: *Jae Hamil, 120 Van Ness Ave, Fresno CA 4:45AM*

JENNIFER CODY

I arch a brow at the text as I lean back in the seat of the car parked outside of the gas station where Ferguson is going to die this morning. Next to me, Bellamy hums in response to the depot's message. We're early by fifteen minutes, which is unusual for the depot—they're usually on the ball with how long it will take us to get from location to location.

The person who drove us turns his head to look at us. He's young-looking and bald on top with the hair he has on the sides grown out long and in a low, blond ponytail. Baldilocks studies me as much as I study him, and when he's decided he's had his fill he gives me a little shake of his head.

"This is the weirdest day of my life," he decides.

Bellamy's face is hidden beneath his dark assassin's hood, but I sense the zero-fucks expression he usually wears when we're on the job radiating from beneath the hood. He's not going to engage the driver, but I don't have the same reputation to uphold as either Bellamy or Fox, so I type out my message and show the driver my phone.

What? You don't spend all day every day with a retired assassin and a Harbinger?

The driver snorts and shakes his head. "No, dude. They warned me you were mute but didn't mention that you'd have anyone with you. Do you guys usually hire drivers last minute? Normally my company requires at least twenty-four hours' notice for out of city drives. It doesn't matter, I was on the night shift anyway, but the guy who needed a ride in was just weird, ya know? I'm used to the freaks out here, but that guy was creepy as fuck—"

"What guy? Did you bring someone to our hotel when you came to get us?" Bellamy questions before I can get the same words typed out.

"Yeah, he said he was meeting some guy named Fox there. He had purple hair. Scary dude. I think he had his teeth sharpened or sharp caps put on them or something. Wicked canines."

Me to Fox: *Where are you?*

Bellamy lifts his phone to his ear and in just a moment he says, "Where are you?"

I lean my ear in close, holding up a finger to the talkative driver.

"I'm just getting to Fresno," Fox replies. *"Why?"*

"Because our driver dropped Tala or someone who looks like him off at our hotel to meet you," Bellamy explains.

"Didn't happen."

Bellamy hums his acknowledgment and tells Fox to be careful before hanging up. "Something's a bit fishy."

A black sedan with dark, tinted windows pulls into the parking space next to us, and a woman wearing a black and white suit gets out of the driver's seat and opens the back door. A man in a leopard print suit and bug-eye dark sunglasses, holding a gold embossed cane, steps out of the car. The woman pays particular attention to me and Bellamy until she, the man in the loud suit, and two other people in black and white suits enter the gas station.

I take a deep breath and glance over at Bellamy.

"Oooh man. Did you see that? That was Ferguson Appleby. He owns a record company. I auditioned with them last time they held open auditions, and I almost made it to the final cut, but my cousin broke my toe while I was dancing and—"

Bellamy gets out of the car without waiting for the driver to finish his story, and I follow him out even though I want to hear the rest of the story. I give the driver a sympathetic frown and hold up a finger to indicate I expect him to wait.

"Oh yeah, sure thing. I got your itinerary right here." He taps the phone mounted to the dash and connected to the radio-gps-map-backup-camera-multimedia-device thing. Whatever it's called.

I duck back into the car and indicate for him to show me the itinerary because that sounds super formal, and considering I've only gotten two texts from the depot, this should be enlightening.

The dude taps his phone and the app that gives him directions shows me a list of…1, 2, 3, 4…17 stops. Seventeen stops from Bakersfield to Fresno to Modesto. Just what the actual fuck is the depot doing? There isn't enough time in the day for this many kills.

I purse my lips and jump back out of the car, moving around the front to where Bellamy awaits with his shorter sword drawn.

That guy has a list of seventeen places we're going all over this part of the state.

Bellamy reads his message, illuminating his face under the assassin hood, and then puts his phone away. "Would you like to bet on who's behind that list?"

I'm mute, not dumb. The last time we went on a killing spree, Santanos was behind it, putting his own people on Fox's list for his own agenda. And since I'm morally gray at best, I do the thing that Fox suggested yesterday.

Me: *I'll pay you a hundred dollars to spread the rumor that Bellamy is using Dakota's phone to avoid Santanos' stalking.*

FuckFace (Darcy, of course): *I'd do that for fun.*

Me: *Make it quick.*

FuckFace: *Something going on?*

Me: *Santanos is up to something again.*

Fuckface: *Text me if you need a tracker.*

Me: *You're the top of my list.*

Fuckface: *I am your list.*

Me: *Only because I haven't bothered to add anyone else to it.*

FuckFace: **laughing emoji**

I put my phone away and make grabby hands at Bellamy.

I grin when he automatically hands me his phone. I'm proud of myself for training my boy so well. I drop his phone on the ground and point to his sword and then the phone with a wide smile.

Bellamy stares at me for a moment before sighing and stabbing his sword through his phone like I told him to. He doesn't even fight me on it, and also, the concrete beneath the sword cracks and shatters. When Bellamy pulls his sword out of it, part of the slab comes up with the sword and the phone.

Gingerly, so that I don't accidentally cut myself because that would be my luck, I help him get the concrete and phone off his sword.

Bellamy wipes the blade on his pants and inspects it. "You're bad for my weapons," he mutters as he jerks his head to the door into the gas station.

CHAPTER 13

I squeeze Bellamy's shoulder before walking into the gas station, squinting against the ridiculously bright lighting inside. The entourage all look at me, then their focus turns to the man at my back.

Look, I know he is perfectly capable, but can I just express how stupid it is to bring a sword to a gun fight?

The three people acting as bodyguards for Ferguson put their hands on their sidearms and come in close to their client.

I wave at them with a smile and go to the cash desk where a giant muscle bro type stands watching the byplay of the tension in the room while completely ignoring an actual customer.

I tap the counter next to the customer's hand, and she startles and whips around to face me.

I lift my hands up, palms facing her to assure her that I'm not armed, and since we're about the same size, I'm barely a physical threat to her. She's pretty, but the smile that comes to her face in response to mine lights up the room with its beauty. Some people are just prettier when they smile, and she's one of them.

I use all my lovely non-verbal communication skills to tell her what's going on. I point to Bellamy, and then to Ferguson, and then make the motion of cutting my own neck with my finger while I make that creaky murder-death sound that accompanies that gesture. I maintain my happy smile and point to the door, and because I'm nice, I pull a twenty dollar bill off my cash clip and push it toward the cashier to pay for her fountain drink and beef jerky.

Her smile has all but faded and her eyes widen as understanding dawns on her. She quickly jogs out, and I look up at the cashier with a shrug.

He gives me a pleading look that's so full of the desperation I'm far too familiar with. "Please don't kill me," he whispers. "If I leave I'm going to get fired, and I just started this job."

I reach over and pat his forearm, empathizing completely with his predicament as I point to the floor behind the cash desk and mime ducking down.

The dude—his name tag says his name is Edovard—gives me a confused look, not understanding my non-verbal cues. He's adorable, if a bit dumb, and Bellamy saves me from testing out his literacy.

"He's telling you to duck behind the cash desk."

"Oh," Edovard falters, starting to lower himself, aborting the move to look at us again, and then giving up and hiding.

I turn, crossing my arms and leaning against the cash desk as I lock eyes on the person Fox will be here in a minute to kill.

He's still browsing the candy aisle like he has nothing to worry about, and his entourage is staring holes into Bellamy, who comes to stand next to me with his sword in hand.

The woman driver/bodyguard wears a neutral expression and watches us like a hawk, which, let's be honest, she definitely should be. I'm a little surprised that she hasn't actually drawn her weapon, considering we're not being subtle about what we're here to do. I mean, I clearly indicated her client's imminent death, soooooo…

Oh right! I nearly forgot!

I turn on my heels and lean over the counter, tapping Edovard, who's in the crash position with his hands behind his head, because that will save him from a bullet wound for sure. He jumps and screams and turns terrified eyes on me, so I give him a compassionate smile and a gentle pat, then point to the phone display and show him my cash clip.

Bellamy needs a new phone. Obviously.

Edovard looks between my money and somewhere in the general vicinity of the phones, and the lost souls of his ancestors paint confusion on his face. Poor guy. He's big and strong and intimidating, but he's a little bit of a himbo, isn't he?

I give him my you're-adorable expression and pat his head like he's a good puppy because he clearly needs positive reinforcement. He smiles at me like he gets that I think he's wonderful and then goes back to hiding in the crash position.

He's adorable.

Honestly, I would adopt him too because he's just so cute and kinda dumb and he might need a keeper. Unfortunately, I can't just claim any adult now that the whole Acolyte thing is defined as a stepping stone to Reaper, but I would if I could, because Edovard is the best kind of puppy: already potty trained and presumably capable of feeding himself.

Since he clearly isn't going to be super helpful, I hop up and over the counter and grab a couple of prepaid phones, patting Edovard's head on the way by. The product in his hair makes my hand a little sticky, but since I'm not wearing one of my nice suits—because I didn't expect to be working—I just wipe it off on my shorts.

As I come back around to Bellamy, the door swings open with a digital doorbell sound and in walks Tala with his sword drawn and a wicked smirk on his lips. He grins at me and Bellamy.

"I thought I was going to be late," he laughs.

Bellamy immediately moves in front of me to a guard position, which causes the entourage of bodyguards around Ferguson to draw their weapons in response.

My ever-polite son sounds almost bored as he greets the Luna wolf that stole Fox's previous job. "Whyever are you here, Tala?"

Tala shoots him a wicked smirk and winks. "Why, I believe I'm here to kill a man, Bella," he teases, taking on an exaggeration of Bellamy's accent.

"Which one?"

Tala chuckles and then his body sort of…um…listen, I don't have a lot of experience with sci-fi in visual media, but there was this one game that the boys in my foster home liked to play called *Borderlands*, and one of the characters that you could play had this superpower where she could turn invisible and then run really fast, and it was called phase walking or phase shifting or something. Yeah, that's what Tala does, but in real life.

Literally, he disappears, a shimmer moves from the door across the gas station, and then Ferguson's head is no longer attached to his body and Tala is standing behind the line of bodyguards holding it in one hand with his bloody sword in the other.

I kinda feel like that's cheating, but also, not gonna lie, it's almost as sexy as Fox—

Who just walked in. Yay.

The bodyguards are sort of a mess. Like, they see that their client is dead, obviously, but then there's a guy with a sword behind them and another guy with a hundred pounds of guns and ammo walking in, and it takes them, like, point three seconds to decide their lives are in immediate danger, and bullets start flying. At Fox, of course, and Tala, because obviously, but also at Bellamy, who grunts before I get in front of him with my ward to shield him.

Fear freezes up my limbs for a second, but no, I am not going to let these fuckers kill my Bellamy. I tackle him to the ground and cover his body with mine and hope with every atom that my ward protects us both.

Moments after I hit the floor on top of Bellamy, a head lands right next to my face. Gross.

What I wouldn't give to be able to tell these idiots that they could have lived if they'd kept their heads about them…

snicker *side eye*

This is what happens when you enjoy macabre humor.

The next thing that lands is a hand, and then all the thunderous gunfire stops, and the void leftover sounds like ringing in my ears, so I look around to find Fox and Tala going at it with their swords.

The bodyguards are all dead—no surprise there. Do not attack my future husband and expect to be alive on the other side of that.

Poor Tala's going to be dead soon, and I kinda liked him.

Shouldn't have messed with F—*what the fuck!!!*

Tala disappears and reappears right behind Fox. He swings his sword in a downward arc and cuts through Fox's body from his neck to his sternum.

Fox swings around, taking the sword out of Tala's hand, who jumps back and holds his hands up in surrender.

Fox bares his teeth at the wolf and snaps a bite at him. "If you want your sword back, you'll have to come and get it."

Aaand I'm hard. Seriously, my inappropriate boners might be giving me a complex, but growly Fox looking at a wolf like he's prey has got to be in the top three sexiest things Fox has ever done.

Tala tilts his head to the side and lets out a breathy sigh. "Consider it yours, Fox, but the kill is mine and I'm taking the head."

Fox's expression falls blank again, and he kicks the dropped head of the record company owner back to Tala. "You could get paid more as a Reaper."

Tala grins as he picks up the severed head. "I don't kill people for the money."

He dips his chin at me and winks. "You clean up good, Harbinger."

I breathe out a dry, "Haahaa," which just comes out sounding like a loud breath because, ya know, no vocal cords, and Tala does that phase shifting thing out the door.

I turn to Bellamy, who's bleeding from his cheek where a bullet grazed him, giving him an expectant expression because I need to know if he's actually hurt or if the bleeding cheek is the extent of his injuries.

He gives me a sour look. "I was fine until someone decided to throw me to the floor and rip my stitches out."

I scoff at that while lifting his shirt to check on the stitching.

It's fine. He's fine. They are barely weeping a tiny amount of blood, and it's not like the skin around them is hot or flushed. He's just exaggerating.

I roll my eyes at him and drop his shirt, turning my attention to the man with a sword stuck in him. I shake my head at Fox and wag my finger once, because we both know I am very bad with first aid.

Bellamy sighs behind me and pushes ahead, grabbing the handle of the sword behind Fox and lifting it out of his body.

Fox's eyes twitch, the only indication of the pain he's in, and then he checks all the straps of his accoutrements. That's right, my boyfriend makes sure all his guns and ammo are properly affixed to his person before addressing the gaping slash in his body. I will never get used to his priorities.

The *ktchk* of the staple gun Bellamy uses to hold Fox's flesh together echoes through the silent gas station until the entry door opens and our driver pokes his head in.

"Um, we're going to be late if we don't get to the next stop," he lets us know and then grimaces at the blood and gore all around us before disappearing back outside.

I take a deep breath as Bellamy finishes with Fox and turn to check on Edovard, leaning over the counter and patting his arm again.

He startles and screams and jumps up before freezing at the sight of the massacre. Truly, I feel a little bit sorry for him—it's hard when it's your first blood bath. Death isn't always easy to come to grips with.

He appears physically fine, but his rich terra-cotta skin is pallid and wan, and the poor guy looks like maybe he might throw up, so I back out of the line of fire and click my fingers to get my boys' attention.

They both glance at Edovard, then Fox shrugs, winces, and comes over to me, pressing his forehead against mine

"It's already stitching back together," he assures me, and follows that up by taking me by hand to the coffee machine and getting me a hot cup of nasty gas station brew.

Honestly, he's spoiled me on his fancy coffee, but I'll take every cup of gross gas station coffee he offers me because I appreciate the care he takes with me.

He presses a kiss to my lips, turns me around, and smacks my butt. "Go on. I'll meet you at the next one."

I can't help the smile that creeps across my lips as I start walking to the door, pointing my finger up toward the ceiling and waving it in a circle in the universal sign of *Let's go!* and pointing to the exit.

I could step over or go around the head that is currently between me and the door, but someone has put a live wire inside me and all my normal levels of human energy are hyped up like I've been cutting cocaine with caffeine powder, so I kick the head out of my way to use up some of the jitter juice in my muscles.

I know, I should probably have my head examined and spend some time on a therapist's sofa, but I've got way more important things to do than that right now. That's not to say it isn't important to make your mental health a priority; I just happen to be prioritizing the psycho part of my psyche right now.

Outside, the air quality almost startles me—yeah, I am totally nose blind to the scent of a bloodbath these days. Our driver, whose name I should probably learn because convenience is a thing and "the driver" isn't nearly as convenient as something like "Edovard," is standing with his door open, and when he sees me, he jumps into the driver's seat and starts the car.

I climb into the back behind him, Bellamy climbs into the back beside me, and Edovard takes the front passenger seat.

For some reason.

I—I don't know what is happening right now. I am pretty smart, and usually I can figure out what's going on, but Edovard joining us is a total mystery to me. Not that I don't like him; I was the one who thought about keeping him.

The driver immediately backs out of the parking spot and starts heading to our next destination.

Bellamy and I exchange a glance then he leans forward and taps Edovard's shoulder, and the huge man startles and yelps and turns around with wide, terrified golden brown eyes.

"What are you doing?" Bellamy asks the man.

All of Edovard's muscles are tense, but he looks forward immediately. "Nothing. I ain't doing nothing."

"I see," Bellamy sits back and looks at me like this is my fault for some reason, and then that jackass points to the man in the front seat. "That's your problem."

I drop my jaw like I'm shocked—spoiler alert: I'm not. I'm in charge of the crazy that happens in our family, and this counts as family craziness—and bring out my phone, typing a message to Edovard and showing it to him.

Me: *What are you doing?*

Edovard gingerly takes the phone and types a message under mine.

Edovard: *I'm not doing anything. I'm just sitting here.*

He hands my phone back and then deliberately places his hands on his legs, palms up, and shows them to me by pointing his nose at them and bobbing his head.

Me: *I can see that. Is there a reason you're sitting there?*
Edovard: *Do you want me to sit back there?*
Me: *I don't think you'd fit back here, buddy.*
Edovard: *I didn't think so either.*
Me: *Ok. good talk.*

Edovard doesn't respond to that except to bob his head again and put his hands back on his thighs.

I show Bellamy the message exchange.

I have no idea what is happening right now.

Bellamy shakes his head and pretends like the witness to our last murder joining us for the next one is totally normal.

CHAPTER 14

*S*ketchy Liars Who Go Back On Their Word About Vacations (I might have edited the depot's nickname): *Conrad Gribble. 223 N. 1st St, Fresno Ca. 5:15am*

Seriously, this is ridiculous. Does the depot not have Reapers in California? It seems like they would have Reapers all over the world and wouldn't necessarily need to send Fox on an actual killing spree in California because he happens to be here when we were supposed to have a few days off.

Something super sketch is going on.

The bank where our next victim is probably currently making the rounds as a security guard is closed, locked down tight, and also, this isn't a heist movie and we don't have a plan for how to get inside.

What the fuck?

Bellamy hums softly as we both get out. I come around to his side, staring at the locked up bank building while he assesses it.

"Hey, um, should I stay here or come with you?" Edovard asks through the window he rolled down.

Bellamy gives me a pointed look and walks away. Obviously he's sticking to the this-is-my-problem thing.

I pat Edovard's square cheek and then kinda massage it. Would you look at that! Muscle-boy's cheeks are also muscley! His face is hard as a rock! I put both hands on his cheeks and massage them, trying to figure out how he got his face bulked out too. Does he eat actual rocks???

Bellamy clicks his tongue and reaches over to stop me from harassing Edovard, but I grab his hand and force him to feel the cheek muscles on this guy, while my adorable lost little puppy looks up at us confused.

Bellamy hums in surprise and also takes Edovard's face in his hand, checking it out the same way.

Edovard puts up with our fondling until Bellamy lets him go.

"Impressive," Bellamy decides and then turns back to the problem at hand.

Because of course he couldn't tell Edovard to stay in the car or leave or go home or anything. Edovard's *my* problem.

Me: *We're going to be breaking into a bank and then killing someone; do you want to come watch that?*

Edovard's lips move as he reads my words, and then he reads them again before typing out his response.

Edovard: *I kinda got sick when you killed those other people. Can I just stay in the car?*

Me: *Sure thing, buddy. Our driver will look after you.*

Edovard gives me a relieved smile and sits back in his seat, putting his hands in that awkward placement on his thighs. Does he enjoy sitting that way? It's a very...well, I mean, I've recently binge-read a bunch of super cute, sweet BDSM romances and it's a very submissive pose, if you know what I mean. It was last week; I found an author with like a hundred books in her back list between two pen names. I'm *so* into her puppy play books, FYI, and I could totally see Edovard putting on a hood and chasing a ball. He'd be adorable.

Hence why I think he needs a keeper.

I click my fingers at the driver and point to Edovard, motioning for the man to watch him by pointing at my eyes with my fingers in a vee and motioning them toward Edovard. He needs someone to look after him, especially after he got into the car with an assassin and his handler—I mean accomplice—I mean...

Well, I'm a Harbinger, so I guess I'm the advance scout? Hmm, actually, I kinda like that. Makes me seem like a danger-seeking adventurer and ninjaish. Look at me sneak into this bank to let the security guard know Fox is coming to kill him. Or her. Honestly, the only person we know for sure is in the bank is the security guard, and from a distance they didn't have a pronounced gender.

I'm thinking that maybe I should take Fox's idea and just refer to everyone in my head as a they/them until they make it clear what their pronouns are. Seems respectful and less chance of making an asshole of myself.

Look at me go, learning from my life partner like I'm supposed to.

Bellamy lets his shoulder rest against mine as I come to a stop next to him, looking at the front facade of the bank. "Anything we do will set off the alarms, and this isn't a bank owned by the council, Annette, or Santanos. Whatever we do will attract the attention of the human authorities."

So we have to be fast and get out quickly. Which is good because we have another job in half an hour.

"Something is going on with the depot," Bellamy mutters. "Break the glass or the lock?"

I know this is coming from me, but I've never actually known a human who would put up with incessant knocking for very long, so I walk up to the front door and start knocking. It's a rapid staccato, loud as hell, and might actually set off the alarms anyway, but if the alarms go off because of my knocking, then the police are probably used to getting dispatched for high winds, and that won't exactly light a fire under them to get here quickly.

"What are you doing?" Bellamy questions, clearly taken aback by my genius.

I give him a duh-look and use my free hand to emphasize my knocking hand.

"Yes, I can see that. Why are you knocking?"

I roll my eyes and look through the glass.

The security guard is standing across from me and clearly indicating with their body language that they are not opening the door.

I send them a bright smile, wave like an excited kid, and keep knocking. My knuckles are beginning to hurt, but that's ok. The sound of Fox pulling up in our rental reaches me as the security guard starts gesturing in earnest for me to stop, so I give them another, brighter smile like I have no idea what they're going on about and continue knocking.

The security guard's patience breaks and they come marching toward me. I feel more than see Bellamy back away, and just as the person inside the bank stops in front of the glass, the window shatters on the heels of a loud gunshot, and the security person collapses with a dramatic hole in their head. I lean over to make sure they're dead, noting that, even from a few feet away, they still appear completely non-binary.

"Want to guess?" Fox asks me, kissing my temple as he pulls me away.

I shrug and look up at him, because they looked human except for being shiny-bald and androgynous.

He presses his mouth to my ear and quietly whispers, "I vant to suck your blood."

I giggle, huffing out my laughter. I guess he just killed a vampire. But wait.

No stake to the heart or sunlight or something equally unlikely?

Fox stops next to my ride, glancing at Edovard before answering. "Imagine the kind of creature that would have evolved if their ancestors lived in caves, were nocturnal, and their main source of safe hydration and nutrients came from the creatures that could travel far and wide for food and water. They learned to mimic their prey because their prey was smart, mobile, and vicious about survival. Add magic to that evolutionary puddle and you get vampires. They're only hard to kill because they're survivalists, not because you can only kill them a certain way."

I'll never take for granted that my usually breviloquent Fox will clarify in detail any misconceptions I might have because I'm new to his world and my only education is pop culture. It's a gift he gives me, and it makes me feel loved when he does.

I lean up on my toes and peck a kiss to his lips, thanking him for the explanation.

The corners of his lips twitch into a tiny version of his surprisingly happy smile, and then he makes a small gesture toward Edovard, asking without words for an explanation.

I press my lips into a line and shake my head with a dramatic shrug just as my phone dings.

Sketchy Liars Who Go Back On Their Word About Vacations: *Vivienne Solano, 426 N. Figarden Dr, Fresno CA. 5:45am*

Me: *Are you trying to get us caught up in a spree killer manhunt?*

Fresno isn't that big of a city compared to home, so three major murders in an hour is a big deal.

Sketchy Liars Who Go Back On Their Word About Vacations: *Cleaners ETA: two minutes.*

I narrow my eyes at their response and show Fox the message thread, arching a brow and making it clear I'm a little sussed out by the depot right now.

"It's unusual that they aren't directly overhead already," he responds, though he's not as concerned by the weird way the depot is acting as I am.

I look upward, searching the early morning for shadows, but see nothing until a heavy weight lands directly on my shoulder. I do not jump out of my skin—mainly because whatever is on me weighs a hundred pounds, making movement that isn't directly to the ground impossible.

Fox snatches the weight off me as I hit my knees on the asphalt and clicks his tongue at the stone gargoyle cradled in his arm. It's smaller than the gargoyles that usually guard our brownstone, and its eyes are huge by comparison, staring up at Fox under two oversized bat ears sticking up from its bald head. It puts its bony, little, clawed thumb in its mouth and curls its spindly little legs up under its wings, which swaddle it, wrapping all the way around it.

It's the most adorable gargoyle I've ever seen.

Fox taps its snubby nose. "Where's your dada, baby?"

As soon as that question leaves his mouth, we hear the chiming of a dozen church bells all around us, gorgeous in their song but loud enough to make it hard to think. I grin at the noise, delighted to have the gargoyles here and cleaning up after us. They're nothing if not super reliable and just lovely to have around. Their magic will wipe away the evidence of our passing. It's nice to know that we won't ever be caught by human authorities because our friends have our backs.

"What is that?" the driver demands, leaning over Edovard to shout through his open window.

Bellamy leans down and looks in at the driver, shouting over the din, "The cleaners."

"Are they coming in a helicopter?" the driver demands with a note of panic.

"How else are they supposed to get here?" Bellamy asks as if the driver should already know this.

I guess our driver is as blind to magic as most humans. Weird. I mean, Fox is clearly holding a baby and interacting with it, but all the driver notices is the noise.

I point to the baby gargoyle in Fox's arms and motion in a circle at the noise. I kiss my Fox's cheek, blow a kiss into the air, and climb into the back of the car, pulling Bellamy with me. Honestly, we don't have time to fuck around with my favorite guardians, but at least they're here and happy to see us.

As soon as we're settled, I tap the driver and show him my phone.

What's your name?

"Yeah, I'm not telling you that. I'm getting paid to drive you; I'm not giving away any kind of information that could be used to find me when you're done killing random people."

Ok. We're going to call you Buttercup.

Because that sounds as ridiculous as his reasoning for not sharing his name.

"Sure. Call me Buttercup," the driver deadpans.

Bellamy quietly huffs a laugh beside me, making no attempt to hide his amusement. "Onward, Buttercup. There's fuckery to spread."

CHAPTER 15

So. Modesto's nice. Not what I expected based on the one movie I've seen that mentioned it. It's got more touristy things than I expected. Also a really high crime rate if the ten targets Fox killed are any indication. Well, a high murder rate anyway.

Ok, listen—*side eye*—Fox only kills people who have actually upset the balance between good and evil, so killing ten targets in one moderate size city is kinda a lot. A few of them had people loyally protecting them, so between him and Bellamy (who, against my vehement protests, decided to participate in a few of the jobs), we actually ended up killing fifteen people in Modesto before noon.

Fifteen murders *in Modesto* one late summer morning is weird, right?

I mean, when I think of the city, I think of nice neighborhoods and middle-class America, not people so evil that they actually imbalance the entire world.

Anyway, since Edovard decided to accompany us from Fresno to Modesto and all the way back to Bakersfield, we decided to put him in Bellamy's hotel room for the night. My son might be staring daggers at me from across the dinner table, but since Edovard is sitting directly across from me, I'm pretending I don't feel his glare.

I have a lot of questions for Edovard that I haven't gotten to ask since he fell asleep between Fresno and Modesto, and then Buttercup decided to occupy him with stories about the L.A. Lights after that. Apparently sometime before I was born, some UFOs decided Phoenix was a fun place to be, and since then every time something moderately interesting happens anywhere, we harken back to the Phoenix Lights in our naming traditions.

Anyway, back to Edovard.

Me: *Edovard. That is your name right?*

Edovard takes my phone and types out his reply. I should probably tell him that he can talk to me, but I'm mildly amused that he takes the time to type instead.

Edovard: *Edovard Durand Folange. It's French. Can I ask your name?*

Me: *I'm Romily Butcher, and my boyfriend is Arlington Fox, but everyone calls him Fox, and our son is Bellamy Jones.*

Edovard looks between the three of us, visibly confused, and Fox sighs, taking my phone and sending the messages to the group chat. Fox and Bellamy's phone's both chime as Fox hands me back my phone and Bellamy reads the conversation so far.

Bellamy lets out a heavy breath and taps the table next to Edovard's hand.

Side note: Edovard is keeping his hands on top of the table in that weird palm up supplicant-y position.

"Edovard, do you have your phone on you?" Bellamy asks.

Edovard's eyes widen a bit in fear and he bites his lush bottom lip, giving Bellamy a tight nod.

Bellamy gives me the evil eye and jerks his head toward Edovard, telling me in plain Mutese that Edovard is *still* my problem.

Look, if the verbal are allowed to combine words to create new languages like Franspanol and Spanglish, I'm allowed to name my main form of communication too. We are now calling it Mutese. Wait. Mutish. No. Mutiny. *laughing while crying emoji* We'll stick to Mutese.

I stick my tongue out at him because parents should always be an example to their children.

side-eye

I didn't say they had to be a good example; sometimes we are excellent examples of what not to do. Just saying. Parenthood has taught me so many things in such a short time.

Me: *If you give me your phone number then I can just text you instead of giving you my phone.*

Edovard's eyebrows wrinkle with visible confusion, but he pulls his phone out and unlocks it before handing it to me with his contact info on the screen.

I enter his phone number and add him to the group chat.

Me: *So, Edovard. How long are you planning on hanging out with us?*

Edovard moves his lips while silently reading, which I find adorable, if I'm honest, but also makes me wonder if he has a learning challenge like dyslexia or something, in which case we need to accommodate him, because we're murderers, not assholes.

He looks around with visible confusion again before wrinkling his face up and typing out a response. Midway through typing he suddenly freezes up and glances up at me in abject terror.

Puppers (we all knew I was going to give him a nickname, and this one just fits): *I don't know. Am I supposed to choose the day and time?*

I stare in consternation at my phone, feeling like I'm missing something. I don't think I've done anything to make him afraid of me. Well, beyond the whole killing thing, but he came with us. That shouldn't be something that scares him when he *chose* us, right?

Me: *Do you want to go home?*

Edovard looks at his phone with big worried eyes.

Puppers: *Am I allowed to go home?*

Fox makes a noise in his throat and sort of nudges me. "Edovard—" he says the name with a French accent and it just sounds like Edward, but French. "Do you think you're a hostage?"

My jaw drops, and my eyes go wide, and I stare at Edovard agog.

Edovard doesn't take his eyes off his phone, he just nods and two fat drops of sadness hit the table top.

Oh my hell no. This beautiful puppy thought he was my hostage all day? How terrifying for him.

I jump out of my chair and grab him up in a tight hug, giving Fox the saddest expression I can make so he knows what to tell Edovard for me.

"We're sorry that we made you think you were our hostage. You're not. You are free to go home whenever you want. Romily is very upset that you spent all day being scared. He wants you to know that he thinks you've been…a trooper?" Fox scrunches up his face a teeny tiny bit, just enough to show me that he's having a hard time getting a clear read on me.

I nod to assure him he got the gist of it and squeeze Edovard tighter before kissing his forehead.

Edovard gives my arm a squeeze where I'm practically choking him and takes a steady breath. "I thought—" he hiccups and my ward kicks in as the pressure of his grip on me disappears.

Oh, he's still clutching, it's just that apparently he has a grip strong enough to hurt me, and my ward will have none of that.

I kiss his forehead again just to assure him he's ok.

"I thought you were going to kill me," he rasps out, which makes me exaggerate another frown at Fox.

This poor guy. I should have just asked why he got into the car. I should have paid better attention. All the signs of his distress were right there, but I didn't even consider how it might actually look to an outsider. Not everyone comes into this life with three mass killings under their belt like I did. Obviously innocent people are going to assume the worst.

"I only kill really, really bad people. They have to be really, truly evil to get on my list," Fox assures him.

Bellamy slowly reaches over and takes Edovard's hand. "We're very sorry we didn't explain the situation to you. We can take you back to Fresno in the morning, or if you don't want to wait that long, I'm willing to drive you back after dinner."

Edovard shifts slightly to look at Bellamy, but he doesn't release his hold on my ward, so I don't release him either. "I'm probably fired, right? Because I walked out on my job."

Bellamy presses his lips together before giving Edovard a sympathetic nod. "Unfortunately your boss is going to think you walked out. The cleaners are thorough and will obfuscate any video evidence of the execution. It's likely you will have to find another job, but I'm sure we can help." He looks directly at Fox. "Right, Oppa?"

Fox glances behind me and sits back, donning his stoic mask again. I glance behind and release Edovard, taking my seat as our server comes to the table with a tray full of food for us.

I take up my phone and type out the response that Fox failed to give.

Me: *We can help you find gainful employment again.*

Edovard: *What does obfooskate mean?*

Me: *It just means our cleaners will do something to the video feed that makes it unwatchable.*

Edovard reads that twice, reminding me that we might need to be more accommodating.

While Bellamy handles the server, I lean into Fox and type into our conversation thread.

Edovard might have a reading difficulty or a learning disability like dyslexia. We should help him.

"Why do you feel like you want to take him home with us?" Fox murmurs in my ear, reading my emotional output, obviously.

It takes some effort not to let his voice go straight to my dick.

He's like a lost little pupper. Of course we need him in our family. I wouldn't force him, but c'mon, he's so pretty to look at, and he thought he was my hostage. How sad and adorable is that? He's like twice my size, and I don't have any weapons. He definitely could have escaped before we left Fresno.

"You can't adopt every person that catches your eye, Romily."

I shiver at the sound of my name on his tongue.

Eat fast. We'll talk about adopting a puppy later. Right now I need to be naked with you.

Fox nips my ear and releases me from his seductive hold, turning his attention to his food. He still eats with purpose, if not enjoyment, but I ordered the fancy—what the hell is this?

I look up from a plate with very little food on it even if it looks fancy as hell and discover I am not the only person with a tiny portion of food.

*What. The. Hell??? *angry face cursing emoji**

Fox leans into my ear. "The fancier the plate, the less edible food is on it.

This is why I don't let Athair choose our restaurants when the fathers take us out."

I'm going to need a burger after this.

Fox kisses my temple, murmuring just for my ears. "Whatever you want, my love."

CHAPTER 16

Bambambambambam!

The incessant knocking on our hotel door has Fox jumping out of bed and trippingly pulling on his yoga pants on the way to the door. Even though I absolutely abhor being woken up when it's still dark outside, I push myself to sitting as Fox opens the door.

"Something—" Gasp. "Happened." Gasp. "Bellamy." Sob. "Someone—"

My stomach drops as Edovard breaks down in the doorway. I jump out of bed and grab Edovard, pulling him into the room with Fox's help.

"Breathe first," Fox instructs him, as he grabs his gun and a sword. "Then tell Romily what happened."

My boyfriend runs out of our room to the door across the hall and Rambos into it just as our hotel door shuts. Yeah, there's no way even the heavy, thick doors of a hotel can stop a man with superhuman strength and a sword from getting through.

I make sure our door won't latch with the flip-lock and push Edovard onto our bed, grabbing his cheeks and demonstrating how to breathe to calm himself. He takes about four breaths, crying the entire time and staring into my eyes with his Prussian blue eyes. I'm not sure how I managed to not notice that his eyes are so blue. Honestly, I thought they were golden brown. I swear they were golden brown.

"We were asleep. And then I was woken up because Bellamy was cuddling me and he was dragged off the bed. There was a dude holding him by the neck and then—" Edovard takes a stuttering breath and his eyes widen as he starts to freak out. "The air cracked open, and the dude pushed Bellamy through the crack, and then he went through it too, and I ran here."

Fox slams back into our room and rips his phone off the charger. His normally stoic face is a mask of black rage as he puts his phone to his ear.

"Arlington Fox. My Acolyte was abducted through a portal that smells like a Luna wolf the depot had delivered to my hotel last night."

His pause as he listens to the response charges the air inside the hotel room, and outside, thunder cracks overhead.

Holy fucking shit.

Fox is mad enough to summon a thunderstorm in a matter of seconds.

"My Harbinger and I will not take any jobs until we get our Acolyte back, you cocksucking, bootlicking, fartsniffing asskisser. And when I find my Acolyte, *I'm coming for you.*"

He ends the call and tosses the phone onto the desk. "I may have just revoked your ward," he explains as he starts gathering all our stuff into a pile.

I give him my "duh" look and do the come and get me wave, inviting him to test my defenses.

Fox grimaces, but reaches over and flicks my nose like he did Bellamy's the other day.

Thankfully he bounces off my ward—a broken nose would not be a good look on me.

He grunts and picks his phone up, dialing someone on speaker.

"Fox?"

Somehow just hearing Annette's deep rough voice loosens a small amount of the tension currently inhabiting all of my muscles.

"I'm turning in my Kroner."

Annette's significant pause undoes all the relief I'd gotten. She hisses out a slow breath and clicks her tongue. "This is forever, Fox. You've one chance to get it right. You sure about this?"

"I'm turning in my Kroner," he repeats with a mild amount of insistence.

She clicks her tongue. "Very well. I will let the council know you're coming. Make sure you talk to Romily first, Fox."

He doesn't bother with valedictions and hangs up without comment, disappearing back out our door and returning a minute later with all of Bellamy's things, including his weapons. He stares for a few seconds at the pile of stuff he accumulated, and a moment later it disappears, just pops out of existence, or I suppose his father teleported it home for us.

Poor Edovard yelps, and I swear on my life his eyes are golden brown now. I'm not crazy. His eyes changed from blue to brown. I grab Fox's phone out of his hand since mine is on the other side of the bed and quickly type out a message.

Edovard's eyes changed. They were blue and now they're brown.

Fox stills in the middle of his frenetic movement and whips around to examine our little pupper. Ok, I know he's not an actual lost puppy, but if you were looking at him through my eyes that's all you would be able to see too.

"We'd have to have an expert examine him. I can't see internalized magic."

Edovard startles. "What? Me?"

Fox turns back to me, places both hands on my neck and jaw, and stares into my eyes with an intensity I don't think I've ever seen in him. "We're flying home because I am faster than taking a jet. It's going to be uncomfortable, but you can do this. When I shift, you and Edovard need to climb up my back and bury yourselves under my feathers at the center of my back and hold on. It's going to take me about an hour and a half to make the flight, and it's going to feel like you're dying the entire way, but I promise that you will be fine when we land. Understand?"

I nod, squeezing his wrists to assure him that I trust him no matter what he needs me to do. Then, because my incredible boyfriend always aligns his priorities with mine, I give him a reward kiss for giving me permission to keep our newest addition.

Fox takes a deep breath, breathing in the scent of my skin before pulling away. "Come along, Edovard. You're coming home with us for now."

Edovard looks at us both wide-eyed. "What about my apartment? I have a fish."

"Send Romily the address; we'll take care of it."

With that, Fox grabs my hand and Edovard's elbow and hauls us out of the hotel to the rental. While Fox drives us to a place where he can shift, I climb into the back seat and make myself comfortable on Edovard's lap, pulling his head to my chest because he looks like he could use a hug.

He immediately wraps his arms around me and curls in, taking a few deep breaths before whispering, "I'm a little confused and pretty scared."

I pat his hair, which smells like argan oil and peppermint and feels a little slick from whatever product he uses to protect his curls. I pull my phone out of the pocket of my sleep pants and put it where he can see it. I adjust the accessibility options to read aloud for me, then open a new message thread that is just between his phone and mine.

You didn't know about magic before today?

He shakes his head in a silent negative.

I'm pretty new to it too. I've only known about it for about eight weeks. It's hard to get thrown that kind of curve ball, right?

He nods.

I promise that we'll help you understand and answer the questions that you have, but for right now I want you to trust me.

"I do."

Fox, Bellamy, and I work for the good guys. We're a strange little family, but we are a family, and I think you should be a part of our family.

He takes a suspiciously sniffly breath and nods.

We're going to get our kid back. I adopted Bellamy so he's mine and Fox's son, and we are not going to let the people who took him keep him. When we get him back, we will spend as much time as you need helping you adjust to the world where magic is real and most of the people you're friends with aren't actually human.

"Not human?"

I'm human, but Fox isn't, and he's going to shift into a huge-ass thunderbird in a few minutes, but trust me, we're going to be fine.

"Ok. Yeah. We're going to be fine. I heard him. He said to get under his feathers. I didn't understand, and I never heard of a thunderbird, but you're a good guy. I can tell. Thanks for helping me. I'm not a real good reader."

I'm a terrible talker. In this family we do what we gotta do to accommodate our disabilities.

He lifts his head and bites his lip nervously, looking at my mouth. "Can I —well, I just never met someone who didn't talk? Do you, like, stutter or something?"

I give him an encouraging smile and point to the tiny scar on my neck, shaking my head.

My vocal cords were removed when I was a baby. I don't have a voice. I never learned how to talk and I am really, really bad at mouthing words.

"He's so bad at it," Fox interjects with a laugh in his voice. "His idea of making word forms includes a lot of clicking his tongue."

I demonstrate my ability to click with meaning by mouthing *Fuck you* at the love of my life. It basically comes out as me loudly sucking my bottom lip into my teeth, making that ck sound at the back of my mouth, and kissing the air. It's embarrassing how bad I am at this.

"As much as you like, my love, as soon as possible."

I swallow hard as the anxiety I've been suppressing since Edovard explained what happened comes bubbling up my throat. I don't like to entertain what-ifs, but I'm having a hard time not losing my shit about Bellamy being out there without his ward and his weapons.

Tala took him, right?

I ask Fox that question.

"He did, but he's a bounty hunter; he only takes as much of his bounty as he needs to get paid. Whoever paid him to grab Bellamy wanted him alive."

I thought I might like him. It turns out I don't like assholes who steal my family away.

"Tala is like Darcy, a true neutral."

And also like Darcy in that I thought I could like him until he fucked with Bellamy.

Fox huffs out a laugh as he takes a turn into the deserted parking lot of the fairgrounds, which isn't even outside of the city and not all that far from our hotel.

We abandon the rental and Fox strips out of his clothes, handing them to me. "Make sure you hold Edovard tight. Don't hold anything but him, let him hold my quills."

It takes me a second, but I get it. He needs me to use my ward to protect Edovard.

I nod, kiss him, and then he jogs his delicious ass to the center of the parking lot and shifts into a huge white thunderbird. It's magic; the shift isn't disgusting. His bones don't break and pop and whatever else you've seen shifters do in the movies. His shift is one moment he's a beautifully naked man with some rather scary tattoos, and the next we're looking at a pristine bird the size of a small jet while the ions in the air charge up like lightning is about to strike.

"That's—that's—*ohmygod.*"

Edovard's gasp is completely understandable, and now I know he's really not human because of the whole human blind spot to magic thing. If he can see Fox, my pupper isn't human, at least not all the way.

I grab his wrist and jog with him over to Fox's tail feathers, which he lowers for us. We scramble up his back, which takes us both climbing with careful handholds on his stiff feathers. I do, in fact, cut myself twice, because I'm the only person who can damage me, and I'm choosing my hand holds on Fox's feathers. Council wards have weird rules to them.

Fox uses his beak to lift a few feathers at the center of his back where he wants us to lie down. I put Edovard under them first, and move his hands to where I want him to hold on, then I attach myself to him like a baby monkey, and Fox smoothes the feathers back down, trapping us below them with some significant pressure.

When Fox said it would be uncomfortable, he wasn't lying. The quills of his huge feathers dig into my body, and the fluffy feathery stuff at the base of each feather is definitely trying to suffocate me.

Then Fox flaps his wings and we have lift off, which sucks like lemon juice in a mouth full of canker sores as we're knocked around on the hard quills. Fox doesn't even ease us into gaining speed. Honestly, I should have known that everything about this would be awful, because Fox warned me. However, I couldn't have predicted what happens to the human body when the only thing keeping it in place is a magical shield that only protects against flying off the back of the bird zooming through the skies as fast as a fighter jet, but that doesn't protect against the shriek of the wind, the pressure of the acceleration, and everything else about going mostly unprotected at Mach 3.

The wind is deafening, the crack of Fox's wings is terrifying, and the ionic charge all around us creates a tightness in my chest that gives me that feeling of impending doom. On top of that, the sheer force of the acceleration is sickening. Thankfully, I don't have anything in my stomach, because Fox is definitely going to need to clean up after this. Neither Edovard nor I have the strength to keep from gagging, and then my entire body decides that it's going into shock, and black stars dance before my eyes as a faint takes me.

Edovard barely catches me, holding me against his chest as darkness consumes me.

If I never have to fly Air Fox again, it'll be too soon.

CHAPTER 17

*D*on't ask me how the flight back across the country goes. I pass out twice and don't wake up after the relapse of unconsciousness until Edovard is shaking me and quietly whispering my name. By that time Fox has already landed and we're firmly on solid ground again.

The things I do for love.

Nausea rolls through me, but I manage to keep my bile in my stomach this time, though regaining my equilibrium enough to crawl down Fox's back is an exercise in futility. I'm a baby deer stumbling around on wobbly legs like I haven't been walking for the majority of my life. Just call me Bambi.

No, don't do that. Bambi is the name of a buxom, blond sugar ba…by.

You know what? Bambi it is.

Me: *I need you to figure out how I can get my hands on fake boobs.*

Papa Smurf: *Are you planning to wear a wedding gown?*

Me: *I already ordered my tux; why would I also buy a wedding gown?*

Papa Smurf: *So you have something to wear your fake boobs in?*

Me: *Valid assumption, but no, it's so Daddy can call me Bambi since I have no legs after that flight with Fox.*

Papa Smurf: *Oh. We didn't warn you about that, did we? Literally only Dakota likes flying with Dakota.*

Me: *I have no regrets, but best case scenario is never having to do that again.*

"We need to go," Fox urges me, taking my hand and pulling me toward the entrance to a two story building made up of mirror windows. I guess he got dressed while I was talking to Tag. Damn, I hate missing the good parts.

I quickly grab Edovard's hand, using him to keep myself from face-planting because of my Bambi legs. Also, I'm mildly concerned he won't follow us inside without specific instructions to do so. He's very obedient but gets a bit confused if the expectations aren't clear, you know. Like how he thought he was my hostage.

With my hands occupied with keeping me upright, I can't ask what we're doing or what this building is, and since it's a single building in the middle of a dirt field surrounded by wild deciduous forest, I'm just going to have to be very observant to figure out what's going on right now.

My clues: Fox is meeting with the council, so I'm assuming this is the building where the council meets. I could be wrong, but Fox seemed very insistent about turning in his Kroner—whatever that is—to the council. He was supposed to talk to me about it, but even if no one else understands this, I trust Fox. Full stop. He doesn't have to explain jack shit to me right now because I trust him.

Fox jerks open the door, and we're blasted with frigid air as we pass through the doorway. Inside, the lobby looks like any modern business with a long round desk at the center with several people working at it and helping the people in need of direction; most of the front desk workers sound Australian.

Blink-blink.

I don't think we're in Kansas anymore. Not that I've ever been to Kansas. Just how long was I unconscious?

The lobby is busy with dozens upon dozens of people milling about, fast walking from one place to another and keeping the elevator bank in a constant state of catch and release. However, as soon as the first person spots Fox, it's like a wave of awareness hits the people in here and they all still, halt their conversations, and the whole place quiets as all the attention turns to Fox.

He ignores them, of course. I'm sure he's aware of their eyes on him, but he isn't bothered by them and doesn't bother with them. He barely makes eye contact with one of the people at the staff desk, and they immediately pick up the phone, their voice carrying through the now quiet lobby as we march toward the elevator bank.

"Arlington Fox is here with his Harbinger and a guest."

Fox takes a right angle turn to the left and heads toward a restroom where the fathers' butler, Jerome, is standing with three suit bags and all of Fox's weaponry. He grabs the suits and weapons, thanking Jerome with a nod. I kiss the man's cheek because I appreciate him bringing me a change of clothes, especially considering I'm wearing pajamas covered in vomit.

Inside the restroom, Fox hands me and Edovard each a suit bag, and we all strip out of our dirty clothes. I use the sink for a quick wash and smile when I find my makeup bag below my gold and brown suit. I comb and style my hair into a curly side part, then line my eyes with brown liner, then add a neutral shadow and blush and a clear lip balm. When I finish that, I step into my suit, adding all my shinies as I do. The fathers, probably Tag, sent me my set of gold jewelry: cufflinks, pocket watch, tie pin and collar chain, lapel pin, and earrings. The only thing missing is my huge diamond ring, which I make a point to point out when I pivot to show off my good looks to my Reaper. I flourish my arms and do a little curtsy-bow, then hold up my hand and tap my empty finger.

Fox is in stoic mode because this is a public restroom, but the layer of stoicism that flashes across his face when he looks at my barren finger looks a whole lot like guilt and regret, not the amusement I'm expecting because I'm teasing him.

I flatten my expression and give him a questioning look.

He immediately turns to Edovard to help him with his tie, because apparently our puppers has never learned to knot one.

"This is a formal meeting, but don't worry about behaving correctly. All eyes will be on me. No one will be looking too closely at you, so just stand still and keep your eyes on me. I can feel that you're worried, but there's nothing here for you to fear. You are safe here."

My heart goes pitter-patter watching Fox comfort our new addition. Hey, look at that, I'm not totally weird! I get turned on by Fox's soft side too!

Edovard swallows down his worry and gives Fox a slow nod. "Ok. Thank you. Sorry."

"Nothing to be sorry for, little pup. You belong here with us, and we're going to make sure you're as safe as we can make you."

Edovard hasn't spent as much time with Fox as the rest of us, and when Fox finishes with his tie, Edovard hugs him, surrounding my man with his incredible, muscled bulk. "Thank you."

Fox doesn't hesitate to return Edovard's hug, squeezing him tight enough that Edovard feels our love in his bones.

When they finish, Fox dons all his weapons, looking badass in an all black suit with his usual hundred pounds of guns and ammo, plus two swords strapped to his back. I will never not think he's the sexiest man on the planet when he's dressed up. He cleans up so well.

I kiss him quickly, then I grab both their hands and we leave the restroom, heading toward the elevator bank with Fox in the lead.

A tall, bald, portly man with a cheerful smile holds the elevator for us, and Fox actually acknowledges him as we pass into the elevator, patting him on the back.

I push Edovard to the very back and stand in front of him. Fox stands next to me, and the cheerful man pushes the button for the upper level. By the way, there are fifty sublevels to this building according to the elevator buttons, which explains why it's so busy but doesn't explain the empty dirt lot where we landed. There are a lot of people here and zero cars anywhere around the building. No drop off lane. No valets that I noticed.

Who wants to bet there's some kind of open portal? I'm giving myself three points if there's a portal room where people come and go. I'm giving myself an extra point if we leave here and end up in Annette's skyscraper.

The cheerful man with a bright smile speaks softly, shyly, not looking at Fox, but rather staring ahead. "Mr. Fox, I gave my illustrations to Mr. Sanderson like you told me to, and he gave me a contract for three books. I was wondering if you wanted one of my give-away copies that he gave me for my friends."

Fox puts a hand on his shoulder and squeezes it gently. "Send them to me through Dakota. I'm sure he and his husbands will want to see what you've done too."

It's weird to hear Fox refer to Dakota by name rather than relationship, but it's because he doesn't advertise that Dakota and Co. are his parents. Fox values his privacy and keeps his parentage and immortality out of the supernatural gossip rags.

"Yes, sir. I'll do that. Thank you."

Fox pats his shoulder as the elevator dings and comes to a stop on our floor. "You're welcome, Johnny."

Johnny moves against the elevator wall to let us pass and gives me a cheery smile and a wave from the elevator car as the doors close behind us. I guess he was just holding the elevator for us, or possibly he's the elevator attendant.

The doors let us out into another lobby, this one smaller and far more crowded than the one below. Chairs line the walls and every single one is occupied. The people who didn't get a chair stand in groups talking quietly, but there's so many people that Fox literally stops dead, clears his throat, and waits for everyone to figure out they're in our way and make a path.

It takes about three seconds for them all to scramble out of the way.

Not even exaggerating.

I'm not sure exactly what is going on right now, but Fox has the full attention of the supernatural community, and they are acting like frightened mice, scurrying to get out of the way.

It kinda gives me warm fuzzies about my future husband. I'm not sure what it says about me that my heart gets affectionate for him when Fox scares the shit out of people, but I'm not too worried about it either. We all have our character flaws; clearly mine is being in love with a terrifying, happily murderous Reaper, but hey, I also get warm fuzzies when he's not in scary Reaper mode.

Fox leads us on to a double doorway that opens when we're within a few feet of it, and as I glance back to make sure that Edovard is following, I catch sight of all the people in the lobby following us inside. I turn, pressing my lips into a thin line as we walk into the center of a small auditorium with stadium seating that quickly fills with the people from the lobby.

Fox takes me and Edovard to the side wall and stops there.

"Stand here," he instructs us, pulling his phone out and tapping it a few times.

He shows me what he's doing, opening an app I don't have, but it brings up a streaming platform, and Fox starts his own live stream.

"Try to keep the camera pointed at whoever is talking."

I nod my understanding and take control of the camera, pointing it at Fox. I'm not sure why he feels the need to live stream whatever is about to happen, but here we go.

Ignoring the camera, he gives me that intense stare, the one that makes me feel seen and heard even though I have no voice.

"I love you."

That's not a declaration; that's a reminder, and people only do that when they're about to do something that might make their partners question their love.

I shake my head at him and smirk because nothing he will ever do will make me question that. I am completely confident in his commitment to his love for me.

The corners of his lips twitch in his version of a public smile. "I believe you."

He's getting better at tuning into my thoughts.

"Please stand," a voice calls out.

I turn the camera toward the person standing at a doorway that opens with the doors sliding into the walls, and the first person through is Dakota, followed by a train of diverse persons.

The announcer calls out each of the councilors' names as they enter. "Dakota Patervulpis. Sheeva Taylor. Killigan Buzzo, Homer Rivera, Zile Elliven, Falmer Jones, Balgur Plummer, Jeff Gordon, Noe von Dongen, Alexie Hirons."

The councilors file into their seats, and then the announcer continues. "Arlington Fox appears before the council today."

Fox jogs to the center of the auditorium facing the council.

Zile bangs the gavel, sets it down, and peers at Fox over semi-circle glasses. "Mr. Fox, what do you bring so urgently before the council?"

Fox holds up an empty hand, and half a second later a golden disc the size of my head appears in his palm. Someone behind me whistles under their breath and the rest of the audience starts a low murmur.

"That's a Kroner."

"Did we know he's immortal?"

"Of course he is. He's been alive forever."

"No, he hasn't. He's only been a Reaper for a couple centuries."

"I thought it was a thousand years."

Zile bangs the gavel, demanding order. "Silence or you will be removed." They don't raise their voice above the crowd, but the people are quick to shut up.

Fox holds up his disc. "I'm turning in my Kroner," he announces loud enough for the entire room to hear.

Before anyone else reacts, the viewership counter on the app triples.

Zile tilts their head slightly to the side. "Are you sure you want to do that? You only get one coin. Are you certain you want to spend it on your Harbinger?"

Fox takes an intentional breath, puffing out his chest while the sleek muscles in his arms bulge under the strain of holding up the coin. "I am paying my Kroner for Bellamy Jones, not Romily Butcher."

"Holy shit!" someone erupts and immediately, "Sorry!"

The atmosphere is so tense, no one even laughs at the person's faux pas.

"Your Kroner is meant for your mate, Fox. It is our understanding that you are marrying your Harbinger?"

Fox stalks to the councils' long bench, vibrating fury from every atom of his body. He stops inches from the bench directly in front of Zile and slams his golden Kroner onto the table, leaning as close to the council person as he can respectfully get.

Zile barely blinks when Fox shouts loud enough for the entire auditorium to hear him clearly.

"I choose who I spend my coin on. Make my Acolyte immortal. Now," he demands, shoving the coin toward Zile.

The viewership counter hits four million.

Fox takes a few steps back when the security guard points at him.

"You're wasting your coin," Jeff Gordon, the representative of evil, scoffs. He's the brother of Reaper Julia's husband, and though he looks exactly like a serial killer—i.e. completely average—he doesn't really give off the evil vibe the way I would expect from someone representing the entirety of evil. I mean, my step-father was clearly more evil than this guy.

"That coin is specifically for your mate, and he's standing over there if the rumors are true. You are stealing his immortal life by giving it to an inconsequential human Acolyte. Does your alleged mate not deserve your coin? Or are the rumors untrue and Romily Butcher is just a temporary lover?"

Ok, that was—well, mean, but I'm still not convinced he's actually evil.

Still.

I narrow my eyes at him, and because I can't verbally object to him using me to gaslight Fox, I throw him a middle finger that I make sure the live audience can see. The seven point two million and counting people watching this live stream.

I'm not nervous.

If my knees are a little mushy, it's because I just got off the back of a thunderbird and I haven't fully recovered from that flight, not because everyone and their grandmas are watching Fox commit to everyone and their grandmas knowing he's immortal.

"Romily is my soul's mate." Aww. Heart eyes. "Bellamy is the son of my heart. *Give my son his* IMMORTALITY!" Fox roars at the entire council and the atmosphere in the room charges under the pressure of his vehemence.

Zile looks down the line of the council. "Any objections?"

Starting with Dakota each councilor voices a negative, including Jeff, who looks sour, but doesn't argue further. I am telling you, if that guy is evil I will eat...something gross but edible, and definitely not any imaginary hats unless they're made of sticky caramel.

side-eye Not everyone likes having their teeth glued together.

Zile takes the golden disc, presses their lips to it and speaks Bellamy's name and title, "Bellamy Anderson Jones, Acolyte of the Harbinger Romily Capricorn Butcher and Reaper Arlington Fox."

Oh my gawd. I just live streamed to the entire world my middle name. I'm actually going to have to murder Fox now. I did not consent to the whole world knowing my full name. And it's not like Fox has an embarrassing middle name to distract from mine. I guess that's the benefit of naming yourself. I didn't get to rename myself before this live stream. Clearly.

Zile passes the coin to the right, and every councilor repeats the same thing, loudly, so that no one will ever forget that my mother was obsessed with astrology.

Imma kill Fox. There's got to be some way he hasn't died yet.

If I'm really creative, I can definitely kill him, and it'll serve the purpose of immunizing him against that kind of death later. I wonder if he's ever died of heavy metal poisoning? I could take that gold disc and have someone turn it into powder and then slip it into his food. It would take a while, but eventually I'd get my revenge.

Fox turns toward me with a silent, *Really?* on his face.

I give him the brightest smile I own and bat my lashes innocently at him before returning my attention to the ceremony the councilors are performing.

The last councilor is Dakota, he speaks the same words as the rest of the councilors, and then tosses the golden coin into the air above Fox. I make sure the camera is on Fox when he catches the coin and presses his lips to it. "Bellamy Anderson Jones, the son of my heart. My coin is yours now."

As soon as the words leave his lips, the Kroner disintegrates into less than gold dust, disappearing altogether. Damn, I guess my plan for heavy metal poisoning will have to wait, because I'm not donating any of my lovely jewelry to the cause of revenge. It's not poetic justice to kill Fox with the gifts he's given me; don't you dare even think it.

Zile bangs the gavel as Fox stalks toward me.

My Reaper locks his direct, intense, formidable gaze on the camera in my hand and stops with his face filling my screen. "I don't know who took my son, but I'm coming for him now."

His dark eyes target me and Edovard, and he jerks his head toward the exit, beckoning us on.

It's time to get our boy back.

I turn the camera around and stare into it with the same confidence that Fox has. I hold up a finger gun, a warning that whoever stands in our way is going to die.

"Choo," I sibilate, then I cut the live stream and follow Fox out with Edovard on our heels.

CHAPTER 18

Ugh. The comments section on our video is so dumb. Everyone knows I'm mute, but make a sound with your mouth one time and suddenly they're questioning the very fabric of reality and whether I'm a liar. I pinned my own comment to the top of the comments section, which is basic instructions on how to make sh sound like a ch and then breathing through your front teeth so it sounds like you're saying choo-choo like a train or pretending to shoot a finger gun.

So far everyone agrees it's possible to make the sound without the use of their vocal cords, but they're debating whether I would know how to make that sound without ever having been able to speak.

On the plus side, there's only been one comment about Fox's immortality, so that's news that's likely to fall into oblivion. On the other hand, everyone not wrapped up in whether my mutism is a cry for attention is making fun of my middle name, and some of them are doing both.

Even in the non-human community, people are trash when they can hide behind their screen names.

Jostein is super tense as he navigates the streets, taking us back to the brownstone. I earned myself four points with my guesses earlier, by the way. There was a portal room the size of a warehouse on the second sublevel of the council building, and the portal we took let us out in Annette's basement.

Next to me in the back seat, squished in as cozy as can be, Edovard peers over my shoulder at Fox's phone as I scroll through the hundreds of thousands of comments on the video, but he must get a little peeved because he covers the phone screen with his massive paw and takes it out of my hand.

"You shouldn't feed the trolls," he mumbles, holding the phone out to Fox.

Fox takes the device and immediately starts scrolling through the comments.

I huff at the double standard, but Fox shakes his head.

"I'm looking to see if anyone's seen Bellamy."

I mean, I wasn't actively doing that, but I was reading every mention of Bellamy, and if someone had left that kind of clue I would have pointed it out. It's not like I've forgotten the whole reason Fox turned in his Kroner.

No, we haven't discussed it, but I don't need to. I'm good at intuiting things because conversations take a long time for me, and I choose to spend my words on things I can't necessarily intuit. Fox made Bellamy immortal just in case the people who took him decide to kill him. Immortals can die, but it doesn't last for long. They resurrect after each death and then they can't die by that means again. If someone shoots Bellamy in the head, his immortality will fix it and then the next head shot won't kill him at all.

That's why Fox did what he did. And the reason he live-streamed the event? Because he wanted Bellamy's abductor to know that Bellamy would live, he wanted Bellamy to know that we're taking care of him, and he wanted everyone to know that no one is safe until Bellamy is.

I've never for a single second doubted Fox, but watching him literally put his money where his mouth is, seeing him do everything in his power to keep our family as safe and intact as he can in this situation—well, there was a tiny, tense ball of anxiety inside me that melted into a puddle of less anxiety after that. It was super tiny. Like, not even noticeable, which is probably why I've been on edge but didn't really understand the reason.

It's like that whole having a house thing.

I take a deep breath and lean into Fox, resting my head on his shoulder and closing my eyes.

I've been waiting for the bottom to drop out of this dream come true scenario I've been living for eight weeks. My experience of life always includes losing the things that are mine or having them forcibly taken away and being thrown away myself. I wasn't wanted as a child, I skipped from foster home to foster home, never staying long enough to get settled, and then I aged out of the system into homelessness. I've never gotten to keep anything for long—not even friends or family; death has taken all of those types of people away from me—and the worry that I'm about to lose everything I've gained since meeting Fox has been hanging out in the back of my head, taking up space, living rent-free.

Of course I've been scared about losing it all. I've never gotten to keep it before. The two mass murders I survived before meeting Fox taught me that death is never far and life is fragile. I survived, of course I did, and I'm an absolute delight because deep in my bones I know that life is short and death is always a hair's breadth away.

So yes, life did the thing it always does to me. It took what's mine away by force. But guess what, fuckers. Whoever took Bellamy can suck my dick because Fox isn't going to let them keep what they've taken from me. I'm safe and my treasures are safe, because Fox is making us safe.

I've been worried, but Fox has shown me that I genuinely don't have to live with that fear. I can let it go, because the worst case scenario might happen, like it has, but Fox will raze the world to give me back the things, the people, that matter most to me.

Bellamy is going to be fine because Fox is going to find him, and he will happily eviscerate anyone standing in our way. And yeah, I'll be watching from the sidelines with a chubby, ready to spring into action the moment we find our son.

Fox makes a deep, lusty noise in his throat—he's obviously reacting to my thoughts on how sexy he's going to be getting Bellamy back—that startles Edovard, who flinches beside me.

I reach over and take Edovard's hand, giving him a comforting squeeze. He's kind of like a nervous dog, isn't he? I'm his person and he trusts me, but he's still getting used to the rest of the family. Although, if him and Bellamy snuggling in their sleep is any indication, he's the kind of pup that will take a substitute person when his isn't available.

JENNIFER CODY

No, I am not reading into a Bellamy-Edovard ship. There will be no Bellavarding in this house. They're not at all complementary. Hard pass. Bellamy needs someone more assertive who appreciates his assets. Clearly our Edovard is not that person. They're more like brothers.

My phone buzzes, and all three of us look to see who's messaging me.

The Sketchy Liars Responsible for Abductions: *Did you claim an Augur?*

Daddy (in a different message thread): *Did you claim an Augur???*

Me (to both of them and Dakota): *What's an Augur?*

McQueen: *How should I know? I've never even heard of an Augur.*

"Forgot that Omp lost his phone, didn't you?" Fox teases softly.

I really did; I need to change that guy's nickname so I don't do that again.

The Sketchy Liars Responsible for Abductions: *An Augur is the person who decides on the contracts that Reapers are given.*

Daddy: *They're the people who tell the depot who, when, and where.*

I take the thief out of the message thread and add in Tag's phone since he's rarely apart from Dakota.

Me: *Athair, can you ask Omp if a Harbinger can claim an Augur like I claimed an Acolyte?*

"I don't think so," Fox murmurs while we wait for either Dakota or Daddy to answer.

Daddy: *I've never heard of that rule.*

Papa Smurf: *Dakota: It's not a rule. Augurs cannot exist in a vacuum; they have to be found and claimed by someone in the community or they never become Augurs. Did you decide to keep that kid you dragged into the council meeting?*

Me: *Do you even know who you are talking to? I would never accidentally claim or decide to keep some random human I barely know. Never. Not me. I don't do that kind of thing. Hey, do you think that maybe Edovard could be this Augur thing since he's going to be living with us from now on?*

The Sketchy Liars Responsible for Abductions: *Name of the new Augur?*

I hand Edovard the phone.

Edovard via me: *Edovard Durand Folange.*

The Sketchy Liars Responsible for Abductions: *Augur Edovard Durand Folange confirmed. Status: Inactive.*

Papa Smurf (in a different thread excluding the depot): *All you need to do is find an Arbiter and you'll have the whole set of people that affect Fox's job.*

THE TROUBLE WITH TRYING TO SAVE AN ASSASSIN

Fox explains a bit further. "An Arbiter is the person that works for the depot. Your Sketchy Liars are Arbiters, and you should keep your eye out for one. They're going to need a new hire pretty soon."

Because Fox is going to kill the person who set Bellamy up. The person who arranged for Tala to be delivered to our hotel in Bakersfield, who's been telling that wolf where he should go to steal Fox's kills. Whatever Arbiter decided to fuck with our family is going to conclude their short life with a bloody end and regret.

Me: *I'll let you know when I find our Arbiter.*

Me: **Contact card for Edovard*

"Who's Papa Smurf and what's your dad's name?" Edovard asks, pulling out his phone as it buzzes twice in a row.

Me: *Papa Smurf is Tag; you can call him Grandpa Athair. He's older than dirt even though he looks like he's forty, so he's way old enough to be everyone's grandpa, but he's actually one of Fox's fathers.*

Papa Smurf: *I DO NOT look forty. Thirty-three max!*

Me: *Daddy's name is Annette, and she's my sugar daddy. Guess what, Daddy! You have another sugar grand baby!*

Daddy: *My wife will be as thrilled as I am. Now stop fucking around and go get my other grand baby back! Welcome to the family, Edovard.*

"Tell, uh, her? Um, thank you."

Me: *He says, "Um, thank you." And I will message everyone when we have our boy in hand.*

"Darcy is meeting us at home," Fox says, showing me a text thread with the tracker.

Fox: *Come to the brownstone. Now.*

Dumbass: *I'm busy.*

Fox: *You will be at the brownstone when I get there in three minutes.*

Dumbass: *OMW.*

My heart pitter-patters in my chest at that exchange. Have you ever been involved with someone so commanding that they don't even have to resort to threats?

It's sexy, and now I've got another inopportune boner.

Me on Fox's phone: *Gawd, I want to fuck you so hard.*

My stupid fingers automatically and without my permission press send on that.

Fox takes his phone back, suppressing his laughter at me.

Fox: *Ignore that.*

Dumbass: *I'm an exclusive top anyway.*

Fox: *Not if you were the last man on earth and all the dildos had disappeared too.*

Me: *Anything is a dildo if you're brave enough, and you, my fated mate, are the bravest man I know.*

"I'm not sure if I should be complimented," Fox hums softly.

Edovard: *I think you accidentally sent me a text about dildos.*

Me: *I would never accidentally add you to a personal thread between me and Fox.*

Also me: *That's a thing Fox does.*

"One time," Fox huffs as the taxi pulls to the curb in front of our brownstone.

He exits the cab and I follow him out, and instead of getting out on his side, Edovard scoots his huge body across the seat and climbs out behind me. It looks as awkward as it sounds. The guy is the kind of huge that would make other guys ironically nickname him Tiny or Itty Bitty Eddie or something stupid like that.

Clearly he's a Pupper. Speaking of which...

I turn on my text to speech since we're in the privacy of our domain now. It's not that I don't trust Jostein, but he's an outsider, and Fox doesn't give outsiders more than his stoicism.

Me: *This is where we live. Welcome home.*

"It's really pretty," he comments, staring at the home.

I think people who aren't around brownstones all the time think they are prettier than they are, but to be fair, this one has been remodeled inside and out to be a comfortable enough family home, and it actually is rather pretty for what it is.

Fox jogs up to the front door and bangs his way in, but I stop to greet our resident gargoyle guardians and introduce them to Edovard.

I touch each one, patting them affectionately, and then take Edovard's wrist and pull his hand to the gargoyles, making him pet my stone friends too. The gargoyles' language is completely vocal and magically sounded, and they can't read, so we communicate through touch and trust. I trust them to have my best interests at heart, and they trust me to prioritize theirs too. Everything else is what it is.

"Your statues are terrifying," Edovard whispers.

I huff a laugh and pat his bicep and then squeeze it because the man has some pretty impressive guns, and someone other than himself should be admiring them.

They're gargoyles and they protect our home, clean up after our crime scenes, and sometimes they transport things and people. Once they detoxed Fox after a fight with one of the lower classes of demons. They're kind of the jacks of all trades in the supernatural community. When they're in stone guardian form, they're called grotesques. They can become animate stone, but mostly they aren't visible to the naked human eye when they do that. I can see them as a swarm when they fly in groups, but I can't make out details of the swarm. I've probably misinterpreted gargoyle swarms as bats more times than I've seen actual bats.

"Oh, that's—" He stops mid-sentence and curls in on himself, bending to whisper in my ear. "Actually, I'm a little overwhelmed by all this."

I give him a sympathetic smile and press a kiss to his forehead, hugging him a little tight to make this big ol' teddy bear feel safe. When I'm done, I take his hand and pull him into his new home.

CHAPTER 19

Fox and Darcy are having a staring contest. Understandable since Darcy is currently eating the jalapeno frozen custard I made specifically for Fox about a week ago. The jalapeno plants in our back garden are, according to Fox, excessively productive this summer, and I've been looking up recipes to use them.

To say that Fox might be a little annoyed by Darcy spooning his special custard out of the carton would be a lie. Fox doesn't really enjoy food, so he doesn't care that Darcy is eating our food. What is probably annoying him is that Darcy is eating something I specifically made for Fox as a gift, and we all know that gifts are my love language.

And now I'm annoyed too.

I storm over to Darcy, grab the carton and spoon out of his hands, and smack his hand with the spoon before tossing it in the sink and trashing the frozen custard. No one gets to eat it but Fox and whoever *Fox* chooses to share it with.

I point my finger at Darcy's face—it's a very attractive face even if it's heavily make-upped with the emo teen goth look—and exaggerate a scowl so he knows he's done bad.

Darcy, a tiny, less than five foot man of Korean and Hawaiian descent gives me a slightly apologetic shrug and speaks in an always startlingly deep baritone with an accent straight from the foothills of the Ozarks. "What's got y'all bowed up? Ya called me just as I was fixin' to grab a root, and now you just threw that perfectly good custard away."

I know a lot of regionalisms because I read all the fucking time, but Darcy's speaking hillbilly just to confuse me. I'm not ashamed to google shit, so I do, and I send a group text so everyone knows what he's talking about.

Bowed up = angry or defensive. Grab a root = eating dinner.

"Oh, see, I didn't know that," Edovard mumbles almost too low to hear.

Darcy, meet Edovard. You may not fuck him. You may not flirt with him. He's mine.

Darcy looks up, and up some more, and grins. "If you're opening your relationship to include a giant, why wouldn't you want a night with a little person? Might be fun, ya know?"

We don't slut shame, but you've had your one hoorah in this house, and you aren't getting more. Fox will explain while I heat up dinner, which I will kindly share with you out of the goodness of my heart, even though I'm not really sure if I like you or not.

"How very kind," Darcy deadpans.

As I start grabbing prepared meals out of the freezer to heat up, Fox explains why we need the best tracker in all the dimensions.

"Tala Sunderland abducted Bellamy through a portal while we were in Bakersfield. Find him."

Darcy snorts from behind me as I unlid a dish for microwaving.

"I could find Red in my fucking sleep," he scoffs, but when I turn around, the Asian twink with a baseball bat between his legs is gone, replaced by a feral, fire-dancing warrior.

No, really, the man is on fire. In his tiny hand, he holds a small, double-edged, silver ceremonial athame dripping with blood from a cut on the hand holding it. The rest of Darcy is covered with an almost invisible flame, the fuel for which must be magic, because his clothes and hair (blue highlighted, black fauxhawk in case anyone cares) aren't burning up.

The most startling thing, and remember that I have seen him tracking in action before, is that his eyes change from normal human dark brown to terrifying black holes of nothingness. It's not that his eyeballs turn black, which I've seen in movies enough not to freak out much. It's that his eyeballs go away somewhere else and instead there is nothingness in the sockets.

To be honest, it's kinda putting me off my dinner. That might just be Darcy, though. I have to be honest with myself that he isn't my most favorite person.

Darcy drips his blood onto Bellamy's clean floors, freaking out Edovard, who takes two jogging steps to hide behind me.

I reach back and squeeze his waist, shooting him a look that says, *Don't worry. I'll protect you from the big, bad Darcy.*

Edovard clenches the back of my shirt in his meaty fist and makes his giant self as small as possible while we watch Darcy do his tracker thing.

Except, Darcy's expression darkens, and I can practically feel the anger coming off him in waves. His voice sounds like it's emanating from the depth of an actual volcano when he demands, "Who the fuck severed the blood bond I have with Red?"

No one here is surprised that the broken blood bond Bellamy had was with Darcy. And I'm kind of proud of my boy for letting that shit go once it was gone, except that now Darcy can't just find him like he did when we were looking for Santanos.

Great. *flat expressionless emoji*

Fox glares at Darcy. "We're not sure who gave Bellamy nutmeg poisoning."

Darcy, this petite man, tiny in everything but ego and cock, emanates a growl so deep it might as well be coming straight from the Mariana Trench. It rattles the windows and vibrates every table in the house, knocking over several of my mini tables.

"I am the best fucking tracker in all the worlds and realms—" He's not talking to us. He's making a fucking announcement, and even though I can't see or really feel magic, even I can tell that his words aren't staying inside these four walls. "I will find you, and I will deliver you to Fox."

And then that fucker disappears, leaving behind a vacuum of silence in his wake.

The microwave beeps, startling Edovard and making him yelp and jerk me by my shirt around to face the threat of cooked food for him. Gawd, he's such a floofer. I pat his waist again and reach to open the microwave.

Edovard releases his hold on me. "Sorry. I guess I'm a little jumpy."

I shoot Fox a smirk, and he speaks for me.

"Romily and I will protect you. And he really likes being useful, so feel free to use him as a shield anytime. He cannot be hurt, so hiding behind him is the smart thing to do."

Oh, wait.

I put the next dish into the microwave and set it to reheat, then pick up my phone.

Me: *Does our Augur have a ward too?*

Papa Smurf: *Dakota: No, because Augurs are not supposed to be in any more danger than they would be living a normal life. Augurs are basically office drones, not field agents. Very little risk, so they don't get special benefits.*

Me: *You realize that if evil people find out who an Augur is that they are likely to target them because these are the people who decide who dies, right?*

Papa Smurf: *I'm aware. Handing out council wards requires a unanimous vote. Guess who doesn't want to protect Augurs.*

Me: *It's Zile, isn't it?*

Papa Smurf: *Or the representative for evil. Could go both ways. *unimpressed emoji**

Well, this is full-on bullshit. Time to bring out the big guns.

Me: *Tag, how would I go about making my kid immortal if I didn't have a Kroner?*

Papa Smurf: *Tag: You will get a Kroner when we make you immortal, but Bellamy is already immortal.*

Me: *I'm talking about my other kid, Edovard, the Augur that I claimed with full knowledge of what I was doing.*

Papa Smurf: *Of course you knew what you were doing. I would never think that you might accidentally adopt an adult person and give them a job specifically designed to support your mate. I would never think that. Ever.*

Me: *I don't know why it's so hard for everyone else to understand how intentionally I live my life. You get me better than anyone except the perfect son you raised, of course.*

Tag: *I really did a good job with that one. Let me discuss with your fathers whether we have the juice to immortalize your new adoptee. Dakota and Co. just did Bellamy, and it takes some time to recharge from that. I doubt Fox will have enough juice to even shift for at least a week. I'll let you know when we're ready.*

Me: *I will keep Edovard safe until then.*

The text to speech mangles Edovard's name, of course. Eee doh vay r d. He says it Frenchlish, so it's pronounced eh d uh v ar d. No, I don't know the symbols for phonetic spelling, why do you ask?

"Eep!" Edovard yelps, grabbing my shirt again and putting me between him and the sudden reappearance of Darcy on fire.

Still.

He's still just burning away, but now he's on an invisible array like the one he used to move us through the world when we were tracking Santanos, and he's brought with him a terrified teenage girl with dyed gray hair and black goth make-up. "I found the cunt responsible for poisoning Red," he announces in that terrifying volcano voice.

I do not have words for how weirdly off-putting it is that Darcy sounds like a volcano monster right now and is somehow burning without actually burning. I mean, sometimes I like the guy, like right now when he's brought the culprit who poisoned my kid, and then other times I just want to throttle him, like right now because he's brought what looks like a terrified teenager.

Although, with magic, age is literally just a number, so she might be a scared teen, or she might be a scared teenage cherub, in which case she would be around five hundred years old.

"I'm sorry, I'm sorry, I'm sorry! I was just doing my job!"

"Your job description includes putting enough nutmeg into a man's drinks to sever his magical bonds?" Darcy scoffs, shaking her arm a little.

I quickly extract her from Darcy's grip; he's clearly not to be trusted with youths right now. I pull her away and click my fingers in front of him, pointing to his face sternly.

"You don't shake the prisoners," Fox informs him for me.

I give my boyfriend a flat look and push the teenage girl—she is *not* our prisoner—behind me and my ward with Edovard.

Fox's stoicism takes on a threatening air when he ignores me and sets his piercing gaze on the girl behind me. "Why did you poison my son, cherub?"

Yeah, he called out her species just for me, because my Fox loves me even when he's trying to pretend he doesn't see me telling him to be nice.

Although I am very interested to know why the girl poisoned Bellamy too. I turn to her and roll my hand to indicate she needs to answer the question, putting her between me and Edovard and placing myself between her and the men who might not have any qualms about killing her.

"I was told he was a special customer. He didn't even have to give us his order; he walked in and we started his drink. Our manager told us he didn't even have to pay, like he was friends with the owner or something. We were told how to make his drinks, but he only came when I was working, so I always ended up making his drinks. I didn't know he didn't know he was severing bonds. I *thought* he was doing it on purpose."

Holy. Fucking. Shit.

I turn to Fox and Darcy with my eyes widened in disbelief. This cherub just lied to our faces, and she expects us to swallow that crock of shit?

The expressions that greet me when I turn are not the faces of men who can see through the lies someone is spinning. Um.

She's lying.

Darcy's flame gets a bit hotter and somehow when he looks back at the cherub he's even more threatening and scary than before. "Listen, you lying sack of shit. You knew you were poisoning Red, and you made the decision to do it knowing what would happen. Don't lie to the mute boy; he can read you better than a projector, ya get me?"

I honestly didn't think Darcy knew that much about me. Huh. I guess he's been paying better attention than I thought.

The girl's fear melts off her and she straightens her posture, clasping her hands in front of her. "We weren't sure if you'd be able to see through a believable story. The fact is, I'm not going to tell you the truth. You can threaten me, you can follow-through on those threats, you can kill me, but what you can't do is make me break the blood oath I've taken that binds me to silence. Unless you sever my bond—and I will eat as much nutmeg as you require of me—I won't be able to speak the truth to you."

Darcy's athame appears in his hand and he slices his arm open. "I don't need nutmeg to break your bonds, child. I'm Darcy fucking Hellspinner, jinn, hearth witch, and fire dancer."

JENNIFER CODY

The girl stares at him and for a moment, genuine concern flashes across her face, then she turns to Fox. "I want my mommy."

Fox's face twitches, Darcy jumps toward her, Edovard cries out, "What the fuck?!" but by the time I get my eyes on what's happening, the teen who'd been standing there is gone and in her place is a tiny infant in a pile of clothes, screaming mad and almost purple in the face.

"Godsdamned cuntybastards," Darcy screams, turning away from the baby.

I also kind of want to back away from the baby, but that's only because it's screaming and I'm not exactly the comforting type. Also, it's a bit weird that the teen turned into a baby, right? Like cherubs are really slow to grow up, so this girl lost like five hundred years of growing up in a few seconds, and why? I have no idea.

I stoop down and pull the baby out of the pile of clothes. I grab her shirt, lay it on a table, and put the baby into it, using the t-shirt to swaddle her up. Why yes, I do in fact know how to swaddle an infant in a t-shirt; I watched a tutorial after meeting the adorable baby cherubs that we saved in the last book. And also because it makes Bellamy uncomfortable when I watch parenting vids.

Sigh. I miss him.

Anyway, as soon as the girl is swaddled, she calms down and I put her up on my shoulder, patting her butt with the intention of putting her to sleep.

While I do that, Fox gets on his phone and Darcy storms out the backdoor into the garden (after tripping on the table Fox put in front of the door *snicker*).

"I'm sending a cherub to you with the gargoyles...She reverted to infancy because Hellspinner threatened her...He's the best tracker in all the realms." That last sentence is said like that's the only explanation required.

He disconnects the call and takes the baby from me, kissing the corner of my mouth. "It's perfectly natural for her to revert when threatened. The greatest physical weapon a cherub has is their cute factor. Her parents will help her grow back up if they want her to."

I give him a weirded out look at that.

If they want her to grow back up? As in, they can decide to keep her a baby forever?

Fox shrugs one shoulder. "They can, but most parents would rather not have a helpless infant for very long. Diaper duty and midnight bottles are a bitch."

Which is why we're not chancing a pregnancy. I can do other people's babies, but as cute as it would be to have a little Fox baby, I'm way too selfish to give up my full night of sleep for any reason other than work or sex. And work better not be calling me every day. Once in a while when it's an actual emergency is fine, but I have limits, and the depot has a plethora of other Harbinger/Reaper teams.

Fox takes the baby out to our gargoyles, and I turn to Edovard to check in on him.

You ok, buddy?

Edovard listens to my text to speech and nods, then shakes his head, then shrugs. "I'm pretty hungry and think maybe I need a nap."

Totally understandable. Why don't I make you a plate and then I'll show you to your room? You can do whatever you want to do with it except move the tables. Fox gets grumpy when anyone moves his tables.

Edovard frowns and nods with an accepting shrug. "You do have a lot of tables."

Fox is a bit of a collector. Thunderbirds are a bit like crows. They see something shiny and they have to have it. Tables are shiny for Fox.

"And they're fun," Fox adds, deadpan as you like, returning from his short trip outside.

Edovard looks around at all the tables everywhere and furrows his brows. "Do you play table tennis or something?"

I whip my head around faster than a thunderbird can fly and my eyes go wide at the smile that spreads across Fox's face. Dammit.

We do not need a ping pong table!

Fox is already tapping on his phone. "Oh no, I hit the one-click button. Did you know you can pay to have someone come and set up a perfectly level pool table?"

I shake my head at my fated mate, shocked at how quickly the idea of game tables caught him and wondering where he's planning to put a pool table.

"I have plenty of room in the basement, and we still have three units we can expand into, which if you keep bringing people home, we're going to need."

Fox doesn't say this as a criticism of me; he's making plans. He needs tables, and I need people. He's planning for both.

I might have stars in my eyes and a boner as I start plating food for everyone, including the scary ass tracker pitching a fit in our backyard. He better not burn up our vegetable plants; I'll sic the dads on him if he does. I'm sure between a demon, a thunderbird, a fairy, and Bear they can find a suitable punishment for the scarily overpowered asshole.

Am I planning to ask him if he grants wishes now that I know he's a jinn?

Yes. Yes, I am.

CHAPTER 20

The silence as we shove food into our face holes is tense. Darcy radiates fury as he stands at the table where the rest of us sit, and he burns my perfectly cooked food with his magical fire before forking it into his mouth. Like, no joke, every bite he takes is burnt on the outside, and the guy doesn't seem to notice at all.

I think I'd be insulted if I wasn't used to Fox, who doesn't really have an appreciation for good food. Plus, Bellamy makes a point of telling me what he likes about a meal if I've cooked it. He's very polite, and words of affirmation might be one of his stronger expressions of love.

Edovard, on the other hand, is vocal about his appreciation. Really, *really* vocal. Have you ever bottle fed a baby who's been screaming for food, and when they finally get their bottle, it takes them a little while to stop vocalizing how upset they are, but they're also just going to town on the bottle, so it sounds like *suck-grunt-suck-grunt-suck-grunt*? I saw a baby do that on the subway once. It's adorable, just like Edovard, and he's very happy about his food.

Darcy finishes his plate first, drops it onto the table with a clatter, and leans forward on his palms, focusing on Fox. "Where was Red taken from? I've never interacted with Tala, but he's my next lead. I need to get a taste of his magic to track him."

Fox shoots him a text with the information, but says, "Edovard was there and hasn't had a shower since it happened."

Edovard freezes, looking up from his plate. "Do I smell bad?"

I shake my head, reaching over to pat his arm. Honestly, we could all use a shower, but he doesn't stink worse than the rest of us.

Darcy jogs around the table, leans in close to Edovard, and sniffs him from the top of his head down his neck and arm and back up. Then he licks the back of Edovard's neck, which visibly freaks Edovard out.

"Oh, that cocksucker thought he was clever, didn't he?" Darcy growls, with a wicked grin. "I got him. You want to come with me or should I bring that beta-fucker here?" Before either of us can reply, he shakes his head and decides for himself. "You best come, who knows where I'll find him, and I can take care of myself, but that doesn't mean I can take on a whole pack of lunatic mooners."

Fox stands without finishing his meal, though it's mostly gone. Edovard gives his plate a sincerely regretful look and sets his fork down, and that's all I need to see.

I turn the sound on my phone off and send a message to Fox, who reads it aloud for me because I'm pretty much done with having a mechanical voice again. I will always accommodate Edovard, but Fox's voice is much sexier and pleasing to the ear.

"I'm going to read what Romily says," Fox explains and then points to me as he does. *"I am going with you two to get my son back, but we are not leaving until we've settled Edovard in. He doesn't need to come and we are not putting a new Augur in the direct line of fire without a ward. And honestly, I think we all need to take an hour or two to prepare before we head off into an unknown situation. Darcy needs to calm the fuck down at the very least."*

"Agree," Fox confirms. "Darcy, prepare the array and get your shit cooled off. Edovard, finish your dinner while Romily and I prepare your bedroom. One of my fathers will come look after you in the morning if we aren't back by then."

Edovard's tension bleeds out of him and he releases a pent up breath. "Oh good. Thank you. That Tala guy was really scary."

I scowl at that and Fox reads the text I send, pointing at me again so that Edovard won't be confused about who is talking. *"Did he hurt you?"*

Edovard shakes his head and shrugs. "No, but he could have. He had a really big sword."

"*That's good. If anyone ever hurts you without your permission, you tell me.*" Because I will defend my family with extreme prejudice. Via Fox. He's my weapon of choice, and he's really good at killing people that need dying.

Edovard's face wrinkles up in confusion. "Why would I ever give anyone permission to hurt me?"

Darcy snickers, finally regaining some semblance of his normal humor. "Oh my sweet summer child…"

Fox shoots me a subtle smirk. "Ask your father."

Edovard turns his confusion back to me. "Father?"

I squeeze his forearm, nod, and type out my explanation. "*When I claimed you as a part of our family you became something like an adopted son, like Bellamy. You're mine now. I'm Papa and Fox is Oppa. Congratulations on winning the family lottery—we are the best family you could have gotten into.*"

Edovard stares at me for a second as his eyes water up. He blinks the tears out of his eyes as he scoots his chair away from the table, sort of folding in on himself like he did before.

I jump to my feet and sit in his lap, pulling his head down into a tight hug.

"*Why are you crying? You don't have to be part of our family if you don't want to. We aren't abducting you. You aren't our hostage.*"

Edovard squeezes the breath out of me, but the fact that he's clinging is enough for me to not complain, and then when I desperately need air, my ward kicks in, giving me breathing room.

"No. That's not it. I just miss having a family. My parents got sick and died last year, and my grandparents died when I was just a kid, and I don't have any aunts and uncles that include me, and my sister hates me and won't have anything to do with me. You guys really want me?"

"Of course we do," Fox states firmly. "We have to get our other kid back, but you are ours too now. When we get Bellamy back, we'll spend some time helping you get settled into this family. You belong here now."

Fuck, I love that man. Listen to him! He says exactly the right thing when I need him to say it. This is what it's like when you find your soul's mate, as Fox likes to call me. They're the puzzle piece that fits exactly with yours.

Sure, we're all jagged edges and hard lives, but his jagged edges fit perfectly with mine, and around us we're putting together the puzzle of our family—jagged puzzle pieces that fit with us too.

Eventually we'll create a beautiful picture made up of puzzle pieces that fit perfectly together.

But yeah, even I can admit that it's a little weird that everyone I decide is mine is perfectly, conveniently suited to just packing up their lives and starting a new one and also happens to have some kind of connection to the community. If I believed in actual fate, that would be a super convenient coincidence, but I don't. Not beyond the whole being Fox's fated mate, even if he insists that humans don't have fated mates.

It's something to cogitate though. First Fox finds the most perfect Harbinger in all the worlds, then his perfect Harbinger grabs up the best Acolyte and now has found an amazing Augur, a functional member of the community that can't happen unless they're found by someone in the community.

Pfft. Convenient, amiright? Convenient enough for an overarching plot line in a multi-book series. *side eye*

CHAPTER 21

Fox tucks the flat sheet into the bottom of the mattress like this is a hotel room while I fluff up the pillows at the top. His grim expression carries with it the weight of the missing; we both know we're going to find our kid, but we've been going without the usual breaks for hours, and as much as I need to get out there to find Bellamy, I also need to take care of my future husband.

As soon as the bed is made, I push myself into his space, looking up at him because he's just a few inches taller than me. I stare into the windows of his soul and give him an unobstructed view into mine, pushing all my love and faith in him to the forefront of my feelings for him.

Chest to chest, I slip my hands around his waist and do whatever I can to give him unfettered access to my heart and mind. Fox is telepathic and can sometimes read my thoughts. It's not like he can hear my inner monologue in his head; I think he mostly just gets impressions and images—my thinking thoughts are often vague, but I make an effort to order them to project them to him.

I want to fuck you before we go white knighting for Bellamy.

It takes him a second to parse that out, but he huffs out a low chuckle and his amazing smile graces his face for the first time in days. He hasn't felt safe enough to be expressive like this since…I can't remember the last time he gave me the gift of his full smile. I treasure this smile because of the rarity of its appearance.

"I think we can make time for that," Fox replies quietly.

In his eyes, I see a burning inferno that he's kept banked because he's had to. There's need there. Desperate, aching need. He needs this more than I suspected, more than I would have guessed.

I lift up on my toes and press a kiss to his lips, then I let him lead me into our bedroom. He stops short as the door latches closed behind us and pivots to face me with an almost challenging arch of his right eyebrow. "You smell like my thunderbird right now."

An amused smile splits across my face as I try to suppress my silent laughter.

Does the caveman like that I smell like him?

Fox's expression morphs into that possessive caveman lust that I love seeing on his face. He backs me up against the closed door and cages me with his arms, leaning in close. "You smell like you belong to me. What's not to like?"

I do belong to you.

Fox growls deep from the heart of his chest, a primal command that triggers the need to bare my neck to him. It's an ancient demand and evolutionary response, the reason humans have universal fears that exist beyond the borders of culture and mythologies. I've never heard him do this, and I don't even try to resist. I lift my chin and tilt my head to the side, giving Fox what he's demanding of me.

He caresses my neck with the tip of his nose, drawing into his lungs the mix of our scents, licking at the trail left in the wake of his scenting. The growl that emanates from his chest softens and sends a rolling wave of pure arousal crashing over me. My cock, already ready—always ready for Fox—twitches, wetting my pants with copious amounts of precum.

Please.

I can't beg like I want to. I don't have a way to voice my desperation, but I'm nothing if not an excellent communicator. I grab his shirt with one hand, neither pulling him close nor pushing him away, just holding on because I need something to ground me. With the other hand I tap on his ass cheek like I'm asking for entrance.

Fox huffs out a breath in my ear. "Romily."

My brain and body spasm in a schism of responses trying to figure out if I'm supposed to orgasm when he says my name or not. My brain thinks, "Go, go, go!" while my body draws up tight and flinches just shy of the edge, because Fox and I have spent eight weeks learning each other's rhythms and needs, and I'm getting better at delayed gratification to give Fox the best experience I can every time we come together.

Panting with the effort to remain still for the possessive man caging me against the door, I jerk and shiver when Fox scrapes his teeth on my earlobe. His clever fingers race through all the buttons on my clothes. He takes care with my jewelry, but doesn't take off what he doesn't need to. When he finally helps me out of my jacket, vest, and shirt I'm so riled up, I need a break or I might come before he even touches my dick. He gives me the shortest reprieve in the history of sex as he tosses my clothes onto a table, then he's back on me, pushing my pants off my hips with my help. He grabs my throat with one hand, forcing me to tilt my head back, and kisses me, passionately, with lots of tongue and intense, feral growling.

I don't have a fear kink, at least I didn't until the last few minutes. Fox's growl triggers that instinctive need to freeze and hide, but it also makes me leak like a precum fountain.

God. Damn.

He just keeps getting sexier.

Captivated by his kiss, by the wild consumption of my lips, tongue, and breath, I'm shocked out of my reverie when he jerks back and grabs my hips, spinning me and throwing me onto our bed. The fire in Fox's eyes ignites, burning as he stalks toward me, ripping his clothes off his body. Something…there's something going on with my lover. He's unusually ferocious right now, and the fire—I don't know why that happens sometimes, but it's unusual enough to pique my curiosity.

Fox pounces on me, straddling my hips and leaning over me, one hand on my throat again and the other holding him off me, braced beside my head. "Need to fuck you," he whispers, staring into my soul, showing me the fire, heat, and need in his.

I move my hand toward my dick, and Fox snaps his teeth at the movement, giving me a brief glimpse of sharp teeth, sharper than his usual set.

I freeze, projecting as loudly and as clearly as possible my intentions, and Fox narrows his eyes, studying my face until he understands my intention. His chin dips ever so slightly in a permissive movement that has me reaching between us to hold my cock up for him.

He grunts, lowering his ass to my cock and rubbing the slick he produces all over it. His eyes roll closed as the crown of my dick catches on his rim over and over until the slick smoothes the slide completely. When that sensation ends, Fox slides the hand on my throat to my collarbone and braces himself on that hand as he aligns my cock to his entrance and pushes me inside his hot, wet channel with a loud, growly moan—Fox has never been a silent lover, and his enthusiasm always puts a fire in my lust.

My nuts draw up tight, already ready for my release, but it's not time yet, and my body knows that. I come when Fox is ready for me to come. I never want to reach my peak before he's ready; I want to please him because he's my Fox, he's my person, I love him, and I always want him to feel that from me. I want him to feel as sexy as he is. I want him to know in his very bones that he's important to me.

"I know," he rumbles as his ass sits flush on my cock. "I love you too, but I need to come now. Don't—" He lifts up and drops, growling loudly as he does. "Don't come yet."

The pressure on my chest increases as he shifts to get his feet under him and then disappears altogether as he sits up, bouncing furiously on my cock. Before I can reach for his cock to help him along, his face scrunches up like he's concentrating, and suddenly he shouts, shooting cum all over my chest in long ropes that pulsate out of him over and over for at least twenty long seconds. By the time his balls stop twitching, I'm covered in cum. Way, *way* more than his usual amount.

I'm drenched, and as soon as the last spurt lands on my chest, he starts fucking himself on my cock again, leaning back, bracing his hands above my knees. His cock bounces side to side, slapping his abs as he pistons on my dick. His eyes fly open, and the fire in them burns bright and hot as he stares at me, and his mouth drops open almost like he's shocked. He throws his head back and that growl that hasn't paused for even a moment since it started intensifies and gets louder. He roars this time, shooting jets of spunk all over me, him, and our bed, thrusting his untouched cock into the air as he fucks himself through it.

I need—my cock hurts from holding my orgasm back, but Fox whips his head back down, baring his teeth, *his extremely sharp teeth*, at me. He slaps both hands on my chest, flipping onto his knees and pushing his face into mine.

"One more. We come together. You can hold off for that."

That voice sounds like Fox, but there's a monster in it. A primordial creature. Something that makes the little hairs on my body stand on end. That could also be the thunderbird calling on lightning. The mix of species in Fox means that the monster talking to me could be a shifter or a demon or whatever kind of Fae he is. It could even be an actual caveman. Whatever it is, it takes every ounce of my effort to hold off from coming right now.

Fox gyrates his hips, grinding my cock into his passage, rumbling his growly pleasure as he does. He keeps his gaze locked on mine, giving me the connection and intimacy I crave. His movement takes me straight to the edge of orgasm and keeps me just this side of shooting off.

"Touch me now," he rasps.

I race for his cock, gripping it just the way he enjoys, loose enough to slide through, tight enough to give him some friction. He thrusts slowly at first, then gains momentum until he's shuttling his cock through my fist at breakneck speed.

The coil of tension inside me winds up until it feels like I'm going to implode if I don't get to come, and then Fox says the magic word, "Romily," in that ancient, needy voice that roars through me and sends me shooting into the oblivion of pleasure and release. His spunk hits me in the face and lands in my mouth as I silently scream at the explosion of cum out of me. Fox's insides milk every ounce of my cum out of me, and it feels like this orgasm goes on for ages before the tension finally drops out of me, replaced by intense aftershocks—

Oh my fuck, I think I could—it feels like I could come again? What?

Fox must catch my thoughts because he immediately starts moving his hips again, fast and hard. It hurts, but that feeling at the base of my spine, the tingly arousal, the culmination of stimulation, intensifies until a lightning orgasm strikes and my balls turn themselves inside out to empty every last drop of cum inside me. My eyes water at the intensity of a second orgasm right on the heels of the first, and when I drop out of that high place, I crash hard, exhausted and almost immediately limp, falling out of Fox's perfect ass.

Fox grabs my hand and puts it on his cock, holding it there and using my hand to get himself off one more time, adding an unbelievable amount of spunk to the cum already covering almost every inch of me above the waist. He snarls, pricking that instinctive fear in me, but I'm too spent to react, and when he finally collapses over me, my hand falls limp to the side.

Not gonna lie, it's gross when Fox squishes the cum between us and a little disturbing when he starts rubbing his chest on mine, basically playing with it. Like, I'm not going to kink shame anyone, but playing with lukewarm cum isn't on my kink list. Apparently it is on Fox's.

Aaaand now he's purring.

And sniffing me.

I grimace when he licks up the cum he flung onto my face. I grimace less when it makes the purring rumble more contentedly.

I guess he really, really, *really* needed sex.

"When you're done fucking like bunnies, the array is ready to take us to Tala."

Fox's purr turns into an angry snarl at Darcy's voice, especially when it doesn't come from the other side of our door.

We both look at the man with a death wish standing in our open bedroom door. Edovard stands behind him with a very confused look on his face, and I just…how is this man that strangely innocent? He surely knows what sex is, right? Right? Someone tell me I don't have to have the sex talk with an actual adult.

I just know, something inside me knows, that Fox is about to do something we're both going to regret, so I slap my hand over his mouth and he lets me push him off me so I can stand. Yep, I'm naked and covered in Fox's cum, but if the guests in our house won't have any shame, neither will I.

I hold my arm up like I'm checking a watch, point to my wrist and then hold up five fingers. They can interpret that to mean 5 minutes or 5 hours, I don't care. I grab the door and push them into the hall, shutting the door in their faces and taking care to lock it. Then I turn back to Fox and point to the bathroom, because Darcy's methods are irritating, but he's not wrong. We've had our break and it's time to go.

"What was that stuff on Romily?"

OMFG.

CHAPTER 22

The tension bleeding off Fox sets my teeth on edge. Fox isn't ever tense. He's calm and competent; he's not tense and whatever this is. He's clenching his jaw and his fists, and every muscle in his bare arms is flexed while the veins stand up like they're eager to start donating to the Red Cross. He looks like he's one someone-else's-wrong-move away from a bloody, violent, deadly outburst.

Darcy is on fire. Again. And he looks about the same as Fox. If I didn't know better, I would think that Darcy caught the feels for my Bellamy, but we know he didn't; that would be incomprehensible because THEY. ARE. NOT. COMPATIBLE.

Remember?

I remember. I remember grounding Bellamy to make sure he worked toward losing his crush on this tracker.

"Why're you looking at me like you just found my jizz in your favorite pocket pussy?" Darcy sure does have a way with words. You're not even imagining how that sounds with a hillbilly accent, are you? I'm listening to it, and it's always just astonishing how gross he makes things.

Mainly because I'm worried I'll have to let Fox kill you for catching feelings for Bellamy. You are not allowed to have feelings for my kid.

Darcy scoffs and unabashedly flips me off. "I'm not a relationship person. I will never be a relationship person. You will never find me 'catching feelings' for anyone, but let me make this perfectly clear. Red was mine first. My friend, my fuck buddy, my colleague, and *most importantly*, my blood bond. I am annoyed as shit that someone severed that bond. I was ok with you adopting him because he still belonged to me. I am not ok with you having him without me." Darcy cuts himself off and rolls his hand to me, indicating my phone. "It's your turn."

That brings me up short. He could have bulldozed this conversation by monologuing, but he's interrupting himself to give me a chance to type out a response. It makes me almost like him again. Fuck me.

I don't like that you had a blood bond with him, and he made the decision not to tell you about the severance because he didn't want it anymore. He wants to get over his crush on you, and absence is the best way to do that. He's not yours anymore, and you can't act like he is because that's bad for his mental-emotional health.

Darcy reads that and spits a glob of saliva and blood onto the magical, invisible array we're traveling on. Now it looks like we're standing on nothing and there's a bit of bloody spit hanging out with us. Nice.

"I'm toxic as fuck. I know this, and I don't give a flying monkey fuck about it. You're not going to keep me away from Red, because he's a grown ass adult who's going to make his own decisions. I'm going to find him, Fox will kill everyone standing between us and Red, and when we get him back, I will re-establish the blood bond with Red, and whatever else happens is between me and my friend. Your turn."

Goddammit, I hate that he's being considerate. And yes, I know I can't control Bellamy's decisions, but seriously.

Don't lead him on. If you have even an ounce of respect for him, just stop offering sex. He can't say no to getting to connect to the person he likes. That's just not fair to him.

"Unless sometime between now and the last time I talked to him you've decided to include him in your relationship and you have an actual romantic claim on him, you have less a say in his sex life than I do, so don't get on your high horse about how I don't respect my friend. I'm not responsible for his crush. I laid out manageable expectations before we ever slept together. I respect Red. I respect his skill, his person, his character, and his fuckin' autonomy. If he wants to fuck, I'm down. The answer is yes. It will always be yes. But in the name of peace between you and me, I won't offer. That an acceptable compromise?"

I grimace at the man and huff out an annoyed sigh, then offer him my hand with a curt nod. It's a perfectly acceptable compromise.

Darcy grabs my hand and pricks my palm with the tip of his knife, then turns it on his own palm and clasps out hands together with a wicked grin. "There, now that's a blood oath I can get behind."

I stare at my palm where there's a mix of my blood and Darcy's. My stomach clenches at the sight and the color drains from my face. I turn my wide eyes on Fox as stars explode into darkness at the edge of my vision.

Fox catches me around the waist, pushes me onto my back on the invisible array, and elevates my legs above my head. His expression tells me he's barely holding back from continuing the fuck fest from earlier, but then he notices the position we're in and that barely able to hold back becomes hanging on by a thread. Fire ignites his eyes again, but he quashes it as soon as Darcy starts speaking again.

"What is happening here?" Darcy questions—ugh, the man sounds genuinely concerned.

I'm beginning to suspect that even though I don't want to like the tracker, I might end up doing just that. Hopefully he'll do something to make it stop before it's too late.

"Puke on my shoes and you're cleaning them up. These are limited edition and thirty thousand dollars a pair. You will pay for a proper magical cleaning."

Ah, there's the Darcy I enjoy disliking.

I'm not going to puke on his shoes. Fox's elevation of my legs has actually made a significant impact on my stability.

Feeling better, I type out the answer to Darcy's question.

You pierced through my ward.

Listen, I am not a fighter. I can scrap like a good street kid, but under this much stress and with the knowledge that more than a few things can steal my ward away from me; I'm allowed to have a moment of panic when the unthinkable happens. The last time I saw Darcy destroy a ward, Belaphor Betelgeuse had kidnapped Santanos, and it did not end well for him.

Darcy reads that and bobs his head like a K-pop star dancing in their first music video. He also looks like one—just saying. "Yeah, I was establishing a blood bond and ally agreement. Your ward wouldn't consider that an attack or the intention to do harm."

I had to shoot the chip in my hand myself.

Darcy shrugs and nods in agreement. "Sure, the technician wouldn't have an established non-violent reason for shooting you. They didn't have any magical reason that would hold them back from taking that gun and putting the chip in your brain instead of your hand. My blood magic won't let me cause harm to the subject of a blood bond, so your ward recognized the intention of my magic and let me through."

Simple, easy, reasonable explanation, and he's not even lying according to my mute boy spidey sense.

I'm not sure that I like you having access to my blood like that.

Darcy smirks and offers me his bloody hand even though I have a whole Fox to help me to my feet. "I only use other people's blood when necessary."

I smack Darcy's hand away and let Fox pull me back to my feet. He immediately moves me so my back is to his front and buries his nose in the crook my neck, whispering for my ears only, "As soon as we have Bellamy in hand, I am tying you to the bed and fucking you dirty again."

And my fancy slacks that are tailored to fit my body perfectly are now a bit too tight in the crotch.

I'd tell the sexy man right now is not the time for this, but we've never really limited ourselves to appropriate times and places, so it'd be unfair of me to scold him for being turned on by his soul's mate. Plus there's something going on with his libido. It's definitely more rapacious than usual, although it could just be lack of opportunity during the last twenty-four hours.

So I rub my ass on his hard-on and shoot Darcy a wicked grin when he arches one of his manicured brows at us. Fox snarls possessively and tightens his hold on me in uncomfortable ways. Sure his dick is poking me, which I like, but so are the ammo belts strapped across his chest, which isn't as pleasant.

Fox went all out for this trip. He's wearing two swords, four handguns, a shotgun, and a crazy amount of spare ammo for his guns, because appar-

JENNIFER CODY

ently we're going into war. Fortunately, Fox is actually a one man army and can't die, though now that he's announced that to the world, I wonder how the Luna wolf pack will react to us showing up.

"Thirty seconds," Darcy warns us. "I'll have to drop the array as soon as we get there if I'm going to backtrace Tala to wherever he stashed Bellamy. All I need is a taste of him."

I don't understand what Darcy is talking about, and I don't have time to type out all the questions I have about how his magic works before the array we're traveling on comes to a sudden stop and drops us on top of a banquet table at the center of a ballroom with a clear glass dome over the top, through which I can see more stars than I have ever seen in my life and the crescent moon hanging over the top of a mountain peak.

Also, we are surrounded by at least two hundred people in varying stages of shift, from fully human-looking to bipedal beast mode to actual wolf monsters that are as tall as I am at the shoulder. I'm really glad I have my ward, but I am slightly concerned for Darcy's health.

Fox announces our arrival by drawing his weapons and shooting the huge woman who jumps to her feet at the head of our table. Her head explodes behind her as she drops. "Give me Tala," he orders into the eye of the hurricane we just landed in.

The calm lasts half a second longer, then the room explodes into bloody action all around us. Fox fires off rapid shots, hitting his targets with perfect accuracy. Wolves, people, and beasts start dropping like flies as he shoots them in the face over and over.

"Go to hell you unfuckable mooner!" Darcy's deep bass has me spinning away from watching Fox, fear crawling up my throat.

Darcy punches the wolf attacking him, and the wolf's head caves in on itself.

Uh.

That's—Darcy just crushed a wolf's skull with his fist.

And then he does it again on the next wolf that attacks him.

One punch is all he needs and the bones under the force of his tiny, twinky punches cave in like they're made of candy glass or something. I am not even exaggerating how tiny this man is; he is short and skinny as hell. I'm pretty sure his cock is thicker than his biceps.

Sometimes I am genuinely jealous of magic users. Don't get me wrong, I have magic of my own now, and I am grateful for it, especially when it sends Luna wolves flying off in random directions after they charge me, but look at that tiny little Asian boy from Arkansas and tell me it wouldn't be amazing to be able to crush a wolf skull with one punch.

Sigh. I'm never going to be magical that way, so I take a deep breath and let that shit go. I don't have the energy to dwell; I'm way too busy making the most out of my life as it is.

Pushing away my jealousy, I start scanning the room to make myself useful. If Tala is in here, I can keep him alive until Fox gets his hands on him; if he's not, well, it would be remiss of me to not wander around to see if I can find him or Bellamy, right?

I'd prefer Bellamy.

Tala's a'ight, but I'd skip the middleman given the choice.

I jump off the table, sending another couple of wolves flying away from my ward, and make my way through the onslaught coming after Fox and Darcy. No, I'm not thinking about how bad the odds are when it's 200 wolves against 2 magical men. I mean, we all know the story of Fox taking out a nest of vampires in Paris several hundred years ago before he had really good guns to kill them all with, so I'm sure he'll be fine.

And even if he does die, he'll be right back. Fox never stays dead; he just gets more immune to it. Yes, I do have to remind myself of that occasionally, because I do not do well with Fox looking like death warmed over.

Bellamy would probably be upset if Darcy died, though.

I glance back to find the man leapfrogging over wolves while simultaneously one-punch-man-ing them to death and figure he'll be fine without me. If something happens, I'll just tell my assassin that we didn't even think to contact Darcy in order to find him and have no idea where he could possibly be.

I'm not scared of my kid; you're scared of my kid.

Another wolf bounces off my ward as I scan the walls to find the doorway out, spotting the double wide banquet doors standing open at the back of the hall. There are a lot of wolves between me and the doorway, but as long as I'm not actively fighting, my ward will stay intact. At least, that's the way it's supposed to work.

When did I get paranoid about my ward?

Oh right. It started when I watched Darcy melt Santanos' ward way back when, and Bellamy losing his ward just reinforced the fear, so now I have to decide if I'm going to let my insecurities keep me from walking to the back doors or if I'm going to trust in the council's magic.

To be honest, I'm not sure which side of that fence I'll fall on this time.

And then I see that fuckface Tala limp-jog right out the doors, and suddenly I'm not too worried about my ward anymore.

I run after him, relieved that the ward keeps up and clears the path for me. I have zero intention of engaging; I'm just going to see where that guy is going. He's injured, so that means that one of the boys got their hands on him—good job Fox or Darcy!

I skid through the doors, thankful the blood hasn't gotten flung this far from the center of the hall so I don't slip and slide through. My combat boots are fantastic, but they're not exactly prime no-slip material.

The corridor is one of those long, wide spaces you find in school buildings and hospitals, and Tala is only fifty paces ahead of me and slower than me. I run, catching up with him pretty quickly, and I just match his pace. Because he's not stopping. He's not even a little worried about me joining him. He sort of side-eyes me and grunts.

I mean, what am I going to do? Nothing. That's what. I'm just going to keep up with his limp-jog. Maybe he'll take me to Bellamy; more likely I'll just leave a trail Fox or Darcy can follow.

"My pack called me home after Fox's little announcement, ya know. I was going to lay low, cover my tracks, make sure you never found me. And then Fox decided to announce to the whole world that he's an immortal and show us that Bellamy is now an immortal, and suddenly there were ten contracts for Fox's life. The lowest payout was a million dollars, and my pack decided it could use the infusion of wealth. Do you know what it's like to be a slave to your own magic? Our alpha ordered me back, and when I told her you would come and kill everyone, she laughed and said, 'Let them try.'"

I'm living in a werewolf monster movie. Clearly. Cheesy dialogue and bad special effects galore.

"I have the power to teleport myself anywhere I can picture. I can create portals in a blink that would get you wherever you wanted to go as long as I had been there before. You want to know why I'm running through the corridors instead of doing that? Because my alpha ordered me to remain in the compound until she kills Fox. Fun times. Fox killed her before she could rescind the order, and now I'm going to die here, imprisoned by my own magic."

You can always consume copious amounts of nutmeg. Dakota informed us that is how Bellamy's wards were disrupted.

I let my phone read those words aloud even though I am not digging the digital voice at all.

"Nutmeg poisoning. That's a pretty dirty trick. It takes a lot of nutmeg to sever a person's magic like that. Where am I going to get it? Are you going to bring me nutmeg? I have zero friends, Harbinger. Bounty hunters like me don't get to have friends. We have contacts, we have people we pay for information, we might even have fuck buddies, but we don't have friends because we have no loyalty."

I give him a sympathetic frown. It's almost a lie. I do think it's sad that he doesn't have friends, but also he made his own bed, and it's not unreasonable to expect him to lie in it.

So, where are we going?

Tala points to an elevator and hurries up to hit the down button. "I thought I'd keep moving away from the battle."

I nod and shrug, following him into the elevator.

Let's go see if the kitchen has nutmeg.

Tala looks at that and furrows his brow. "Why are you suggesting things that would help me?"

Well, I mean, when Fox gets his hands on you, you're going to wish you hadn't taken the contract on Bellamy, but if you suddenly change your mind about loyalty and want to be my friend, then there's no reason for Fox to get his hands on you, amiright?

Tala gives me a skeptical look and shakes his head, hitting the button for the next floor down. "I'm not built for loyalty."

I reach out and pat his shoulder.

You just haven't found the right people to be loyal to.

CHAPTER 23

The kitchen has nutmeg. Copious amounts of nutmeg. I don't think Tala needs to worry about having enough to break his bonds since there's enough here to make like ten thousand pumpkin spice lattes. I might be exaggerating, but barely. There's three fifty pound sacks of whole nutmegs, almost like someone knew we would need copious amounts of nutmeg.

So. Convenient.

Also, I think it's about time for me to ask how much nutmeg it actually takes to poison someone's magical bonds in the least amount of time, because this is a lot of nutmeg, and now I'm wondering if Tala can break his bonds in one dose. Psst. That would be bad for me and finding Bellamy.

Me to Dakota via Tag's phone: *Dakota, how much nutmeg can a person like a Luna wolf consume in one go if they wanted to erode their magical bonds as quickly as possible?*

Unknown number: *Nutmeg is a therapy, not a quick fix solution. No one can eat enough for it to work in one go, even if it didn't kill them. I think if I didn't mind dying, I could probably eat 3 nutmegs every day for a month and it would have the same effect as one nutmeg every day for three months. Bellamy was likely protected by his ward from the physical poisoning that consuming that much* nutmeg would have done to him, but as soon as the ward broke, his next dose would have made him ill if not killed him.

Me: *So what I'm hearing is that an immortal who was immune to nutmeg poisoning might be able to sever their bonds pretty fucking fast.*

ThunderChicken (I updated my nickname for Dakota's new number): *Luna wolves are not immortal. There are actually very few immortals hanging around; you just happen to have the good luck of knowing a significant percentage of them.*

Me: *I think I know eight.*

I'll give myself half a point if I'm right. Although I know that Fox and Bellamy are immortal and that his fathers are too.

ThunderChicken. *You know six, that I know of. Fox, his fathers, and now Bellamy. You have seen a few others: the council has four immortals on it. There are a few scattered here and there across the realms, but I think all in all the actual number of immortal people is a hundred or fewer.*

Oh, damn.

Me: *What about the Avatars?*

ThunderChicken: *Effectively immortal like you are, but not actually.*

I grab Tala's hand just before he puts a handful of whole nutmegs in his mouth and shake my head violently at him, mouthing, *No!*

Yes, I do click my tongue trying to mime the N, thank you for noticing.

Tala has the smarts to realize he should do what I say, so I show him the text thread between me and Dakota. He reads it through, huffs out an exasperated sigh, and pops one whole nutmeg into his mouth. "Magic is all about balance. I can shift between my forms, but it takes a lot of energy. One nutmeg isn't going to give me any physical symptoms because I'll burn through it too fast."

Brilliant. Let's bag up ninety more of these, that way you can see the countdown. It helps, trust me.

"Yeah, good idea," he agrees, and we start making piles of ten nutmegs that we can bag up for him.

When we have a pile of ninety nutmegs, Tala pulls out one of those purple Crown Royal bags from a drawer full of them, we put the nutmegs in it, and he ties the strings to his belt loop.

I examine the aesthetic on him. He's wearing his leathers, like he was before, and his sword is still strapped to his back. He's put his ropes of silver hair up in a ponytail the same diameter as my hands if I put the tips of my thumbs and index fingers together to make a circle. Granted, my hands aren't huge man hands, but they aren't small either.

All of that with purple lipstick, red eyeliner, and a purse hanging off his hips...he looks like a space pirate, and I'm so here for it, so I give him a thumbs up and a wink.

Tala puffs out his chest and a crooked smile appears on his face, wicked and flirty. "Not too bad yourself."

Are we friends yet? Can I ask where you took Bellamy?

Tala's smile disappears and he grimaces. "Might as well wait for Fox."

I sigh and jump up onto the counter, taking a seat, because my inner sense of Fox, the instinct that knows my lover as well as I know myself, tells me that he's about done upstairs and will find me in a minute or less.

You don't have to do this the hard way.

Tala shrugs and leans against the counter next to my leg, crossing his arms over his chest. "I really don't have a choice."

I lean my head against his bicep and just offer him some support because I know the next few minutes are going to be hard on him, and maybe that's a little hypocritical of me because I'm not going to stop either Fox or Darcy from getting what we need from him, but that doesn't mean I can't just let him know that I recognize his personhood and struggle.

Maybe next time we can be on the same side of the contract.

Tala chuckles as Fox and Darcy come slamming into the room, and the next thing I know there's a machete in his hand and he's pressing the blade into the skin on his throat.

Goddamn it.

"So I took a contract that requires me to die before telling you anything," Tala explains. "I didn't read the contract carefully enough before I took payment."

Fox stares a hole into the bounty hunter's hand. He's drenched in the blood of the dead pack above us, steaming from the heat coming off him, and he's furious. So angry that he's barely holding it back.

Darcy is on fire, also covered in blood and gore, and he steps forward, studying Tala with a tilt of his head as he looks up at the giant Luna wolf. "I ain't going to let you kill yourself, Tala. And don't worry, you don't have to say a motherfucking word."

A drop of blood wells up under the blade at Tala's throat and rolls down his almost bare chest. "It's getting harder to fight the magic, Darcy, so you might want to hurry the fuck up."

Darcy's volcano voice releases a deep, dark, instinctively terrifying chuckle. "I hope you're faster than the mooner," he announces and immediately darts forward.

What happens takes less than two seconds:

Fox is suddenly right there, grabbing Tala's wrist and pulling it away from his neck. Darcy jumps behind Tala and pulls his head back, biting into the wolf's neck or something. It looks like a vampire bite, except Darcy isn't a vampire. His teeth are totally normal, and he didn't mention vampire in his list of things he is. Do jinn have sharp teeth? Because Darcy is definitely chugging right now, and there's plenty of bloody leakage from the corners of his mouth.

I might be sick.

Actually.

Yeah.

I jump off the table and grab the trash can, emptying my stomach into it.

There's got to be something wrong with me.

I am not the guy who faints at the sight of blood. Or gets sick when there's a blood exchange. At least I wasn't until Darcy showed up in my life.

The rumble of Darcy's volcanic laughter shakes the cabinets around us, and I stop heaving enough to glance at him with a bloody mouth—definitely plain ol' human teeth there—and Tala staring at him wide-eyed.

"Blood bonds are my domain!" Darcy roars into the air, louder than the human voice is capable of being.

Magical microphone. But why? Is he loud enough to be heard by the people holding Bellamy?

Darcy looks down at Tala with a scary, *terrifying* smile. "Tell me, bounty hunter, where did you take Red?"

CHAPTER 24

So. Anyone want to explain to me how we ended up here again?

Neither of my companions reply to the message I send in our group chat. It's a rhetorical question anyway.

The damp alley smells the same as it did six weeks ago, which is kind of amazing in this city considering things get smellier the hotter the summer gets. It's pretty disgusting, but today it's just normal levels of gross. Not that it matters, but it is a red flag if you're looking for them.

The dim stairwell we descend leads to a creaky metal door that opens into a brightly lit corridor, which is lined with doors that Fox kicked in when we rescued the cherubs weeks ago. Everything is strangely the same as the first time I walked into this basement. The doors are shut and locked, the dome cameras are still in the ceiling and presumably working, and the hall is completely silent except for the squeak of our shoes on the polished, white linoleum flooring.

Darcy pushes ahead of Fox, raising his nose into the air and sniffing. He follows his nose to the T at the end of this corridor and shoots us a wicked grin, pointing to the right and down. "Can you smell our boy, Foxy?"

Fox grunts and pinches my ass on his way by to take the lead. "Call me Foxy again," he dares the super badass tracker who I might begrudgingly be coming to respect.

"That's your nickname in my phone."

"I saved you as 'Dumbass.'"

I nod, confirming that because it's true, and then I show Darcy what I saved him as: Fuckface.

Darcy snorts a chuckle as we follow Fox into the stairwell and down.

"I'm not even mad because that just proves that you're a worthy family for my Bellamy."

My Bellamy. I do not recognize any claim you think you have on him.

"As long as Bellamy recognizes my claim."

I sneer at that and make a scoffing sound.

He's not going to let you reform the blood bond. Also, I'm going to need you to explain how blood bonds work since I now have one with you.

"It's pretty basic blood magic. You and I now have a thread of magic connecting us. We didn't agree to consequences for breaking the oath between us, so it would just break the bond. The benefit is that I can find you anywhere in all the realms, and you can summon me from anywhere in all the realms. All you have to do is think my true name and I will come to you. No, I'm not going to give you my true name; only one man knows that, and if he tells you what it is, he isn't the man I know and respect. Other than those two things, it's inconsequential except for a few rituals where your blood would be more potent than other kinds of blood. I don't usually do those kinds of rituals, so you don't have to worry about that."

What can I do to break the oath between us?

Darcy gives me a wicked grin. "The only person under contract is me. You'd have to consume copious amounts of nutmeg."

I've been snookered by the best tracker in all the realms so that he can keep tabs on me. I—I don't know how I feel about this. On one hand: snookered. *x for eyes emoji* On the other: aww, he cares enough to want to keep tabs on me. *smiling with floating hearts emoji* On the other: he wants to keep tabs on me. *grimacing emoji*

We pass the first two flights of stairs downward, and Fox stops us outside a door labeled SL3, holding a finger to his lips to silence Darcy.

Gosh, it's nice that no one has to shush me. *snicker*

The corner of Fox's lips twitch and he shoots me a covert wink before carefully turning the knob on the door and pulling it open just enough to

JENNIFER CODY

peek through. He does a quick check and pulls back, opening the door fully and leading us through.

This corridor is much like the first, except instead of linoleum for our shoes to squeak on, there's high traffic steel gray carpet.

As soon as the door to the stairwell shuts behind us, a door at the end of the hall to our left opens, and a person steps out holding a toddler. Jeff Gordon, the evil council dude, not the other one—well, I mean, they could be the same person; I don't know what the other one looks like and have zero knowledge except in passing of the famous drivers in Nascar—holds up his hand like he's waving us down. He really doesn't need to do anything to get our attention; he has one hundred percent of our focus.

"Ah, I see Tala's contract ran out before his loyalty." He looks a bit sour-faced by this information.

"Jamie Gordon. Does your wife know you've stepped out on her?" Darcy questions, pushing past Fox again as he cuts his wrist with an athame dripping ethereal smoke in clouds that pool at his feet as he walks, obscuring them.

So this is Sexy Mama's hubby?

I snap a photo of him and shoot it to her as Jamie responds.

"Julia and I work because we aren't in each other's pockets."

Me: *Your hubs is standing between me and my son.*

"You probably would be in less danger if you'd stuck close to your Reaper," Darcy threatens him.

Sexy Mama: *If you can keep Fox from killing him, I'll be there in two minutes.*

Might not be Fox who's the problem here.

Me: *No promises.*

I show Fox the text exchange as Jamie kisses the cheek of the toddler in his arms. "Even you aren't so corrupted by life that you'd do anything to traumatize this cutie," he proclaims confidently.

I would just like to point out that Darcy had no problem scaring a teenage cherub so much that she reverted, and Fox, the love of my life, the man of my wet dreams, the person who fits me perfectly, does the thing.

"Darcy caused a cherub to revert to infancy less than eight hours ago. He's not the person you should put your confidence in. He's lawful neutral at best."

Jamie pauses at that and really looks at Darcy, who is now on fire again, up to his waist in that smoke dripping off his athame, and also still carving some kind of design into his arm.

You know, I think I've decided that blood magic mixed with fire dancer is probably the creepiest type I've encountered. There's just something inherently heebie-jeebie inducing about watching a man on fire carving himself up. I can see why humans demonized blood magic users.

Oh hell. I just realized: Darcy's part demon!

And now I just really need to know if that means he's the same sex as Fox.

Fox gives me a look that speaks volumes about time and place, and how I need to learn to stay on task in the moment, and to be fair, it's not really a great time to be thinking about Darcy's physiology. Although a bit hypocritical of my man when he was the one poking me with his dick on the way to kill a pack of Luna wolves.

"Darcy's a meanie!" the toddler in Jamie's arms suddenly exclaims.

Darcy snorts. "I remember you from Roswell. You're the little scamp that hid behind the servers. I almost broke my face trying to pull you out." He holds up his knife, pausing his ritual self-mutilation as he considers the cherub. "Daisy? Dandelion? No. Dahl! Your name is Dahl."

The toddler folds their arms over their chest in the cutest pout ever. "I didn't want to go home."

Yeah, the Roswell thing was weird. Some of the cherubs weren't exactly excited about going home.

Darcy resumes cutting himself—hurk. This is kind of, uh, gross. "Unfortunately, sometimes we just have to do things we don't want to do. I told your parents that they needed to find more stimulating activities for you; I can see that they didn't take my advice."

The cherub gives him a flat look as Julie and Gavin both come flying into the hall through the stairwell door behind us.

"Jamie Gordon, just what the hell are you doing painting a target on your chest for Arlington Fox?" Julie demands, pushing past my party and running at her husband.

Jamie sighs, rolls his eyes, and puts the cherub down, bracing for impact from his wife.

Julie tackles him to the ground.

I squat down and hold my arms out for the cherub, who toddles over to me and lets me pick him up. He squeezes my neck in a tight hug. "Hello, Harbinger. I'm happy to see you."

Awww. I love these little guys. I don't even remember this one specifically, but I appreciate him. He's so cute. I just want to squish him.

"Still older than you," Fox reminds me before stalking toward the door Jamie came out of.

On the floor, Julie holds Jamie's face in her hands, whispering intensely in a language I've never heard. It's a hissy language like that snake language in Harry Potter. Super hissy and both beautiful and creepy.

"It's not *Parseltongue*," Dahl giggles. "It's the language of the Saurians, the lizard people who live in the Earth's mantle."

I cock my head at the Reaper and her husband, wondering which of them is the lizard person. I can't always see through glamour, so I guess whichever one of them is a lizard person has better glamour than what I can see through.

"You should follow Fox," the cherub interrupts, pulling at my shirt.

My feet move before I've even decided to follow. I'm three steps behind Darcy before I think about putting Dahl down, but he reaches for Gavin, who takes him with a kind smile, radiating pure joy at the adorable little cherub.

Darcy and I follow Fox through the door, and I nearly run into the back of him when he comes to an abrupt stop. It's not like I can't see over the top of Darcy's head, so there's nothing to protect me from the display that Fox is staring at when we enter the…

Wet room.

This—jesus*fuck*.

Jamie was in this room with the cherub when we came through the door. With. The. Baby.

Fresh and congealing blood stands in pools that trickle toward a drain at the center of the concrete floor. Blood spatter drips from the walls and ceiling, and a cut rope hangs from a meat hook mounted just off center, like the person who designed the room specifically didn't want the blood of their victims to drain away too quickly.

Tacked on the back wall are printed out photos of Bellamy in various states of torture—hacked up, eviscerated, dismembered…

I can't look at the photos.

I can't…

Bellamy isn't still in this room, even if his blood is all over it.

I slip Fox's short sword out of its sheath and turn on my heels, walking back out of the room and straight to Gavin. I take the cherub from him, walk him to the closest door, peek inside to find a clean office, and put the baby in there, pointing at his face and then at the floor.

He nods. "I'll stay here."

I stand again, backing out into the hall and shutting the cherub into the office. I turn back to where Julie is still talking to the man who knows where Bellamy is, stalking toward the couple.

No one expects a Harbinger to fight back. We have a ward meant to keep us out of the fight, so when I kick Julie off her husband, everyone is too shocked to react quickly. I drive the sword through Jamie's chest just under his sternum, staking him to the floor. Numb with fury, I punch him in the face three times before anyone has the sense to stop me.

Gavin tackles me away from Jamie and Julie flies at me, attacking in a flurry of fists.

I take a knock to the face that hurts less than I remember punches hurting. Survival mode kicks in for me, and my body moves in accordance with the scrappy skills I learned in street fights with foster boys and the territorial homeless.

I get two good hits in, then Julie and Gavin both are torn off me.

Fox holds both by the front of their outfits, Julie's corseted top and Gavin's leather harness. His face reddens with violent rage as he roars, primitive, rabid, and oh so terrifying. It's a primal scream rooted in the predator that lives inside him, the creature born of blood and air that makes him the most feared Reaper on the planet.

He tosses Julie and Gavin one after the other down the corridor with enough force to overcome the drag and push them to the opposite end away from us.

I jump to my feet, storming back to Jamie and kicking him in the face, secure in knowing that Fox has my back.

Darcy joins me staring down at the man who glares up at us like he doesn't feel pain and is more annoyed than afraid. "Where is Bellamy?" Darcy demands, dropping into a squat and grabbing Jamie's wrist, yanking his arm out straight.

Fox offers Darcy a double edged dagger, and Darcy takes it, slamming it through the man's wrist, pinning his arm to the floor.

"I can't tell you and wouldn't even if I could," Jamie rasps.

Darcy laughs, dry, humorless, and scary. "Like I said before, blood bonds are *my domain*." Then the man starts carving up Jamie's arm in the same pattern that he put on his own.

And I thought blood magic wasn't my thing. Turns out, I'm fine with it. Look at Darcy go.

Jamie hisses when his arm starts steaming and the blood welling up from where Darcy cuts him starts boiling. "What are you doing?"

Now there's the fear I would expect from a man facing down my Reaper and our fire-dancing, demonic, blood witch.

Fox moves beside me, and I turn just enough to catch him meeting Julie head on, sword to sword.

Gavin stares at us, agog, and shakes his head, holding up his hands in surrender. "Julie! Stop! You're going to get yourself killed!" he tries to reason, but if I was the one on the floor and Fox was the one fighting to get to me, nothing could stop him but death itself, and only if he wasn't immune to it.

Jamie screams.

I glance down at where Darcy continues to cut the man, about halfway done with whatever he's doing.

Darcy growls as he continues cutting the man. "It only hurts because you let an amateur magician fuck you up, so suck it up, buttercup. Darcy's going to fix it so that you'll never do this again."

Jamie screams again, causing Gavin to startle and Julie to make a critical mistake. Fox runs Julie through, pulls his sword out, and knocks her blade out of her hand as he catches her, staring her in the face as she fishmouths at him.

Fox grabs Gavin's attention with a click of his fingers. "Take her to the gargoyles," he orders, stoic but firm.

Gavin immediately takes her out of Fox's arms and runs for the door.

Fox's attention snaps back to Jamie as Darcy finishes carving up the man's arm.

Darcy speaks in the demon language, which requires some interesting vocal gymnastics that always fascinate me, because humans cannot make a lot of those noises. It sounds like Darcy is chanting, but that language lends itself to chanting, so he could just be speaking normally. I wouldn't know. I don't even have the right kind of hearing to hear all of the sounds demons include in their language. Both sub and super vocal noises are a regular part of the demonic language.

Are you wondering why I don't call it by name? It's because Fox said the name of the language once, and I couldn't even hear it because the sounds that make up the name of the language are beyond my hearing range. The neighborhood dogs can hear it though. So there's that.

Jamie screams again, but this time it's a bit wet and gurgly.

"You're going to lose him," Fox warns Darcy.

Darcy doesn't say anything, but the cocky smirk that splits his lips tells me Fox is either overly worried or Darcy is exaggerating his skill—I love my future husband, but I might, maybe, perhaps trust that Darcy knows what he's doing. Possibly.

I cast Fox a side glance and immediately look away from his accusatory stoicism.

Sorry, love of my life, the jinn who sometimes sounds like a volcano monster seems like he knows what he's doing.

I don't type that, but Fox must still be in tune with me because he reaches out and hooks his fingers in mine, giving them a squeeze.

Jamie gurgles again, but then he convulses and violently coughs out a black glob of…

Well, I don't know what it is. Could be a blood clot, could be some kind of manifestation of magic.

Darcy pulls the sword I pinned Jaime to the floor with out of the man's torso, grabs the black mass off his face, and burns it up. He hands Fox back his dagger after pulling it out of the man's wrist, and then he stands with a manic smile on his face as he gazes down at a blank-faced Jamie.

"Now, Jamie Gordon, tell me where Bellamy is," Darcy rumbles—no, that's not volcano-Darcy voice, that's just normal-Darcy voice, but his normal voice is deep enough to hit those lower bass notes that sometimes blow out speakers.

Jamie stares up at Darcy completely blank, and the sounds that come out of him are stressed, like he's fighting to obey, like there is something holding his voice hostage. He opens his mouth and tries to push the word out. "P-p-p-ri-sss-on-nnn." That's the only word he gets out before he stiffens like someone just hit him with a taser and his eyes roll back into his head.

Darcy screams down at whatever is happening, and the cloud of smoke that had been contained to swirling around his lower half flows out from him and into Jamie's nose and mouth. A moment later, the smoke comes rushing out of the injuries we caused the man, and with them comes a thing.

It's a thing. It looks like a translucent, white, little gremlin with spindly legs and arms and a big head, but it came out of Jamie. I don't know how it fit inside him because it's about a foot long. I'm no medical expert, but it seems like it would be hard to hide that big of a parasite.

Darcy grabs the thing, and it screams like a dying tribble before poofing out of existence.

Fox grabs Jamie and tosses him over his shoulder, stalking toward the exit. He clicks his fingers at the door behind which I hid the cherub as he passes, so I swing open the door and catch Dahl when he jumps into my arms.

"Oh good. I was a little worried someone was going to die," Dahl giggles, hugging me hard again.

Me too, baby. Me too.

CHAPTER 25

"There is only one prison I can think of that could stymie me as a tracker even with access to that amount of Bellamy's immortal blood," Darcy says after we hand off Jamie and the cherub to the gargoyles that follow us around everywhere we go.

The gargoyles divided into two groups, one went into the building to presumably clean up the wet room, and the rest took off with Jamie to presumably make sure he doesn't meet an early death.

Fox makes a noise from his throat and looks upward past the tops of the roofs over the alley. "I can fly there in a few hours. Time doesn't move the same inside the prison as it does outside. If he's in that prison, and we need to be prepared that for him, time will have passed in excess by the time we get him back."

How much time?

The expression on Fox's face makes my heart sink in my chest. "It depends on where the prisoner is. Some experience one day per hour, some experience a month, some a year. It depends on how deep into the prison the prisoner is housed. In the depths of the prison, every hour that passes is a lifetime. Hope Bellamy is near the top, but if he's further down than the second level, we have to be prepared for getting back a different man than the one who was taken from us."

"Based on the pictures Jamie decided to display for us, I'd say there is little possibility of getting back the Red we know and love the way he was before he was taken." Darcy's grim announcement wants to plant a seed of hopelessness in my mind and heart, but I'm not going to let these two do this to me.

I take a fortifying breath, straighten my suit, and step into Fox's space, peering into the depths of his intense, ancient brown eyes.

I'm going with you to get our kid back, and it doesn't matter how deep he is in the prison, he's coming home with us.

Fox dips his chin, acknowledging my unwritten message. It's hard to maintain this level of communication with him; it's easier to text him, but right now, we're both growing, we're testing our limits, pushing our bond, and getting stronger. Stronger as a couple, stronger as a family, and stronger as psychics.

Ok, only one of us is kind of a mind-reader, but we're both working on becoming really good at that form of communication.

Fox and I turn in unison to Darcy, who takes a slight step back.

I will not laugh. I will not laugh. I will not laugh.

Fox doesn't have that kind of discipline, and he huffs out a breathy laugh. Oh how the tables have turned for the two of us.

"Are you coming or will you wait at home for us?"

Darcy flattens his lips as he considers his choices. "I'll wait with Edovard. Bring Bellamy back; you aren't the only people to whom he matters."

Fox dips his chin again, grabs my hand, and we jog out of the alley toward the street, where we flag down a cab.

We climb into the first one to pull over, and Fox tells the driver to take us to Annette's building. Not sure why, but I'd follow Fox into hell itself, and if he's taking us to see Annette before we go to prison, I trust him.

Just as the cabbie pulls into the road, Fox and I both inhale, catching a familiar smell. I can't place it right away, but Fox doesn't seem to have the same problem, because a deep, feral growl erupts out of him and he whips his dagger out, pressing the blade against the cabbie's throat.

A hand grabs Fox's wrist from the seat beside the driver as Santanos appears in the front passenger seat with a grim set to his mouth. "Please don't kill Hassan. He's still recovering from his last encounter with you," Santanos drawls with a level look at us.

The corner of Fox's eye twitches, but he slowly pulls his dagger away from Hassan's neck. "We wouldn't have gotten in the cab if we'd known it was on the way to the dump."

Santanos lifts the side of his mouth in a half smile. "Don't worry, we'll drop you off safe and sound. I just want an update on Bellamy. I didn't know he was missing until your livestream. Do you need help finding him?"

I tilt my head to the side, giving him a skeptical look and making a disbelieving noise.

Santanos blows me an air kiss and winks at me. "I know it might seem unbelievable, but I didn't have anything to do with Bellamy's abduction. I didn't hire the Luna wolves to take him, and I do what the council tells me to do, not the other way around. I might want my assassin back, and yes, I am more than willing to take him out from under you by any reasonable means, but I'm not going to let some upstart take away the pleasure of stealing Bellamy from you away from me. So, if you need help, I offer my assistance, and I swear that until he is safe in the bosom of his family, I will cease all attempts to seduce him away from you."

Fox takes a moment to stare at the Avatar of Evil before he responds. Me? I may not like Santanos, but I respect that as the Avatar of Evil he is actively working toward bringing the right balance back to the earth. So he's bad, but he's not *that* bad.

"We're going to the arctic prison. I want to know how someone got my son into that prison without raising any flags."

Santanos' expression hardens to stone, and the atmosphere in the car takes on a heavy, dreadful air that makes it almost hard to breathe. "I will have a detailed report for you, the council, and Annette as soon as possible along with as many of the culprits as I can reasonably get my hands on."

Fox dips his chin once, slides his dagger back into its sheath, and pulls me under his arm.

Santanos turns in his seat, facing forward as he begins sending out messages, and before long Hassan pulls up in front of Annette's building.

Santanos turns to us as I open the door. "Get the boy back and let me know when he's safe behind your ward again."

Fox grunts a non-committal acknowledgment, and we debark from the cab. He grabs my hand and leads me into the high rise where Annette keeps her offices. The elevator opens as soon as he hits the up button, but instead of hitting the thirtieth floor where Annette's offices are, he pushes the button for the top floor.

The elevator zooms upward without stopping, and in a few seconds we're alighting on the top floor to an open space with rows of shelving filled to the brim with so much stuff. Fox walks with confidence through the shelving as I trail behind him, studying the rows of clothing, weapons, camping gear, books, non-perishable food stuffs...It's an altogether amazing assortment of things.

Fox stops in front of a shelf full of winter gear, which makes sense if we're heading to the arctic, though the last time he went north, he went naked, so now I'm concerned about how he dealt with the cold last time.

Fox pulls a pair of insulated coveralls and a huge coat off the shelves and hands them to me. "Your ward will protect you from the worst of the chill, but it won't keep you warm."

I flatten my lips at him, asking without words how he plans to deal with the freeze.

He caresses my cheek and pecks my lips. "I've already frozen to death in the arctic; I'm immune, my love."

Well, I guess there's that, but it makes my stomach clench at the idea that Bellamy wasn't immune before he was stolen away from us and what he might have to go through to become immune to the cold.

I am not ok with this. Bellamy better be ok when we find him, or I am going to let Fox go completely berserk avenging our boy. I might do that anyway.

Fox can get away with not threatening people; I'm not that scary. Give me another few thousand years and maybe I'll get there too, but let's be realistic, I'm a bubble of pure sunshine—it's unlikely I'm going to ever be scary enough to not have to threaten to sic Fox on people. I've accepted this fate; Fox deserves my sunshine and delightfulness, and it's a fair trade to take his intense loyalty and protection.

If he's willing to raze the world for Bellamy, imagine what he would do for me. I am never, ever, *ever* giving my Fox up, no matter how long it takes him to give me my diamond ring.

I don the winter weather gear, including a pair of goggles to protect my eyes and a scarf to protect my face, and then Fox takes me up a flight of stairs to the roof access.

Outside, I'm immediately too hot and sweating in my gear, and at first I don't notice that, blocked by the hood of the coat, my sugar Daddy is waiting for us.

"Get my grand baby back." The sound of her whiskey-rough voice startles me into spinning to find her.

She stands with a cigar smoking between her power red lips. Her recently cut, short, strawberry blond hair blows to the side in the wind, and her pale blue eyes squint at us through a furious mien. "I'll work with Santanos to find out how they got Bellamy into the arctic prison, and then we'll plug the security holes."

"I get any contracts or executions," Fox tells her as he starts stripping off his gear and storing it in a duffle bag I didn't notice he brought with him.

"If it is possible, I will give you first choice," she replies, watching him without seeing him; her gaze is distant, distracted.

Fox drops to a squat to unlace his boots. "No. I get them all. There is no choice, Avatar. Every person who violated the security systems to put Bellamy into the arctic prison will face me."

He puts his boots in the duffle and stands, revealing his ice-cold expression as he faces Annette. "This world will tremble when it remembers what happens to those who fuck with my family."

Annette's breath stalls for a moment as she stares into the face of the Reaper that other Reapers fear; the man who people want on their side because going against him is a good way to get dead.

"I will let everyone know," she says after a long pause. "Just make sure you're not tipping the scales."

"Even if I do, I'll be the one who fixes it."

He says those words, backs to the center of the helipad, and shifts into his magnificent bird form—the one Tag said he might not be able to take for a week. Look at my Fox being more powerful than even his father gives him credit for.

heart eyes *drool* *eggplant* *waterdrops*

Don't try to kink shame me. This is a kink shame free zone.

He lifts a couple of feathers on his back and then offers me his wing as a ramp this time since his tail is hanging off over the edge of the roof.

I give Annette a quick hug, but she stops me, holding me tight. "I'm not sure who's scarier, the Reaper or the Harbinger who loves him."

I huff my laughter at that, back up, and point to my face. It takes a special kind of crazy to love an unapologetic murderer, and I have it in spades.

Now to put it to good use getting back on the back of my thunderbird.

I will not puke. I will not puke. I will not puke.

CHAPTER 26

I hit my knees as soon as I manage to slide down Fox's feathers and rip the scarf covering my face just in time to empty my stomach onto the ice.

It steams for a few seconds and freezes, leaving my mark on the arctic just like I never hoped to do.

Gross.

Fox helps me up to my feet and steadies me. He's naked and ice is forming on his hair as I look at him, but he considers his discomfort secondary to my well-being. I cover my face back up with the scarf and point to the duffle bag he carried in his talons all the way here.

He takes another second to study me to make sure I'm ok before ripping the zipper open to redress and don his weapons again. I watch him, spending the short time he takes encouraging my body to recover from the trip up here. I spent the majority of it unconscious, but I managed to wake myself up when he landed instead of having to be awakened. Yay for getting better at flying with my boyfriend.

I am so not looking forward to the flight back.

As soon as Fox is dressed in his normal black yoga pants and A-shirt, ya know, appropriate summer weather clothes, not frozen arctic clothes, he points his boots toward a section of the landscape that looks melted and marches us toward the hole in the ice. Without pausing, he steps past the ice into the hole, but instead of falling into the ocean, the illusion hiding a smallish building that looks like a shack in the middle of the ice sheet falls away and the door swings open, held for us by a pretty blond woman in a colorful jumper with a bright smile on her pink lips. "Welcome back, Mr. Fox!" she enthuses.

Fox pulls me inside and stops long enough for the woman to shut the door. She gives me the same bright smile and starts helping me out of my cold weather clothes. "You must be Mr. Butcher. Hello. I'm Kristie Finster; I'm so happy to meet you. I wasn't expecting company. What can I do for you?"

She takes my coat and hangs it up while I pull off my coveralls since it's plenty warm in here.

"We're here for Bellamy Jones," Fox explains curtly.

Kristie's eyes blink at us blankly. "The assassin?"

I nod.

She looks between us. "We haven't had a check in since the last time you were here."

Fox gives her a steady look but says nothing.

Her expression grows genuinely concerned. "You think Bellamy Jones is here?"

I nod again.

She furrows her brow, glances between us for another half second, and then hits the button on the elevator, hopping into the car as soon as the door is open. She barely waits for us to join her before hitting the only other button.

The elevator descends super fast, and when the doors open, Kristie runs out into a short corridor, banging through a door at the end to the left.

Fox and I join her in a room full of screens, most of which are blank, but I count seventeen tuned into prison cells with people inside them. It's weird looking at them, because some of them are at normal-ish speed, but the rest are in various states of fast forward, and two of them are hardly recognizable as images fly by with just brief flashes of stills.

She scans every screen, even pausing the ones that are moving too fast for us to see the person inside it, but none of them show us Bellamy.

"Check the empty cells," Fox orders.

She does as she's told, turning on the cameras in the empty rooms one at a time, but none of them show us Bellamy.

Fox taps on a screen.

Kristie pauses the recording.

Fox points to a tiny, blurry anomaly at the edge of the screen. "Which cell is this?"

Kristie gasps and looks at us in a panic. "G-seven."

Fox storms out of the monitoring room, and I follow on his heels through the door to the left of the monitoring room at the end of the corridor. It leads to a set of metal stairs that we run down with Kristie right behind us.

"How did he get in here?" she calls as we race down. "How long has he been here?"

"Hours," Fox erupts, losing his stoicism to fury.

"Oh fuck," Kristie pants.

We descend fourteen half-flights of stairs before Fox rips open the door labeled G. We run down a gray-painted corridor with numbered doors and stop at number seven.

Kristie places her hand on the door and it immediately disappears, opening up the cell.

Fox pulls me in with him, leaving Kristie in the hall. I don't see Bellamy right away, but when I do—

Bellamy stares at us from the ceiling above where the camera watching this cell is mounted. Whoever brought him here staked him to the ceiling. Railroad spikes hold him in place away from the camera's view, and the only reason we saw him is because his hair grew out long enough to block part of the camera, it's so long.

"Took you fuckers long enough," Bellamy croaks, voice rough from disuse. "Mind getting me the hell out of here?"

Fox starts pulling stakes out, opening wounds that have long since healed around the metal. Bellamy doesn't react at all, clinging to Fox as he falls away from the ceiling one stake at a time. When Fox gets him down, carrying him in his arms because there's no way Bellamy can stand on his own, I rush to him, grabbing his ginger Merlin beard and making him look at me.

"I'm over it, *Papa*," he assures me a bit derisively. "For a while I was angry that you two made me immortal, but after a couple of centuries one gets some perspective. You didn't know what had happened and you had to do what you could to make sure you would get me back alive. It's exactly what I would have done too."

Centuries.

I kiss his forehead and look at Fox, projecting the depth of my wrath so he knows he better make the world tremble for me as well.

Fox kisses Bellamy too and indicates it's time to go. I lead them out, back into the corridor where Kristie pulls us out of the room, gaping at Bellamy.

"I am so sorry, Mr. Jones! I don't know how anyone got past me!"

Bellamy groans softly. "It was a direct deposit. Fuckers dug a tunnel into that cell."

Kristie sucks in a breath, looking into the cell. I follow her gaze, but I don't see any holes.

Kristie, on the other hand, must see something, because she spits. "Fuckers! Who did this?" she demands.

"Humans," Bellamy replies softly. "Mostly. There were some from the community, but non-magical, blind, fucking humans did most of the work. I don't know who tunneled in; I didn't see them. They were invisible even to me."

"Someone with strong enough glamour to hide from you? That narrows the suspects down. The Avatars, the council, maybe some of the royal families? Can you see the Mab?" Kristie asks as she leads us to the stairs.

"As far as I know, I've never been in the presence of a Mab."

Fox makes a negative sound. "Athair is a Mab."

Bellamy snorts. "Has he ever succeeded in hiding from me?"

"I don't know that he's ever tried."

"Sounds about right," Bellamy hums, closing his eyes and leaning his head against Fox's shoulder. "Home. Food. How long have I actually been gone?"

"About a day."

"Fucking humans," he slurs, drifting.

The rest of the journey back up is done in silence. I almost give up halfway, but the need to get Bellamy home spurs me onward. Ugh, living with Fox has spoiled me; I should be able to walk up seven floors without needing a break. Am I going to start stair-stepping? No. I'll just avoid buildings that don't come with working elevators, thank you very much.

When we get to the top, Kristie provides us with enough blankets to insulate Bellamy for the flight south, and then Fox and I take our Acolyte home.

CHAPTER 27

Things one does not want to see when walking in one's front door after a long, tiring, but successful twenty-four hours, a list by Romily Butcher:

1. 4 future fathers in law making a huge mess of my kitchen
2. 3 randos
3. 2 Avatars
4. And 1 pupper staring at the Avatar of Evil like he doesn't quite understand what he's looking at.

All of the people occupying our common rooms stop talking as soon as we walk in, and in an effort to stop the dramatics, I step in front of Fox, who's carrying Bellamy, and hold up my hands in the universal sign of DO NOT APPROACH.

When everyone freezes in their tracks, I pull out my phone and add everyone in the room to a group chat.

You thought it would be a good idea to descend on an injured, traumatized, professional assassin? I like most of you, some of you I love, not sure why Santanos and co. are here, but none of you except Darcy and Edovard should be here.

Bellamy will see you when he's good and ready. Except Santanos and Hassan, obvs. GTFO.

The crowd of our family and Santanos erupt into protests, but Fox kicks one of the small tables over, interrupting the cacophony. "Out. Darcy and Edovard stay."

With those words, Fox carries Bellamy upstairs and the rest of our visitors leave, whispering to me on their way by. Mostly they just say they're glad that we found Bellamy.

Tag gives me some instructions for the food that the fathers were prepping for us.

Santanos tells me he left me a file on the living room coffee table, and then he clarifies he means the one in front of the couch.

Annette kisses my cheek and her wife does the same, apologizing for letting Annette drag her along.

Then finally it's just the people who belong here and Darcy, but I think he's earned a place to lay his head today.

Edovard wrings his hands as he steps toward me. "They just kept showing up, but Darcy knew them, so I didn't say anything."

I turn up the volume on my text to speech again.

It's fine. They are all important, well except Santanos and Hassan, but it's not the right time. People need to learn to be happy for us from a distance.

Edovard nods. "Santanos isn't important? He was the little blond guy, right?"

Darcy snorts.

He's not important to our family except as a foil.

Edovard's confusion is adorable, but I just don't have the energy right now. I'm crashing hard, but I need food for Bellamy, so I start moving to the kitchen and smack Darcy to get him to explain to Edovard what I mean.

"Santanos is the Avatar of Evil. Romily stole Bellamy right out from under him, and he's trying to get his assassin back. He's only important to the Foxilys because he's the comparison. Fox and Romily are the good guys, Santanos is the bad guy."

Foxilys. Ha! I should have thought of that ship name myself.

"Santanos can't be evil. He was nice to me," Edovard argues with a stubborn tone as I start serving mounds of food on four plates and setting those on a tray to take upstairs.

"He's the Avatar of Evil. The council imbued him with the magical authority over all evil. His job is to make sure that the evil that persists in the world doesn't get out of control." For some reason Darcy's voice sounds like he's trying to placate Edovard, which is weird because Darcy is not the placating type.

I move my eyes away from the food to the two men just to make sure everyone is ok. Edovard's face is damp and he's wiping away tears, and Darcy has the same look of panic that Fox gets when he sees people cry.

I shake my head at him, frowning as if to say, *Look what you did.*

Darcy backs up, holding up his hands in surrender. "I didn't do it."

Edovard grabs a napkin off the dining table we usually eat at and wipes his face. "Santanos isn't evil."

"Of course not," Darcy agrees, grabbing another napkin and offering it him.

This is going to be a whole story, isn't it?

I'm not narrating that one.

I put four bottles of water on the tray, grab Edovard's wrist, point to the tray, and direct him to carry it upstairs.

Edovard gives me that lost puppy look, but Darcy saves me having to type it out.

"I think he wants you to take the tray up to Fox and Bellamy."

I nod, and Edovard's confusion clears. "No problem."

He takes the tray up, following Darcy, and even though I want nothing more than to cuddle Bellamy and Fox and sleep for hours, I pick up the report Santanos left and shuffle through ten pages of a dossier on three humans and an unknown person no one has ever seen and whose name we don't know. The only things we know about the person are that they have enough magic to tunnel through the wards of the arctic prison without tripping any alarms and the humans call them the Prophet.

Because it totally makes sense to worship a magic user if you can't actually see magic.

Jesus-fucking-Christ, people are gullible. I really don't know how we've survived on this planet for so long. We're evolution's version of that one mistake we all make that haunts us for the rest of our lives.

You know what I'm talking about. You're going along minding your own business, and then BAM! Suddenly you're in the middle of the biggest mistake of your life that everyone will bring up at the family Christmas dinner every year for the rest of time because it's the funniest shit they ever heard, and it'll embarrass you every time, but eventually you'll be able to laugh too.

That's what humans are to evolution, I'm pretty sure.

It's embarrassing how dumb we are when we get in groups.

I put the report down, huffing my frustration into the empty space.

We might not know much now, but we will keep poking at this thing until we figure it out. Even my sunny disposition has its limits, and I refuse to spend more time than necessary worrying about a human cult and their enigmatic magical lead. We got our boy back; it's time to leave the rest for another day.

I take a deep breath, pushing away all the fear, worry and stress, put the food away, turn off the lights, and head upstairs.

Bellamy is sitting against the headboard of his bed, and Fox sits next to him, feeding him one bite at a time like the perfect father I know him to be. Edovard is reclining right next to Bellamy, helping to steady him so he doesn't fall over before he can regain his strength, while Darcy takes up space on the table under the window, cross-legged, staring at Bellamy with a hard, angry look.

I drag the one chair in the room over next to Bellamy and sit, holding his hand. I know it won't take long for him to recover, but seeing him so very weak and damaged after only one day is fucking with me.

"Stop staring at me like that," Bellamy grumps between bites.

It's the hair. You have the perfect face for shaving.

Bellamy chuffs, tired eyes closing. "I spent so long growing this magnificent Merlin beard. You'd think you'd have a little respect for it."

"It is weird how fast you grew that beard. Is it a magic thing?" Edovard asks, completely clueless as he reaches out to run his fingers through the long ginger beard.

"Yeah, buddy. Just magic. Don't worry about it. I'll shave it off in the morning," Bellamy sighs.

I also stroke Bellamy's long, luscious beard.

You could pull off prickly emo hipster if you kept eight inches.

"I've heard the teen years *are* the hardest," Fox agrees with a teasing smile in his eyes.

Bellamy snorts softly, looks straight into Fox's eyes, and deadpan as you like, "Hey, Papa, did Oppa ever tell you what happened to your rin—"

Fox slaps his hand over Bellamy's lips, silencing him as he leans in close enough to press his forehead against Bellamy's. "I will send you more unsolicited dick pics than you could possibly handle. I will get everyone I know to send them. Constantly. You will get so many that you'll genuinely consider going on a dick fast because you'll be so tired of seeing dicks every time you have to look at your phone when Papa talks."

That is…wow. I'm just gobsmacked that Fox is resorting to threats right now. Fox doesn't threaten people, but damn. When he does?

Well, if the genuine worry in Bellamy's eyes is any indication, Fox is pretty good at hitting the right note for them.

Also,

What happened to my ring?

I make sure my text to speech is enabled so no one can pretend I didn't ask that.

Fox blows out a frustrated breath through his nose and pushes himself back upright. "Ok, everyone but Edovard out. It's time for Bellamy to sleep."

Bellamy huffs out an exhausted chuckle, reaching over to squeeze my knee. "He's right. I need sleep."

Darcy rumbles his annoyance. "I want to fix the blood bond, Red. Before anything else happens."

Bellamy sighs softly and turns toward Edovard. "Not tonight, Darcy. Let me recover first, my friend."

I grimace at that, but Bellamy reaches out and squeezes my hand. "It's amazing what a few centuries of perspective can do, Papa. Truly, I'm over it, and renewing that blood bond would mean not having to go through this shit again."

He has a point, and even if I don't like it, it doesn't mean he's not right.

Fox puts the leftover food well within reach so that if Bellamy wakes up hungry he has something right there. He and I kiss Bellamy again and leave him with Edovard. Fox points Darcy to the guest room and then takes me back to our bedroom, to our shower, to a couple of orgasms, and to ten solid hours of sleep.

CHAPTER 28

(The epilogue, because y'all seem to think I end stories too abruptly)

So. The non-human community has a gladiator arena. I wouldn't have ever guessed that we still let people fight like this, but here I am sitting in the covered platform where the movies taught me that Caligula sat with his sister-wife when he oversaw the arena. Because, ya know, Hollywood is always super accurate with their historical films.

Admittedly, I'm pretty stoked that we've kept up the tradition of the gladiators being naked! Wait, that was the Olympians, wasn't it? The gladiators fought bare-chested. Also acceptable for my lusty eyes, but since Fox is actually just wearing a little loincloth, I'm calling it naked. He has his favorite sword, one of the curved ones that drips the ethereal smoke that means it's filtering out all but his demon magic.

Bellamy stands with Fox in the sand, also bearing his favorite sword dripping with filtered magical smoke, and a hardness in his lavender eyes as he scans the thirteen people he and Fox plan on killing today.

We rented out the arena for the executions of everyone we decided needed dying as an example of what happens when you fuck with the Foxilys.

Yes, that ship name is happening now; just go with it. I love the fuck out of it, and next time we change our government IDs it's going to be our surname. For all four of us, including Edovard, who's sitting next to me staring across the arena at Santanos, because there's another covered platform where the Avatars and council members are observing the goings on.

Darcy, Tag, Amos, and Bear are all with me on this side, but Dakota is on the other side, and when he sees me noticing that Santanos is also staring at Edovard, he reaches over and smacks the twink upside his head, breaking the uncomfortably awkward stare-off between Edovard and Santanos.

The event today is being live-streamed to the worldwide audience, but like the council meeting before, the arena is overpacked with standing room only. Someone with a microphone calls out the reason each person in the sand is there, starting with Fox and Bellamy—revenge, obviously. No, this isn't justice. Justice is a fair trade; these people are going to die as an example. One of them is the human photographer that took the pictures of Bellamy in various states of dead or dying.

I don't think photographing macabre shit should end in a death sentence under normal circumstances, but this isn't normal circumstances, and I've learned that some people just need killing, especially the ones targeting my family. Call me callous.

Or pissed.

We captured and contained the three cult leaders and seven of their minions, the photographer, the Arbiter that put out the bounty for Bellamy for the humans, and Jamie Gordon. Yep, the council unanimously voted to allow us to kill Jamie. The man has a magical life-insurance policy, so the death won't stick, but he's still in the arena, and this is his one and only resurrection. After this, if someone kills him, he's dead-dead.

Fun, right?

I kind of hope he fucks with us again.

Me: *Are you watching the livestream?*

DB Cooper (the thief who stole Dakota's phone): *How did you know I still have this phone?*

Me: *Because Santanos hasn't told me that he picked up the idiot who stole Dakota's phone.*

DB Cooper: *Am I an idiot if I'm still running around with Dakota's phone? Cell service is expensive, you know.*

Me: *You see that man with the red hair?*

DB Cooper: *Can't take my eyes off him.*

Me: *I would do anything for him, including having you tortured and killed in his stead. Stay safe, and watch what happens when someone fucks with my family.*

DB Cooper: *Your boys have my rapt attention.*

The story will continue in Murder Sprees and Mute Decrees book three, but I'm not narrating that one. That's all on Edovard. *side eye* Me? I'm going to watch my boys eviscerate a group of no-good-doers, get horny watching my future hubby work, then take him home and fuck him into the mattress. We might stop for ice cream on the way—Bellamy deserves his treats after all he's been through. Don't worry. He's fine.

-Romily

NOTE FROM JENNIFER

Dear Reader,

Thank you for reading The Trouble with Trying to Save an Assassin (henceforth, Trouble 2).

Obviously, since writing book one, things have changed for me. I planned on a trilogy following Fox and Rom through their epic love story. I didn't plan on making this series a big thing. I wrote Trouble 1 on a whim because I binge-watched with unadulterated delight a bunch of Keanu Reeves movies and thought to myself, *This but gay and funny.*

I underestimated how much people would enjoy reading Romily's irreverent narrative. I just thought I'd write myself a little treat of a book and figured that fans of my Diviner's Game universe would enjoy a fun little diversion from the norm (plot heavy, low angst, PNR). I was taken aback by the response to Trouble 1, and so my publishing plans changed drastically.

What I think will be happening with this series:

1. Edovard x Santanos novella (untitled yet…)
2. The Trouble with Trying to Get Engaged (working title, I'm not thrilled with it; if you have other suggestions, shoot them to me)
3. Darcy x Elijah novella (also untitled…)
4. The Trouble with Trying to Marry a Reaper (I like this title)

NOTE FROM JENNIFER

After that, I expect to start Bellamy's series, but that's so far in the future I can't pretend to know what's happening with him yet. Well, I have a small clue, and you do too, if you were paying attention to DB Cooper.

Speaking of paying attention, any guesses what books Romily and Fox were reading in this story? The only hints I can give you is that I am friends on Facebook with all of the authors of the books I vaguely described, and they are all indie published authors. Feel free to stalk me there to try to figure it out. Romily will let you know if you got it right next time he pops up for a foreword.

Or you can email me, jennifercodymm@gmail.com. I'm happy to let you know what books I recommend.

Thank you again for reading Trouble 2. I hope you enjoyed it. I hope you stick around to find out what is happening with the most innocent pup of all time and the Avatar of Evil. Please leave a rating and review, if you would be so kind. Word of mouth is the best marketing an author like me can get, so tell everyone about the Trouble series if you like it.

For the love of MM,
Jennifer Cody

MURDER SPREES AND MUTE DECREES BOOK 3

SNEAK PEEK

Edovard

The air here is really hot compared to Fresno. It's like I'm getting baked in an oven like a chocolate vanilla swirl cupcake. Or one of those German chocolate cakes. Actually, I'm probably more like a gingerbread man.

Gosh I'm hungry.

We flew all the way to Arizona yesterday, and it's been at least two hours since breakfast, and now we're sitting in an arena like they used to build in the olden days when there were Roman emperors. Except there aren't any vendors trying to get me to spend eight dollars on a hot dog. I would, though, if there was.

My stomach rumbles as my new Oppa (that means "Dad"), Arlington Fox, shuffles his bare feet in the sand of the arena. It makes me wince, because that sand is probably really hot.

I don't really want to look at what is going to happen, because I get a little sick when I see people die, so I look away from Oppa and Bellamy (my new brother) to the crowded stands of the arena. There are a lot of people here to watch the guys who did bad things to Bellamy die. Papa (my other new dad, Romily Butcher) told me that we're making a statement to the community of supernatural people: Don't fuck with the Foxilys.

I'm a Foxily, or I will be when we all change our names. Oppa says he needs to change his identity in the next five to ten years, and when he does, we are all getting new names. I haven't picked out a first name yet, but I'm excited about getting to be a Foxily. I like how it sounds, and it's nice to have a family again.

My eyes fall on the guy everyone keeps telling me is evil, but I've learned not to judge people before I get to know them. Look at me. I'm over six feet tall, I'm brown skinned, I have a square face, and I'm super buff. I like being a bodybuilder. I don't need to compete with anyone else; this is purely for fun, and people judge me by my looks all the time. They assume I'm some kind of tough guy, or a criminal, or whatever. I'm not. I'm just strong because I like being strong.

The blond curls on top of Santanos' head shine like a real halo, and the way his pretty blue eyes look at me makes me feel tingly sometimes. I don't know why everyone thinks he's evil. He's been nothing but nice to me. He saw how distressed I was when my new dads were gone saving my new brother, and he gave me a cup of hot tea he said would relax me. It tasted like the tea my mother used to drink before bed, so I know he was trying to help.

No one is going to convince me that a guy who gives a stranger hot tea like that is a bad guy.

The tingles are weird though. Never felt anything like that before.

"Here you go, baby boy."

One of my new grandfathers—I can't remember what I'm supposed to call them all yet; this one is blue—hands me a really big glass full of sparkling ice water.

Immediately I feel thirsty and smile gratefully at him. "Thank you, Grandpa."

His love for me shines out of him and he pats my head, telling me he's happy I'm a part of his family now.

I like how all the people in my new family let their love for me shine like they do. As long as they're with me, I'll never be alone in the dark again.

I chug about half the water, and when I look in the glass to see how much is left, it magically refills, which is pretty cool. I didn't know magic existed until recently, but some of the things that magic does are incredible.

Like refilling my glass so I won't get dehydrated in the Arizona summer heat.

The announcer guy starts telling us about the reason we're here today as my eyes catch on Santanos again, staring at me. There's a lot of light in him, too. He has a lot of love inside him; I can see it. I don't think it has anything to do with me, but I like looking at people who have lots of love inside them. My sister doesn't have any love inside her. She never has, especially not toward me.

I don't want to think about that.

I'd rather look at Santanos, because even though I don't judge people based on their looks, I do like how pretty Santanos is. He's really nice to look at.

My other grandpa, who's sitting with Santanos, reaches over and smacks the back of his head. Santanos spins around, glaring at—um, I think that one is Dora, no Dorito? I can't remember. Some kind of D name I never heard before—and I can almost hear his loud protest at being smacked by my new grandpa. Almost. He has a really nice voice, and I kinda wish I could hear it again.

Instead, the announcer tells us that the executions can begin, and despite not really wanting to watch, I end up watching my Oppa and brother kill the people in the arena with them. It's kind of amazing, even if I get a little sick seeing the blood. I've never been around people who use swords like Oppa and Bellamy do. They're fast and strong and look like they're dancing as they kick up sand and turn it into crimson mud.

A lot of heads end up separated from their bodies, but I guess that's the point of this. Oppa and Bellamy are telling everyone not to fuck with our family in the bloodiest way they could think of. Most of the people die fast, but two of them are left fighting after the others are killed.

One of them is a big lizard guy with a mohawk made up of spikes like rosebush thorns, but the spikes are made of bone instead of wood. He's got a long metal pole that he's using to defend himself against Bellamy. I've never seen anyone defeat one of the lizard people in a fight, but I trust Bellamy. He can defeat this one because he's a trained assassin, and I've watched him sparring with Oppa, and he's really good. Better than the lizard guy, that's for sure.

Oppa is fighting a really fast, mostly naked girl with long, black claws, wild messy hair that I think has an actual wasp nest in it, and a dark splotch on her chin like she's spilled so much grape juice while drinking it's become a permanent stain. She looks ferocious, and she's fast enough that Oppa can't kill her right away.

Both Oppa and Bellamy fight fast and hard, and within just a few seconds of Bellamy cutting open the lizard guy's gut—the water I've drunk tries to make an escape, but I choke it back down and look away from the intestines—Oppa kills the wild girl by cutting off her claws and then her head.

It's so sad, and gross, and sad. I don't like watching people die.

I close my eyes to remove the sight, but instead of the usual red from behind my eyelids, I see the face of a person. That really startles me, because I don't ever see things when I close my eyes. That's why I close them! But this face. This guy is really dark, scary-dark. Dark like he has no love inside him at all.

"Seth Adam Hultgren. Thirty eight victims—no, no, no!" I cut off the monotone recitation coming out of my mouth without my permission because it's really scary. "Papa!"

Papa is already in my lap and hugging me hard as tears start pouring down my face. I can't stop them from coming. I don't see faces; I don't randomly have names and stuff like that come spewing out of my mouth.

"Shhh, it's ok, baby boy," the blue grandpa says as he takes my hand and starts rubbing my back too. "That's just your Augur abilities kicking in. I guess they were waiting until the right time before they started up. You're ok. Now we have the name and a reason to investigate them. Did the magic tell you anything about the victims?"

I choke on that. I knew I was supposed to be some kind of helper for Oppa, but it's been a couple weeks, and I haven't been at all helpful, except when he wanted some help clearing out one of the apartments next to our house (he's going to remodel it so that whenever me or Bellamy decide to move out of the main house we can just move in next door). Unfortunately, I do know more about the victims.

It's really hard to get the words out, but I manage to. "They're all dead. He killed a bunch of college girls from a university in Milwaukee."

All three of my new grandpas hiss at once, and then somehow Papa isn't in my lap anymore, and instead I'm looking at another blond, but this one has blue eyes instead of brown, and he looks pissed.

"What happened?" Santanos demands, putting his hands all over my face and shoulders and arms. It feels like he's touching me everywhere, and as soon as I realize that he basically wormed his way into my lap, the tingles start up again all over my body, especially where he's touching me.

"Why are you touching my son?" Papa's digital voice from his phone reads the words he writes aloud. I like it better when he lets one of the others read his words to me.

Santanos completely ignores my papa.

"Stop feeling him up! He's just been through a traumatic event," the digital voice reads.

"I don't mind, Papa." It's kind of nice anyway. The tingles are a little fun.

"What happened?" Santanos repeats, this time looking me in the eye.

Weirdly, along with the light of his love that shines out from him, he smells like the smoke from the sage smudges my grandpa used to burn to help clean out his house.

"I guess I got my Augur powers," I explain, relating the information that my blue grandpa said. "Seth Adam Hultgren. He killed a lot of college girls in Milwaukee.."

The burning sage smell immediately starts smelling like a stinky fart and the light inside him dims. "Then I guess it's about time for Fox to make a trip to Wisconsin."

HAMMER & FIST

SNEAK PEAK, CHAPTER ONE

"Have a nice afternoon." The previously perky waiter's voice comes out husky as he slips me the receipt for my lunch.

I smile up at him, taking the receipt without touching his lingering fingers. Glancing at his name tag, I return his well-wishes. "You too, Daniel."

He saunters away with an attractive wiggle, which I watch because it'd be rude not to enjoy a performance meant for me. When he rounds a corner out of sight, I unfold the receipt to find his phone number and the total charge for my meal—discounted.

I lay a bill on the table for his tip and slip the receipt into my pocket. I don't need it for the phone number; I have to give it to my agency's accounting department to get my per diem. Government bureaucracy is a bitch, but we deal with it if we want our paychecks.

I walk out of the cafe into the bustling streets of the downtown area of my current city of the month: Knoxville, Tennessee. I check my smart watch, then my pocket-compass, and turn left, heading north.

A young man heading toward me trips over a cobblestone and catches himself on my shoulder. Before he can touch me further, I steady him and put him back on his feet.

"Sorry," he apologizes with a recognizably northern accent, cheeks flushing with a pretty blush.

I smile to reassure him. "It's fine. You ok?"

"Oh, yeah. I'm fine. Thanks for not letting me hit my ass." His accent delights my ears, but his smile quickens my pulse.

I squeeze the hand he's holding, only now realizing that I connected to him skin-to-skin.

Shit.

I failed to put my gloves back on after watching that distracting waiter's ass.

My dick throbs and twitches, trying to derail my plans for the day.

Fuck me.

I hate my magic sometimes.

"Hey, you want to grab a coffee?" I offer, pulling my hand from his to grab a card from my vest pocket. "I'm off at seven this evening. I'm not from around here, but your company this evening would be better than sitting in my hotel room alone." I slip the card into his hand, tracing one finger over the pulse point in his wrist. We both drag in a gasp of air like we've suddenly run out of oxygen. Arousal and need flood through me, and as much as I want to drag him into the nearest alley and have my way with him, I can't. Not yet. I will because I must, but it will be sweeter and less frustrating if I wait a few hours.

"Sure, but I don't drink coffee," he breathes, leaning toward me as the magic enthralling me prods me to become his slave.

Gods, he's beautiful.

I take a deep breath and focus on the magic enthralling me, pushing a tiny bit out to enthrall him back. I don't like doing this, and it physically hurts me to do because it goes against the point of the self-sabotaging magic, but I do this every time this happens, because my desire to live in freedom is stronger than the compulsion to dedicate myself to one person.

"I'll think of something. Call me at seven-fifteen," I instruct, rubbing his pulse point as the magic puts him into a light hypnosis; if he truly doesn't want to call me, he can choose not to, but the magic will remind him if he does. "Not a minute later."

"Yes," he agrees, looking up at me with attraction and lust on display in his pretty brown eyes.

I smile warmly and kiss his cheek. "I look forward to seeing you tonight," I murmur in his ear, then drop his wrist and step back.

He gives me that pulse-pounding smile again as we part ways.

As soon as I'm far enough away, I pull my phone out of my pocket and dial my handler. She answers on the first ring. "What's up?"

"Man tripped into me. Got a date at seven-fifteen."

The sound of her typing clatters in the silence between us before she responds with a curt, "Noted," and ends the call.

I put my phone back into my pocket then jog north, weaving through the pedestrians, annoyed with myself for forgetting my gloves and conversely delighted by the stirrings of false love. I don't even know his name, but I'm enthralled and in love with him. My logical mind and the part of me that craves absolute freedom knows that I'm not in love with a stranger, but the magic that binds me to anyone I touch doesn't know the difference between true love and obsession. It just wants me enslaved.

On a side street off the main thoroughfare of downtown, five steps down from the sidewalk, I push open the door to Dorian's Antiques. The bells above jingle, announcing my arrival, but one of the bells must have split at some point and the sour note makes me wince, sending a shock of pain down my arms. Discordant noises have always caused me nerve pain; as a kid, I'd sometimes blackout if a harsh enough sound caught me off guard, but now I can mostly deal with it without even flinching.

Dorian sits behind the register and looks up at the sound of his bells. "Sexy Lexy! How you doing, man?" His broad smile and teasing tone fail to hide the faint scent of fear coming from him and the tension around his eyes.

"Hello, Dorian," I greet him, pulling my favorite cold iron dagger from its hiding place. His eyes go wide as the stench of fear permeates the air. "I heard you had problems with a gremlin yesterday. You know you're not an authorized fey dealer."

"Problem? No! No problem. The gremlin got a bit lost, and I took it to the right place! I'm on the up and up! I swear!" Dorian's lies whisper through the air, cocooning me in ephemeral cotton candy. I lick my lips, unable to resist the sweetest treat a person could ever give me.

"We both know you're full of shit, Dorian. Get up, let's go." I point my dagger toward him and wave it at the back of his store. "Inspection time."

Dorian swallows hard but gets up and leads me to the back of the store. "I swear, Lex, I didn't do anything. Whatever you heard, I didn't do it."

Delicious. Cotton candy again. I breathe it in through my mouth, salivating for more. I say nothing, but Dorian keeps talking. I don't hate the guy. He might be a bit of a crook, but I clean his house out every few months and he gives me a lot of information in exchange for not tossing his ass into the nether realm. It's a system we've worked out over the last few years, and as long as he keeps up his part of the deal, I will protect him from other IDIA agents who aren't so forgiving.

I place a hand on his shoulder, lightly touching the skin on his neck. "Tell me about the gremlin, Dorian. How did it get here?" I demand, pushing a tiny amount of thrall at him—I want the truth this time, no matter how tempting his lies are.

IDIA, the Inter-dimensional Immigration Agency, keeps the peace when non-human crimes happen. Dorian may look like a middle-aged Arab to any human wandering into the store, but he's an immigrant from the Faerie realm. The fey are usually secretive about their subtype, but I figured out during my first encounter with him that Dorian is an earth sprite.

"It came in through the front door, just like you," Dorian replies, opening the door to the back of his shop, then taking me down a set of stairs to another door.

"You know that's not what I mean," I growl, getting annoyed with his prevaricating.

Dorian glances at my dagger before unlocking the second door, using three different keys. "I heard there's a portal in Benson Park," he whispers quietly.

"Good thing you did," I remind him, pushing the backdoor open. He's only useful to me if he can provide information, and an illegal portal in Benson Park is the type of info he's good at relaying.

I step into a small garden that leads to Dorian's real storage unit. A sun that has never shown its light on earth hangs overhead, feeding life into a variety of plants both decorative and useful. Movement among the tall grasses immediately catches my attention. "IDIA, please step forward with your blue identification bracelet held out. Anyone without a valid form of identification will have the opportunity to apply for the appropriate travel documents with Inter-dimensional Immigration."

Unless you run. I don't say that aloud. I'm not required to, and sometimes I enjoy the chase. Right now, I have some excess energy brimming from Dorian's lies. I could go for a round of chase-catch-kill.

Illegal immigrants are always given the opportunity to become legal, though in ninety-nine percent of cases, they're deported back to their respective realms. Anyone who resists detainment is immediately deported or executed, depending on how much resistance they put up and how merciful the field agent in charge is feeling. I'm not in a merciful mood.

Three wood nymphs step into the open, holding out bare wrists. Well, bare everything. Unsurprisingly, they're nude; nymphs rarely wear clothing.

Rage at the sight of them makes me whip around, glaring at Dorian, who's still standing in the doorway. "Slaves, Dorian? You're dead."

"No! I didn't traffic them! I found them. I am not a slaver!" he cries out, and this time I don't taste the sweetness of his lies.

So, they aren't slaves. At least not his. That doesn't mean he's not guilty of capital crimes.

I turn back to the wood nymphs, looking them over for signs of assault. They each have fading bruises around their wrists from being tied up. "How did you get here?"

They all look alike to me. Fey can tell one nymph from another, but I'd never mastered the skill. To me, they all look like innocent, brunette fifteen-year-old girls. Brown skin and brown eyes, eerily symmetrical features—basically identical. They aren't the smartest fey subtype, and their short term memories only hold onto things for a week at most, and sometimes they mix up their memories, but my magic makes me able to tell when they're not speaking the truth, even if they are convinced they're right.

"There was a big bang, and then darkness," the one on the right explains. True.

"Then we were bounced around!" the middle one exclaims, illustrating the bounce. True, again.

"Then we were bounced onto hard ground." The third one takes up the

HAMMER & FIST

story, landing on her butt with her hands together showing how they were tied up. True.

The first one speaks again. "Then there were humans everywhere!"

"And tall buildings!"

"And then there was Dorian!" They all squeal in delight. That's not a good sign. Nymphs getting excited over a person is usually a really fucking bad sign.

I resist the urge to squeeze my eyes shut and turn back to Dorian. "You found them on the street?" I question to confirm that's what their idea of hard ground is.

He nods.

I narrow my eyes at him, ready to just kill him, because I can see the writing on the wall, and it's an execution order. "Speak your answers, Dorian. This conversation is recorded for IDIA." Technically that is true. I have a small crystal that records everything I say and do. I turn it in at the end of every month, and it is stored in case something happens and the agency has to review my case work. However, the reason I want him to speak is because I can only tell if he's lying if he speaks his answers into the air.

Read more about Lex HERE

ABOUT JENNIFER CODY

Jennifer Cody writes gay romance of a variety of sub-genres, though her favorite is paranormal romance/urban fantasy. She uses her husband's vast knowledge of all things man and mechanical to help her write, but takes literary license with her characters because they're romantic heroes, thereby making him shake his head in disbelief almost as often as she causes his incredulous laughter.

With three kids at home, the only time she has for boredom is 5 a.m. when everyone else is still asleep, and coffee usually keeps that at bay. When she reads, she usually binges an author's entire backlist for a few days but has a few one-click favorites she stalks. Her go-to sub-genres are gay PNR (Paranormal Romance) and UF (Urban Fantasy), but she has a soft spot for certain contemporary MM tropes (falling in love with the Manny, and small-town/rural stories).

Join Jennifer's Facebook group, Jennifer Cody's Cocky Cuties, for all kinds of fun shenanigans, live writes, schedule updates and more!

Sign up for my newsletter on my website to get more news and occasional serial shorts.

ALSO BY JENNIFER CODY

DIVINER'S GAME TRILOGY

Bishop to Knight One

Knight to Castle Two

Queen to King Three

DG Short Stories

(Only available on my website. Sign up for my newsletter to get these.)

Loki Adopts a Cat

The D'Aquinos Go to War

SHATTERED PAWNS SERIES

Spinoff of Diviner's Game

Pass

Capture

Promote

Shah Mat (2022)

Houston Hub Shorts

Forgotten Fox

Mr. Monster Kok

Forgotten Fox

A Knot with Santa

Genesis

MURDER SPREES AND MUTE DECREES

The Trouble with Trying to Date a Murderer

For Recruits a Mute Boy

The Trouble With Trying to Save an Assassin

HAMMER AND FIST SERIES

Sledge and Claw: Lextalon

Inferno (Hammer and Fist: Geminatus Book 1)

RECOVERY ROAD SERIES

Forrest's #Win

Gentry's #Doms (MMM)

Jericho's #Switch (Sign up for my newsletter to get this one)

MULTI AUTHOR COLLECTION

Tentacle Tails

LOOKING FOR A BIT OF DARK EROTICA?

Jennifer Cody writes as Cinnamon Sin

Nefarius

Nefarius Too

Matty's Monster:

Captured

Tortured

Turned

Unleashed

Primal Prey:

Catch Me

Printed in Great Britain
by Amazon